DOWN IN DEMERARA

Mike Manson

⟨ **Tangent** Books

First published 2018 by Tangent Books

Tangent Books
Unit 5.16 Paintworks
Bristol BS4 3EH
0117 972 0645
www.tangentbooks.co.uk

ISBN 978-1-910089-77-4

Cover design: Sue Gent
Map: Maggie Moss
Copyright: Mike Manson 2018

A CIP Record is available from the British Library.

Printed on paper from a sustainable source.

Here we sit like birds in the wilderness
Down in Demerara.

Traditional Nursery Rhyme

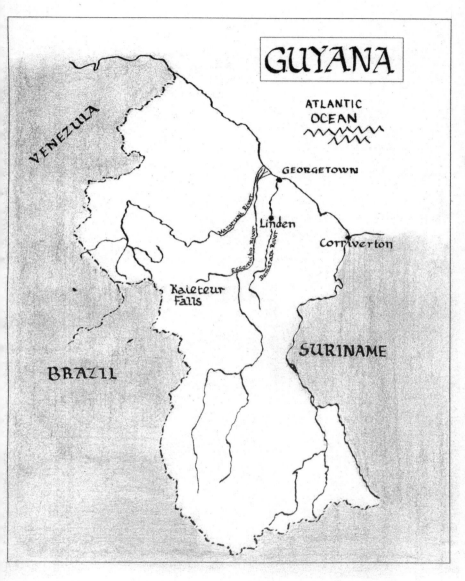

My hand-drawn map of Guyana. What this doesn't show is how hot and sticky this tiny country is.

PART ONE

ONE

Breakfast in a brothel.

Corriverton, Guyana, 1999

I pulled back the dirty net curtain. The pot-holed road was flanked on both sides by a boardwalk. Behind were ramshackle clapboard houses, once painted white in the colonial style, but now a cracked grey. Men sat on door-stoops, waiting, seemingly doing nothing. Women sheltered from the sun under umbrellas at makeshift stalls selling fruit and drinks from cool-boxes decorated with slogans such as 'In God We Trust', '1 Luv' and 'Never Despair'.

Ellis, a petite figure as taut as a wire, strode across the road towards the Sweet Dreams Guest House. Even from this distance, I understood why Gordon wanted her checked out.

There was still a whisper of ocean freshness in the early morning air as I hurried downstairs. In the hotel lobby a table knocked up from a wooden crate was crowned by an ashtray overflowing with cigarette butts. On the wall by the entrance was a condom dispenser, empty.

'Hi,' I said, putting out my hand for a quick, no-nonsense handshake. Ellis had a gamine haircut and a golden tan and wore a tight-fitting white T-shirt and cargo shorts.

She blinked as her eyes adjusted to the shade. 'What's up with the fucking tie?' she said.

'It's top quality Chinese silk.'

'Jesus! Do you want to end up floating in the Corentyne River with a machete in your back?'

'Gordon suggested it.'

'Yeah, well, Gordon's never been to Corriverton. What goes on in Slough isn't necessarily the same as what happens here in Guyana.'

'It's not Slough, it's Langley.'

'I don't care where it is. If you wear a tie people make a judgement.'

'About what?' I said.

'That you're a government spook.'

'Spook! I'm here to help.'

'Here to help! What are you? This isn't Comic Relief, you know.'

'I'm gathering data.'

'That's not what I've heard.'

'I'm researching the labour market.'

'You're stepping into a minefield!' Ellis put her bag on her shoulder. 'I need something to eat,' she said. 'We'll go to Renata's.'

'But...' She was already out of the door.

We left the hotel and walked along a dusty street, busy with early morning traffic. We passed a barber, a fashion retailer and a general store; all closed, their windows protected by bare metal bars.

Ellis moved fast. She had the stringy, pent-up energy of someone about to self-combust. A man staggered along the pavement and bumped into me. I apologised. He glared, and, without saying a word, wandered on.

'Mercury poisoning,' Ellis explained. 'It makes people unsteady on their feet.'

'How do you know?'

'You'll see lots of men like that. They get poisoned processing the gold. Brain damage, it's irreversible.'

'That's tough.'

'So,' she looked me up and down like an agricultural auctioneer assessing livestock, 'you're the Department's latest recruit.'

As we strode along the boardwalk I explained I didn't work for the Department of Development Overseas. I was merely a consultant, zooming in, doing the work and zooming out. Ellis laughed. That's exactly what DoDO had told her in 1996 and she was still here three years later. I was freelance, I said. 'That just means they pay you less.' The pay was good, I insisted. Ellis said I should wait until the money was in my pocket and then decide whether it was good or not. I assured her I was on a swift visit to Guyana and I'd be leaving as soon as I had the information I needed.

We entered Renata's through cowboy-style double-swing doors. Out front, the room was simply furnished, with wipe-clean tables and plastic chairs. Further inside, through an archway, there were scarlet velvet curtains and several softly-lit cubicles.

We sat by a window with a good view of the crowded street. 'Well, this is nice,' I said, surprised by the choice of venue. My work as a labour market researcher provides me with some interesting experiences – but rarely are these experiences as interesting as eating breakfast in a brothel.

'Best coffee in town,' said Ellis. 'Renata looks after me. I get less hassle here. The punters know what's what – they understand I'm off-limits.'

'How do they know?' I could see this was a strategy that could misfire.

'They can tell.' Ellis stared angrily at me. 'And if they don't, they learn quickly.'

Even though it was breakfast time, the personal services side of the business was doing a brisk trade. There was a steady stream of punters leaving the back rooms with a far-away post-coital look in their eyes.

Ellis passed me a stained menu. 'What do you want?'

'What do you recommend?'

'The eggs are good.'

'What sort of eggs?'

'Egg, eggs! What do you mean? You don't want quail's eggs or something la-di-da like that, do you?'

'I've gone off eggs. I'll have a toasted cheese sandwich.'

She winced. 'It'll be processed slices. The tropics aren't exactly famous for their range of fine cheeses.'

I felt uneasy as Ellis stared at me with her sharp, ice-blue eyes. The temperature was rising: it wasn't even 9.30 am and I was sweating like a bastard. I slid a finger between my neck and shirt-collar, trying to loosen my tie.

'So, Felix, what really brings you here?'

'As I said, I'm doing a report on the labour market.'

'That's not some cover for another shady enterprise, is it? It pisses me off when MI6 or the CIA exploit NGOs for their own grubby agendas. It gives genuine development a bad name.'

'I'm applying a new framework.'

'Oh yeah?' she said mockingly. 'Tell me about it.'

'It's about jobs and how people earn their money.'

Ellis laughed. 'Oh my God! No wonder they're not employing you. You're not going to live long enough to draw your first pay-cheque!'

'What do you mean?'

'This is Corriverton, man.'

'So?'

'Look out of the window. What do you see?'

The dirt road was noisy with mopeds, trucks, buses and four-wheel drives.

'I see everyday stuff – people going about their business.'

'Exactly. People going about their business. And it's no business of yours.' Now that Ellis pointed it out, Corriverton had a liveliness and energy I hadn't noticed in laid-back Georgetown. People were talking on the boardwalk, shaking hands, doing deals, shouting across the street.

'But people work here, don't they?'

'They're not going to tell you about it. Especially if you're a government spook wearing a tie.'

'Okay, I get the message.' I slipped off the tie, rolled it up and jammed it in my pocket. I felt better without it.

There was a smell of eggs being fried. Ellis looked at me and shook her head. I couldn't tell whether she was bemused or concerned. 'Felix, if that's really all you're here for, you are on one hell of a fool's errand.'

'So what's going on?'

Ellis took a tobacco tin from her bag and was silent for a moment as she concentrated on rolling a cigarette. Jimmy Cliff was playing on the juke box: Let Your Yeah Be Yeah. She gestured towards her tin. 'Help yourself.'

'No thanks. I gave up smoking rollies a long time ago.'

'Well, you don't live in Corriverton, do you?'

Ellis lit the cigarette and blew a thin stream of smoke into the air. 'Look, listen. As you may have noticed, Corriverton is a busy place. There's lots of money changing hands in the shops, bars and brothels, but no obvious industry – nobody seems to be ... to be working. Okay, you might think the money is being made up-country in the gold mines. Yeah, well, that's probably right, that's where the legendary land of El Dorado was said to be. But that's only part of the story. If you go down to the waterfront tonight you will see it's like a frigging regatta down there. Boats, all shapes and sizes, none of them with lights on, are scurrying over the river. In Corriverton, all you need is a rust-bucket that floats, the night vision of a cat and you're in business.'

I nodded. I was beginning to understand what Ellis was hinting at: what we economists call the informal economy.

'Across the River Corentyne is Suriname. It used to be a Dutch colony. It's now one of the most lawless countries in the world. Guns, drugs, gold, credit cards, women, parrots, you name it, are smuggled over the border. Corriverton is the black-market capital of Guyana – the smuggling highroad of South America. Contraband from Brazil, Colombia, Peru and Bolivia all comes through here.' Ellis paused, re-lit her tiny stub of a cigarette, and stared at me. 'Nobody is able to stop it. In truth, nobody wants to stop it. Certainly not the government. There's too much at stake.' Ellis wasn't doing much to dispel the Caribbean cliché of ganja and gangsters.

This news put an unexpected slant on my project. 'Gordon said you'd be able to show me where to find the statistics I need,' I said.

'Did he? Gordon's such a prick.'

'Do you have any data at all?'

'You really don't get it, do you?'

'I do,' I said. 'I understand. I'll keep a low profile.'

Ellis gave a despairing sigh. 'So what exactly are you after?'

'Information on the labour market. Supply and demand, skills, assessment of local prospects. That sort of thing.' Sitting in a bordello, it sounded an absurd thing to say.

'Oh man! You might as well start here at Renata's. Supply and demand, it's right in front of you. The women have got it. And the men want it. Go out the back and ask the girls about their skills. Combine work with pleasure.' She waggled her index finger provocatively. 'You might learn something.'

The waitress, thin and uninterested, brought our food. Ellis had two fried eggs on a bare white plate. I pulled my dried toast apart to check the contents – a mastic paste difficult to identify as a dairy product.

'What did I tell you?' said Ellis.

She looked over her shoulder before leaning forward. 'Okay Felix,' she whispered, 'we need to cut the bullshit and get down to business.'

'Yeah?' Oh God! I thought. She knows. She knows about Gordon's crazyometer questions.

'So when's the ...,' she cleared her throat, '... the hardware arriving?'

'The hardware?'

'Keep your voice down.'

'I don't know anything about hardware.'

'The shipment. That's why you're really here, isn't it?'

'I've told you, I'm in Corriverton to gather statistics.'

'Yeah, and deliver hardware.'

'Ellis, when you say hardware, can you be a bit more specific?'

She bent closer – our foreheads were almost touching. 'Computers,' Ellis whispered.

I was relieved. She wasn't aware of the crazyometer, after all.

'Why do people keep on asking me about computers? I know nothing about sodding computers.'

'That's why you're in Corriverton. Everybody knows that.'

'Everybody! Who is everybody? Everybody except me! What's going on? Who told you about computers?'

'Several weeks ago I heard a man from DoDO would be delivering some computers.'

'Heard from whom?'

'On the grapevine. Whispers everywhere.'

'They must be talking about somebody else.'

'There is nobody else. You're the first person from DoDO to visit for months.'

'I know nothing about computers, I swear.'

'Are you sure?'

'Of course I'm sure. I was only told to come to Corriverton a couple of days ago.'

'I heard about your planned visit at least a month ago.'

'It's not me.'

'They mentioned you by name.'

'They can't have done. I only signed up for the project just over a month ago.'

'It was definitely you.'

'Who mentioned me?'

'I don't know! I can't remember. It was probably an email from DoDO HQ.'

'This is a case of mistaken identity. There must be another Radstock. It's not an unusual name,' I added.

'You're the first Radstock I've ever met.'

'It depends where you come from. In Somerset every other person is called Radstock. It's almost as common a name as Smith or Brown or Gummidge.'

'What's your contract say?' Ellis asked.

'I haven't seen my contract yet. I'm just zooming in and zooming out.'

'You ought to read it. Maybe there are other things you don't know about. Other trips.'

'What else did they say about me?'

'Depends who you speak to.'

'So?'

'Some said you were travelling round Guyana. That you'd be coming here and then going up-country to Linden.'

I leant back, reassured. 'That's definitely not me. I'm staying in Georgetown.'

'Yeah, so what are you doing here, in Corriverton?'

'It's a mistake. I'm not supposed to be here. And Linden? I've never heard of the place.'

Ellis shook her head. 'I can't believe I have to explain this. Linden is on the edge of the bush. It's a quiet little mining town, though there's plans to build a road to Manaus in Brazil. That'll shake things up.'

'No chance! I'm banned from venturing into the bush. At the moment Gordon is more concerned about things back in London. He wants me out of Guyana as soon as possible.'

The juke box was now silent and the back-room business had slowed. Apart from a lone man, legs stretched out, languidly smoking a cigarette, Renata's was empty. Ellis sat back in her ketchup-red plastic chair and folded her arms.

'Look, it's just a rumour. Ignore it,' she said.

'Ignore it! You've got me worried.' Traffic hummed on the street outside, footsteps click-clacked on the boardwalk.

Ellis continued: 'Others said this person – who is definitely not you

– would be dead within twenty-four hours of arriving in Corriverton.'

'What! Ellis, I don't like these rumours. I don't like them at all. Dead! You're trying to scare me, right?'

When I studied the Quantitative Research Methodology option in Lecture Theatre 4D18 at Bristol Polytechnic, the curriculum was about sampling, the standard curve of deviation and regression analysis. There was no talk, not even the tiniest mention, of threats of violence. Or, I swallowed at the thought, murder.

'Pay no attention,' she said.

'I am. You bet I am. I'm ignoring all this, completely.'

'They were talking about somebody else.' Ellis's voice softened. 'Relax, Felix,' she said as if she was calming an anxious child. 'I'm sure you're right. There're lots of people round here called Radstock. I just haven't yet come across any of them.'

TWO

There may be a few other small tasks.

I'd received the call a month before.

Winter had come early. It was a dark Friday afternoon in mid October and I was eager to go to the pub. The phone kept ringing – I eventually answered. A man who spoke in a charming yet detached voice said his name was Gordon Lewis and he wanted to know if I could help him with a project his department was undertaking.

To speed up the conversation I'd answered yes, yes, and yes, to all of his questions.

'Well, that all seems okay,' said Gordon, 'you sound like just the person we're looking for. Would you be available to fly to Guyana in two weeks' time?'

It was the sort of job with a sizeable income I'd been dreaming of. The Department of Development Overseas (DoDO) would pay me more in a day than I currently earned in a week. At this stage I wasn't entirely clear what the work entailed, but I accepted the assignment anyway.

'It'll take a fortnight, maximum,' said Gordon. 'We'll give you an open ticket. If you finish early you can grab a plane back to the UK.'

I put the phone down. 'Where's Guyana?' I asked Adge, my assistant.

'Africa.'

'Are you sure?'

'Why?'

'I'm flying there is two weeks time.'

Adge wasn't impressed. 'I wouldn't go there, man.'

'What do you know about Guyana?' Adge had never been further than the Tropicana Leisure Centre at Weston-super-Mare.

The dial-up modem was intermittent, so that evening I opened an atlas and searched for Guyana. I scanned the pages on Africa, I decided West Africa was its most likely location, but eventually tracked it down to South America.

By some quirk, Guyana is classified as being part of the Caribbean. For a moment I was excited, I thought of rum and reggae. And I was pleased to read they spoke English – the only English-speaking country on the continent. The one name on the map I recognised was Demerara. So that's where the moist brown sugar I put on my porridge comes from. Further research was not so encouraging. Away from the coast there are no towns, just untamed rainforest, and rather than an azure sea fringed by white sandy beaches, Guyana's shoreline is a sluggish mud bath with mosquito-ridden mangrove swamps. Down the coast was the infamous French prison, Devil's Island.

Even so, in my current circumstances, a visit to Guyana suited me just fine. The money was good but, more importantly, Aurora and I needed time to sort ourselves out. Although we'd been living together for two years, I sensed something in our relationship was shifting.

A couple of months before, for no particular reason - it was a Friday night in 1999, with Top of the Pops and TFI Friday on the TV – we had both got deliciously drunk and stoned. We ordered take-away curries, went to bed, got up again, emptied a bottle of duty-free Thai vodka I had found in a cupboard under the stairs, and painted our faces with Nutella. We howled and moaned as we tried to lick each other clean.

Then I did something surprising. Aurora didn't understand at first.

'What did you say?' she said.

Wrapped together on the sofa, I had asked Aurora to marry me.

Well, I thought I asked her to marry me. The next morning as we changed the bed-sheets, cleared away bottles, roaches, and foil containers, I wondered if I'd made the whole thing up. Had I muddled it with the video, some Nora Ephron fluff-buster Aurora wanted us to watch? I didn't mention the proposal again. Neither did she.

This trip was an opportunity to figure things out; time apart would, I hoped, strengthen our love.

Over the following days Gordon, who said he operated from Langley, filled me in on the project.

'Langley? Washington?' I asked. 'Isn't that where the CIA is based?'

'No, it's Langley, Slough.'

'Slough?'

'Yes, Slough. By the M4, under the Heathrow flight-path.'

'Ah.'

'I understand you have a framework,' said Gordon. 'Is it cross-continental?'

'It should be, so long as the host country adheres to the international standards. Of course, I'll have to tweak some of the variables, but it should be compatible.' In truth, I wasn't sure the Radstock Framework© fully functioned in the UK, let alone overseas.

'Good. Go to Georgetown, get the information, do your forecasting or whatever you do, and zoom out again. There may be a few other small tasks, but I'll tell you about them once you're in Guyana.'

'It would be useful to know in advance what these tasks are.' I was swimming in deep water already. I feared additional activities could well pull me under.

'Certainly, I will give you plenty of warning.'

'I can then prepare the relevant information.'

'Of course. Quick and dirty, that's what we want.'

Quick and dirty was okay by me.

Gordon was more interested in my clothes than anything else. 'You'll need a light suit and you must always wear a tie. The Guyanese respect a man in a tie. And a hat. You can get a very good Panama over there. I will arrange for a hatter to come to your hotel.'

'I'm not a hat wearer.'

'Are you crazy? It's over 100 degrees in the shade.'

'I'll need more than a hat, then.'

Gordon recommended mefloquine as an effective anti-malarial – it didn't interact with alcohol and would help me sleep and get over jet-lag. He said I should take vitamin C. You could prepare your mind, it's more difficult, however, to control what happens to your body. Was there anything else I needed to know?

'I'm not sure,' I said. 'Do they have the right data? I'll send you a list of what I require.'

'Don't bother,' he said. 'On your first day, you will have a meeting with the Minister and his colleagues. They will organise everything. DoDO is providing a vehicle for your sole use and a logistics coordinator will be at your disposal.'

'Logistics coordinator?'

'That's what Human Resources call drivers these days. More kudos but paid the same. I will arrange for you to receive comprehensive briefing papers when you arrive.'

My preliminary investigations on the web uncovered little useful information. The Cooperative Republic of Guyana had an undeveloped homepage with links that led nowhere. The UK Foreign Office offered the usual warnings about being bitten by mosquitoes, dangerously erratic driving, and the need to always travel with doors locked and windows closed. The CIA World Factbook listed pages of statistics, several years out of date, indicating high levels of poverty, chronic infrastructure problems and crippling external debt – 'all signs', it warned, 'of a failing, third world country with socialist leanings'.

'Shouldn't I have a letter of introduction or something?' I asked Gordon.

He roared like a madman. 'You've been reading too much Graham

Greene.'

I felt painfully unprepared, but hung onto Gordon's assertion that all the figures I needed would be available in Georgetown.

On the day before my departure Gordon phoned to go through the final details. What sort of ties would I be taking? Silk was best in high temperatures – though susceptible to being eaten by voracious tropical moths. And did I know how to tie a Windsor knot? An invitation to the British embassy might be on the cards. Gordon had also arranged my hat fitting. I wondered what century this guy was living in? It certainly didn't sound like 1999.

'Bring US dollars with you, the Guyanese currency is less than worthless. You need a wallet-full of notes just to buy a good claret. Mind you, I'm told Georgetown is a nice little place. It's like a Caribbean Isle of Wight, but with guns. If you look after yourself and take precautions, you'll enjoy it. Between you and me I'm rather envious. The Guyanese are a hospitable people – the women are convivial and the cuisine is spicy. Try the rotis: they're the best in the Caribbean. I would have done this work myself, but with the millennium coming up I'm crashing on deadlines.'

Gordon's final comment unsettled me.

'Oh, Felix,' he said casually, 'if you get into any serious difficulties, we can always fly you out.'

Several times over the next few weeks I would find myself pondering the significance of this remark.

Aurora was too busy working on the illustrations for her latest book, Beautiful Butterflies of Wessex, to see me off at Heathrow. 'Nobody does that these days,' she said as we kissed goodbye. She'd recently dyed her blonde hair black and had taken to using heavy eyeliner.

I promised I would be back before Christmas.

'Watch out for snakes,' she warned.

'It's a business trip. I'll be stuck in an office.'

'Okay, watch out for spiders, then.'

We laughed and hugged. She said she couldn't make me out, she could never guess what I was thinking. I looked into her china-blue eyes and felt sad, as if I was going away for a long time and losing something.

'I love you,' I said as she closed the door.

THREE

The Radstock Framework© is born.

Perhaps I ought to explain how the Radstock Framework© came about. As a youth I'd been aggressively unambitious. Until my parents moved to the London suburb of Ruislip I had lived in a remote village on a hill overlooking the Somerset Levels. I had a quiet but happy childhood: bike rides across the Levels, fishing for pike, fighting florid-faced farmer boys and hiding in garden sheds with eager girls. I attended the local school, a Victorian red brick building with a single echoing classroom divided down the middle by a dusty curtain, and was taught by severe spinster ladies who smelled of lavender powder and wore long floral dresses and Clarks sandals. I achieved average marks, but excelled in Maths. Maths was the one constant in my life and my world. I dreamed in a private language of numbers. I may have counted on my fingers, but I could do one hundred multiplications in a minute. I loved to explore how numbers fitted together – I got lost in the figures; I saw patterns and colours and music. Nobody else in my school seemed to get that.

I spent many hours staring out of my bedroom window across the isolated moors, which shimmered green in the summer and flooded in the winter. For a treat, Sunday tea was Shipham's meat paste on Hovis bread while we watched Great Expectations on a black and white television the size of a grocery box.

The highlight of my year was the visit to the Bridgwater Carnival, an extraordinary parade of carts lit with as many light-bulbs as a generator would allow without blowing up. The climax of the festival was the sinister squibbing – a row of macabre sack-clothed men ignited hand-held home-made fireworks. There was no shortage of gunpowder: it wasn't a coincidence there was a government ordnance (bomb) factory nearby. Mishaps were common. There were frequent low-grade amputations. For the local youths it was seen as a badge of honour to lose one of your least useful pinkies.

My parents, CND beatniks who, incongruously, hated jazz, worked on a small-holding growing withies for basket-making. We were jumble-sale poor, but rabbit pie and farmhouse cheese was always on the table. Dad told me contentment was the thing to strive for – happiness was fleeting, and riches inevitably brought misery. To please him I thought I might become a monk, a saddhu or holy man, something like that. But the rigours of the ascetic life put me off and, besides, I didn't believe in any God.

I was about sixteen when the inevitable happened and the withy business ground to a moneyless halt. 'We can't compete with cheap foreign imports,' Dad explained. Why my parents chose to move to Middlesex wasn't made clear. I never asked. Though I did feel it wasn't a good idea.

In Middlesex I felt anonymous, part of nothing. I couldn't get the lie of the land. Where were the castles and churches and abbeys of Somerset? Where were the myths of Avalon? Where was the zodiac landscape of Glastonbury or the Christmas flowering cherry tree? I craved a sense of place. In Ruislip, row upon row of semi-detached houses concealed any hint of the past. There was no fable or poetry in this miserable suburbia, just a nowhereland where nothing happened.

I wandered between education and temporary jobs. I thought of work as entertainment, to be watched from a distance. It wasn't really anything to do with me. Money? I lived on a student grant, signed on at the Benefit Office and pulled pints on the side. This provided enough cash for a roof over my head, a drink and a smoke to help me relax.

For over a decade I did exactly what I wanted, steering clear of life-changing decisions, giving the finger to the Man. I was a Zen master of procrastination. I got drunk, took drugs, had one-night stands with women I hardly knew, and never tidied up. It seemed to me the perfect work-life balance was 25 years of youth and pleasure, then 25 years of work and bringing up a family, followed by a final 25 years of fun.

But five years ago I hit a turning point. I can remember the moment well. I was twenty-eight, and three years overdue for the big shift. Hung-over and grubby, my shirt torn and my wallet missing, I walked along Nelson Street in Bristol. My brain felt desiccated and my breath reeked of sour cider. I no longer enjoyed my unfettered, drifting life. Recently, while drinking pints of rough in the Long Bar in Old Market, I'd had an existential revelation. I'd realised it was me who was out of step, and the world wasn't going to come round to my point of view. As I stumbled down that dirty street, past fly-posted walls and rough-sleepers in piss-stinking doorways, I knew something had to change. If I didn't get my act together I could be one of those doorway dossers, struggling to live even half a life.

So it was time to straighten out and get a job. A proper job, a secure job, a job with prospects and a contributory pension fund. As for bringing up a family, once I'd got a job, I reckoned a visit to the registry office would follow shortly afterwards.

But a position with prospects, how do you get that? How do you choose? Selecting a suitable career could be a full-time occupation in itself. I might not have liked work, but I did enjoy talking about it. I knew I wasn't suited to robust outdoor labour, so I got my hair cut, bought a jacket from Next and became a careers adviser.

At that time there was a national shortage of careers advisers, so I was offered a bursary to pay for my training. It was a generous grant, more money than I'd ever received from the Benefit Office. I studied for nine months at one of the new Polytechnics and then secured employment in a small cathedral city in the West Country, which, for legal reasons, I'm not allowed to name.

I was employed by a local government department. The conditions were modest – I received a small but regular salary, I was signed up to a pension scheme, and every morning, at eleven o'clock, a mug of milky coffee and a Rich Tea biscuit was put on my desk. ¬

One of my tasks was to visit a remote comprehensive school, deep in the nearby forest. The woodland community was isolated and suspicious of strangers – there were murmurs of cousin coupling and Romany slavery. Local career opportunities were limited to tending sheep or working in the drift mines – little more than fox holes in the hillside. Few young people wanted, or had the sense, to move away.

There was a code I wasn't privy to. I noticed nods and winks from the foresters. I bought a Mini car which broke down a day later – the roadside repair man said the radiator had been filled with porridge to stop it leaking. I moved into a house with pigeons in the loft, rats in the cellar and a poltergeist that slammed doors and knocked ornaments off the mantelpiece in the still dead of night. I felt constantly ripped off, short-changed and never given the full story.

And it didn't take long for all this talking about work to begin to rattle my nerves. I felt a fraud encouraging people into a consumerist existence I didn't subscribe to. Day in, day out – even using my newly learnt open-question techniques, I went through the same conversations.

'So why do you like the idea of this job?'

'Coz it's interesting.'

'And why is it interesting?

'Coz I likes it.'

Round and round it went. I noticed there was a crucial element missing in careers advice. It was blindingly obvious. Careers advisers talked about the content of work, but not the context. What people really want to know, is where are the jobs? How many jobs are there? And what are the jobs of the future? Surely there was a mathematical solution to this? I looked at sources of data and current projections. As I studied these figures I began to see patterns and shapes and stories.

Over the following weeks I experimented with government statistics and developed a data model and a basic forecasting framework – largely built on a doubtful predictive tool developed by a team of Dutch social scientists – about how the labour market worked. It was an achingly slow process. After a few months I ran a trial of the projections. I matched my predicted numbers for the construction industry in the South West of England with current Job Centre vacancies. To my delight, the metrics were right and the forecast was spot on. I then did the same for jobs in the hotel and catering sector. Again, my figures for supply and demand (labour market churn) were right on the nail. The numbers were singing, it was like a choir of heavenly voices. I couldn't understand why somebody hadn't come up with this before. The Radstock Framework© was born and I had my own niche specialism.

My employers were impressed by the financial potential of the Framework and employed me as a Labour Force Planning Executive. I planned away to perfection and for the first time in my life I felt motivated, doing something both creative and useful. With the help of a generous grant from the European Commission I was shunted into a corner of County Hall and left to develop the concept.

I was contracted to undertake assessment and forecasting by Chambers of Commerce, Training and Enterprise Councils and other dubious quangos that had more money than good judgement. None of my bosses knew what I did, and they didn't like to expose their ignorance by asking.

Of course, there was great interest among social scientists in the framework. The Journal of Development Economics and the Journal of International Development asked for articles, but even now, four years later, they haven't as yet published them. These academic journals take a long time to go to print. Several universities asked for in-depth details, which I wasn't about to give. You can't copyright a theory – I was going to hang onto this little cash cow and milk it until its udders hurt.

In the end, the local government auditors felt uneasy with a department generating income rather than spending it. The Public Sector making money! It didn't fit within local government philosophy. So my work was put out to tender. Of course, nobody else had the formula, so I was able to buy it back for a peppercorn sum and set up my own company.

People said I should have made heaps of cash, but somehow it never happened and the initial excitement of those early days soon wore off. Now, as I approached my mid-thirties, I'd run out of dreams. After my bungled proposal to Aurora, even that road to the registry office was proving to be rockier than anticipated. To be honest, I wasn't feeling too optimistic about my future. A nagging sense of ennui had crept into my daily existence, my life seemed to have stopped and beautiful things felt just out of reach.

FOUR

As quiet as a country under curfew.

I flew by Virgin Atlantic to Barbados, and then with some smaller airline to Trinidad. Crossing the Atlantic felt like an eternity as I watched the plane's progress plotted on the little TV screen in front of me. Thirty-five thousand feet up, with the nearest land a thousand miles in any direction, I had the unsettling thought that I was just a few rivets and thin aluminium sheets away from oblivion.

The plane was crammed with young and beautiful people heading, I guessed, to the exclusive Sandy Lane resort on Barbados. These over-privileged brats acted like they were already on holiday as they swallowed cocktails and hoorayed across the aisles.

My one-hour journey from Bridgetown to Trinidad was quieter. I'd left the holiday pack behind; the aircraft was sparsely filled with passengers nervously clutching overflowing carrier bags and cardboard boxes.

I was concerned that I had little idea why I was flying to Guyana and what I was going to do when I got there. I'd been so busy arranging visas, anti-malarial tablets, asthma inhalers and suitable neckwear and giving firm instructions to Adge on watering the Swiss cheese plant, that I'd had little time to consider my plan of action and do initial groundwork for meetings. I hadn't seen any briefing papers, let alone signed a contract.

I ordered another bottle of screw-top wine and stared out of the window into the dark, and reassured myself matters would become clear as soon as I got to Georgetown.

I daydreamed and thought of Aurora: her awesomely curvaceous body and her wide, luminous smile. The first time I met her in Bristol

Zoo, nearly two years before, there had been a blizzard. It was a snowy February afternoon and, despite the cold, she was wearing a long, Indian cotton dress.

In the warmth of the tropical house, a large turquoise butterfly, a South American Morpho, fluttered about her outstretched arm. The butterfly landed on her hand but quickly took off again. It circled and re-settled on her palm. It was a serene moment; I'd never experienced anything like it. I swear all the animals went quiet. The room freeze-framed while I walked in the stillness towards her, intending to speak. But I could see from her intense blue eyes she didn't want to be disturbed.

Later that afternoon I spotted Aurora, her Nordic blonde hair pulled back in a pony-tail, drawing in a sketchbook in the zoo cafe.

I stood by her table. 'The butterflies like you. Is it your perfume?' I asked.

'Most people are too impatient. You have to be still and let them get used to you.'

I didn't bump into Aurora again for a while. I'd visit the tropical house every week hoping she'd be there - her calm, fragrant presence attracting those tropical jewels.

At Port of Spain, while I waited for my final connection, I talked to a well-juiced Canadian. He'd worked in a mine in the Amazon rainforest. 'There's a gold rush. And everything that goes with it - booze, prostitutes and violence. The land is up for grabs. It's out of control and dangerous,' he said.

'Tell me about Georgetown,' I asked.

He was silent for a moment. 'I only got to view it from the back of a cab.'

'And Guyana?'

He smiled. 'They have a national pastime. It's called 'liming'.'

'Liming?'

'Hanging out. Man, they take chilling to another level.' He gave a muted laugh. 'Chat and chill, that's what they do all day – lime.'

'It's a pity I'll be too busy to join them.'

'Watch out for the rainforest. It's a freaky place – you come face to face with your inner self. It can be disturbing. Just drink the hooch and go with the flow. Don't fight it.'

From Port of Spain we flew over the Orinoco delta to Cheddi Jagan International Airport, the airport for Georgetown. The pilot was an Indiana Jones type I'd spotted earlier knocking back shots of rum.

The jet engines shrieked as the plane shuddered to a halt on what felt like a dangerously short runway.

'Welcome to South America,' the steward said.

I stood at the top of the steps and breathed in the night air. It was thick and humid with the sweet taste of composting vegetation. I wanted to change into lighter clothes.

Apart from a few yawning officials, the Arrivals Hall was empty. I'd been flying for thirty eight hours across numerous time zones. I had no idea what time it was, but it felt late. I stood in silence by the luggage belt. I could hear the fizz of the strip lights.

'Excuse me, how far is it to Georgetown?' I asked a man in uniform who appeared to be overseeing the baggage collection.

'Georgetown?' The man rolled his eyes. 'At this hour?'

'Is there somewhere here to stay?'

He pointed at a wooden bench. 'You can sleep there. But it is not recommended.'

I'd given up sleeping on benches a few years ago. 'How long does it take to get to Georgetown?'

'It depends. An hour, maybe two. It is not far.'

'Depends on what?'

'Whether the Demerara is in flood. Last year was El Niño. We had very hot weather and torrential rain.'

Before leaving England, I had visited Stanfords travel bookshop to buy some guide books. I thumbed through Lonely Planets and Rough Guides. There was scant mention of Guyana. One guide was diplomatically non-committal, saying that '...there is little to see. Just being there is an experience.' It finished by advising 'it is best not to arrive at night time.'

I was now the last person standing by the conveyor belt which had come to a halt.

'That's it. No more bags,' said the official.

'Where's my case?'

'Come back tomorrow.'

'Tomorrow?'

'It'll be here.'

'I need it now.' All I had with me was my shoulder bag containing my passport, wallet, a book called Under the Volcano and a multi-pack of giant Toblerone bars.

'We're closed.'

'Wait.' I was feeling disorientated and unusually anxious. 'I need clean clothes. I want my wash bag. I have to take my anti-malarial pills.'

'Tomorrow', the official said over his shoulder as he walked away.

Actually, I'd half anticipated this. With all the flight changes it would have been a miracle if my luggage had kept up with me.

I left the terminal and walked outside into the roar of a sticky tropical night. It sounded like the dry squeak of a thousand rusty doors. Mammals? Insects? Amphibians? Whatever animals were making this racket, there were a lot of them.

Despite what I'd been told, the taxi driver assured me the road to Georgetown was passable – the river bank had collapsed, but the flood level was lower now and God willing we would be okay.

I don't know what I was expecting. Even so, my initial moonlit impression of Guyana came as a surprise. The streets were deserted and the single storey shacks dark. It was as quiet as a country under curfew. The driver negotiated his way at frightening speed around potholes, cattle, stray dogs and the occasional car coming directly at us. We passed a factory of silos and twisted pipes that looked like an oil refinery. 'Demerara Distillers', the taxi driver explained. 'Twelve-year-old rum. Very, very good. You must buy a bottle.'

We parked in the courtyard of the Stabroek Lodge alongside a trio of black Toyota Land Cruisers. As I paid the taxi driver I asked him what made the chorus of noise in the night. He cocked his head and listened as if he'd never heard it before.

'I think it is the car engine,' he said.

FIVE

Hat fitting at this hour?

The buzz of the phone by my bedside woke me. Early morning light shone through the window slats. I looked at my clock. 6.00 am.

'My name is Roxy, Welcome to Guyana.'

Was this Gordon's idea of a joke? My hat fitting at this hour? I couldn't think straight. I'd had just two hours' uneasy sleep.

'I'm sorry, I'm very tired,' I said politely.

'I offer the best service in Georgetown,' she said in an oddly seductive tone.

'I'm glad to hear that. Please call me later.'

'I will call you when you are more wide awake, Mr Radstock.'

'Thank you. Oh, by the way, my size is seven and a quarter.'

'Is that in English or French?'

'English, I think.'

I heard her laugh. I put the phone down and lay spread-eagled on my bed, sweating. How complicated could it be to fit a hat? I only wanted to sleep.

The Stabroek Lodge, with its gables and balconies and louvered blinds, was built in the colonial style. Once the private house of a ballerina, it had a wide, elegant staircase, polished teak floors and bug-proof rattan furniture. It was quiet now, but I could imagine the sound of dance and music once echoed around its spacious rooms. Apart from its green tin roof, every inch of the four-storey building was made of wood and at night, as I had discovered, it creaked and groaned like a tall ship under sail in heavy weather.

As I ate my breakfast of tropical fruits and a very large, blue-white hard-boiled egg, I looked out over a garden crammed with fleshy leaved plants and striking quartz pink blooms. A tiny opalescent hummingbird flitted from flower to flower using its needle-thin tongue to drink nectar.

My logistics coordinator arrived to take me to the Ministry. A handsome African-Caribbean man, tall and lean, he was immaculately dressed in a crisp blue and white striped cotton shirt, sharp trousers and shiny black shoes. He was standing beside a white four-wheel-drive. I was pleased I would be travelling in some style.

'Mr Radstock,' he said with a bright smile, 'Xavier Yolando Zeeland at your service.'

These days, I find it increasingly difficult to judge age – I reckoned he was older than me, perhaps thirty-eight. His hand was soft and he smelled strongly of spicy aftershave.

'Pleased to meet you Mr Zeeland.' He stared at me with his keen ebony eyes, as if searching for some secret. I was concerned he might find one.

'Please call me Xavier. My job is to support you in every way I can. For the duration of your visit I will constantly be at your side. If there is anything you want,' he said, giving me a wink, 'anything at all, you must let me know.'

'Do you have my briefing papers?' I said.

'I expect DoDO will have emailed them to you.'

'I'd like to see if they've arrived.'

Xavier glanced at his watch. 'We haven't got time. We're booked to see the Minister at ten.'

'I'm not fully clear about my operational strategy.'

'The Minister cannot be kept waiting. I'm sure, at this stage,' Xavier said reassuringly, 'a standard paradigm will suffice.'

'Good idea,' I said. I was impressed by Xavier's knowledgeable recommendation. 'Yes, a standard paradigm, I'll go with that.'

This was my first opportunity to see Georgetown in the daylight.

The roads were laid out in a grid. Alongside many of the streets were drainage ditches, some big enough to be canals. The limpid water was covered by delicate ivory-coloured lilies. The wooden houses with their sagging balconies, had an agreeable, washed-out belle époque feel. Built on stilts and set back from the road behind green lawns, I liked the look of them.

We drove alongside an embankment, perhaps twenty feet high, with a candy-striped red and white lighthouse on it. 'That's the sea-wall. The ocean is on the other side. It is a popular place for families to walk in the evening.' Xavier spoke with a precise BBC World Service accent. He had a lightness of manner that concealed, I was beginning to realise, a deep intelligence.

Despite the grid pattern of the streets I soon lost my sense of direction. We drove by the overgrown botanical garden, its grand iron gates locked and rusting. A flock of lime-green parakeets skittered from tree to tree. Xavier pointed out the cricket ground, 'the legendary Clive Lloyd's home turf,' and an interesting round, thatched building the size of a circus tent. 'The Umana Yana, a replica of a traditional Amerindian hut, called a benab,' Xavier explained. 'It is used for Amerindian Conventions. It makes the tribal people feel at home.'

We passed Shanta's Roti Shop, 'the best traditional Guyanese food in Georgetown, if not the country,' the Hibiscus, 'good outdoor seating,' and then we were in the vicinity of the Stabroek Market, an area busy with workshops and stalls. The covered market, a vast hangar-like building of iron and corrugated steel, painted cream and rust, was topped by an incongruously large clock. The surrounding roads were swarming with people and vans. There was shouting and loud music – the air was filled with the smell of fruit and exhaust fumes.

Xavier's driving skills were impressive as he weaved in and out of the unpredictable traffic and the ruts in the road. The car's air conditioning kicked in – for the first time since I'd arrived in Guyana

I felt able to think clearly.

Xavier appeared to know everybody. He slowed down outside ramshackle cafes and shouted greetings, pointing at me and laughing. At one junction Xavier lowered the window, reached out and shook hands with a dreadlocked man wearing wrap-around Super Fly shades and sitting in a 1950s American car.

'That was Eddie Grant.' Xavier said as if this would mean something to me. 'He says he likes our wheels.'

'Eddie Grant?'

'He was in The Equals, he's now a very successful record producer.'

Come to think of it I had heard of The Equals. They'd had some hits in the sixties. In those days Eddie Grant had a dyed blonde afro. Later – it was all coming back to me now – he rinsed his hair, grew dreads and re-invented himself as a British Bob Marley singing 'Living on the Front Line' and 'Electric Avenue', pseudo-revolutionary songs about Brixton.

'I thought Eddie Grant was English,' I said.

'English! He's my cousin.'

People looked up from their work and stared at our car, trying to see who was inside.

'This Land Rover Discovery is unique in Georgetown. They think you are someone important,' Xavier said.

'Maybe I am,' I replied.

Xavier looked at me and gave a condescending smile.

'Yeah, man.'

After half an hour of zigzagging across Georgetown – G.T. as Xavier called it – we drew up outside a large, shuttered wooden building. A peeling sign said this was the Ministry of Employment.

As I was getting out of the car, Xavier handed me a cloth.

'Mr Radstock,' he said in his best authoritarian English accent, 'can you clean the windscreen, please.'

Xavier squirted the washers. I wiped the glass.

'Okay?' I said.

'On your side, there is a greasy patch.' Xavier pointed to an area of the windscreen that seemed perfectly clean.

'It's fine,' I said.

'No, there is a smear,' Xavier insisted.

'Where?'

'There,' he said pointing.

'I can't see anything.'

'You can only see it from the inside. You must rub harder,' Xavier said, carefully adjusting a St Christopher medallion that hung from the rear-view mirror.

'Okay, that is good. Now the rear window.' Xavier waved at an armed security guard standing at the entrance to the Ministry.

I was getting hot. 'Perhaps you could do this, while I'm with the Minister.'

'We want the car to be spotless, Mr Radstock. Everyone is looking. It is important for you to create a good impression.'

SIX

Don't go into the interior.

I was shown into an empty waiting room where I could hear the murmur of voices. The floorboards creaked with every step I made. I didn't sit - both the chairs where splattered with what looked like bird shit. I stood and listened to what was being said in the next room - or tried: the words were indistinct. The incessant tone seemed serious, there was no laughter, and at one stage what sounded like a fist banged a table several times.

I studied a Bartholomew's wall-map, the first detailed large-scale map I'd seen of Guyana. I examined it with interest, standing on tip-toe to read some of the smaller italicised names. Guyana is a lozenge-shaped country, bordered to the east by Suriname, to the south by Brazil and to the west by Venezuela. To the north it has an Atlantic shore, which is broken by a number of rivers – the Demerara and the Essequibo being the largest. Where the Caribbean came into all this I couldn't see.

What this map didn't show was how hot and sticky this tiny country was. I wanted to feel comfortable talking to the Minister and his team – but my collar was too tight and a fine rime of sweat was already forming on my forehead. There was a shuffling noise above me. A bird, the size of a pigeon, with a brilliant Van Gogh-yellow chest, was eyeing me from a rafter.

Guyana is an isolated country, rarely visited by outsiders, and really only accessible via the coast. What struck me looking at the map was the lack of paved roads. A highway ran along part of the coast, otherwise there was just one road, as straight as a rod, that led inland and came to an abrupt halt after 150 miles. The interior was either impenetrable, uncharted, rainforest or remote savannah reachable only by plane. The map showed a number of grass landing-strips – useful, I guessed, for the transport of small, high-value goods. Otherwise, there was a dendritic sprawl of rivers, largely un-navigable because of perilous rapids and waterfalls.

I'd been waiting twenty minutes and wondered if I'd been forgotten. I looked up at the yellow-chested bird. It didn't seem to like my stare and with a rustle of its wings flew out of the window.

It seemed the majority of Guyana's population lived along the coastal strip. A text box at the bottom of the map gave a brief historical outline. The land was annexed by the Dutch West India Company and then came under British rule in 1815, due to a treaty at the end of the Napoleonic Wars. Guyana eventually achieved independent rule in 1966 – the same year, I seem to remember, that Ian Smith established his white supremacist Independent Republic of Rhodesia.

At last, after half an hour, I was invited into the boardroom. The green, yellow and red national flag was pinned to a wall, otherwise the white painted room was bare. A dozen men, eleven of whom were formally dressed in dark suits, were sitting round a large mahogany table. The twelfth man, a vast, physically imposing individual wearing a vividly- patterned orange and yellow African dashiki, introduced himself as Doctor Professor Lucas, the Minister of Employment. He had the most impressive weightlifter's shoulders I'd ever seen – his neck muscles appeared to go up to his ears.

'Now, what is it you are going to do for us?' said Lucas. He spoke with a deep, resonant voice that required you to sit up straight and pay attention. I noticed his hands, vast water-melon fists, the hands of a land worker not a bureaucrat.

Seeing this group of unsmiling men made me conscious of how unprepared I was for my assignment. I was glad I was wearing my tie.

'What would you like me to do?'

'You are the expert who has travelled all the way from London, you tell us.'

'My full instructions from DoDO are due to follow,' I replied.

A slight and earnest eager-looking young man sitting to Lucas's right spoke. 'Mr Zeeland has been appointed as your logistics coordinator and aide. He has been instructed to do all he can to help you. He is a good fellow. The best, in fact.' I'm sure I heard one of the twelve men – I wasn't sure which – give a muted chuckle.

'So what is your strategy?' Lucas asked.

'I'm working on it. After an initial assessment I will need to make some adjustments to the standard paradigm,' I said, remembering Xavier's suggestion.

'You have a standard paradigm?'

'Yes, of course. It's based on a complex forecasting framework I've personally developed.' I hoped that might shut him up.

'I see. So what do you need from us?'

'Perhaps I can speak to your Office for Statistics.'

'I am sure they can supply you with all the figures you require.'

'Do you have age, gender and ethnic breakdowns? I'm assuming your figures comply with the International Labour Organisation's classification standards?'

'You will find our statistical data both rigorous and scientifically proven,' said Lucas in a manner that intimated there was no more to be said.

The men smiled; a couple of them clapped. I nodded and grinned in acknowledgement. This was going far better than I had expected. I imagined the surprise on Aurora's face (or, oh my God, shock) when I returned home early.

'Thank you. I appreciate that,' I said.

Lucas shrugged his massive shoulders. 'We are a hospitable country but it is best you do not go into the interior.'

'I will have no need to leave Georgetown,' I assured him.

'Mr Radstock, you must understand some areas are restricted.

Ever since Reverend Jim Jones set up his community we have been wary of supporting settlers going up-country. People become intoxicated by the bush. They hallucinate – they think they are talking to God. And we all know what happens when people think they are talking to God. Reverend Jones thought he was talking with God. But it was the devil he was communicating with. The bush may look like the Garden of Eden but visitors soon find existence is hard, and either return broken-hearted or drink poisoned Kool-Aid. To put it bluntly, they go up-country and they go bush crazy. It is not good for our people. It is not good for our international reputation. We need investment, we don't want to scare people away.'

'I'm a researcher, not an explorer.'

The Minister explained that the Cooperative Republic of Guyana was a rich country made poor by European imperialists with a superiority complex who had plundered the country's resources. Things had changed since the days of the Commonwealth. 'It is now payback time,' he said.

I shook my head, feeling uncomfortable with the implication.

'I hope my survey will prove useful.'

'So, when will our computers arrive?'

I tried not to look blank. 'Ah yes, the computers.'

The Minister stared at me in silence. Everybody stared at me. All I could hear was the screech of footsteps outside the room as somebody walked up the stairs. The Minister looked at his watch, an ostentatious Rolex Oyster. Fake I assumed. If only I'd received my briefing papers. My scalp was moist with sweat.

'I'm sure they are on their way,' I said at last. 'I will find out what's happening.'

The Minister sat back and folded his arms. 'Mr Radstock, we do not care for people who are here on false pretences. I will see you in a month's time when you will report on your findings.' With a wave of his hand he indicated it was time for me to go. I stood up. 'You must know,' Lucas said, 'you won't be permitted to leave the country until we have our computers.'

'They'll be here, I can assure you,' I attempted to say with confidence, but my words came out like a series of high pitched squeaks.

Payback time? I didn't like the sound of that.

SEVEN

I had no idea what I was going to do.

Xavier was standing by the car talking to a security guard. They were both laughing. When Xavier saw me he straightened up and flicked his cigarette to the ground.

'Where next, boss?'

'I need to go back to my hotel and work on my strategy,' I said to Xavier. 'Hopefully, the briefing document has arrived. Meanwhile, I would like you to book a meeting with the Chief Statistician.'

Xavier looked puzzled. 'I have never heard of such a person. I will investigate.'

'And later we'll go to the airport to pick up my missing baggage.'

Alongside gourmet food and the best rum punches in Georgetown, the promotional brochure for the Stabroek Lodge boasted a 'Twenty-four-hour business centre'. In reality, this was a stuffy, mosquito-infested cell, with a low-capacity computer, a printer with no paper, and a sporadic internet dial-up connection.

As soon as I booted up, the screen flashed with a virus alert. Gordon had warned me most computers in Guyana were less than useless, being riddled with herds of Trojan horses and other malicious programmes. Thankfully, Festus, who worked on reception, offered me the use of the work-station in the hotel office.

Gordon had still not forwarded the briefing paper so I spent half an hour composing a well-considered email describing my situation. I was about to press 'send' when the screen faded and the lights went out. Within five seconds the hotel's back-up generator had kicked in, but my two-page report was lost. My second email was shorter and more to the point.

Hi Gordon

I haven't yet received my briefing papers. Please send ASAP.

I met the Minister today and he assures me all the statistics are available.

He also mentioned something about the arrival of computers. Do you know about this?

Best wishes.

Felix

PS Georgetown is charming and there are parrots everywhere!

Exactly why I mentioned the parrots, I'm not sure. I suppose I wanted to add colour to a dull email.

After eating a chicken sandwich, I began to map out my strategy. I needed Xavier to procure data on mining, sugar and rice production – also the low-down on any other significant farming and fishing activities.

Surprisingly, for a former British colony, there was no apparent railway network. Good roads and railways oil the machinery of the labour market, but in Guyana transportation appeared undeveloped. I was disappointed by this. The train with its dense socio-interactions is the preferred mode of transport for economists. The railway carriage offers a perfect microcosm of society and provides a temporary bonding experience: passengers are rendered equal and have a shared destination[1].

From what I could gather, most inland transport was by boat. But even then, the possibility of long river trips appeared to be limited. The forest was said to be rich in minerals and exotic hardwoods but

---

1 Noitall, I., Terminal Experiences, The Illustrated Economist (1970),Vol.3, p.111–147.

with few reliable methods of transporting these natural resources they remained largely untapped. I was going to have to tweak the Radstock Framework© accordingly.

I wondered about Guyana's potential for tourism, but with no current access to the internet, all the information I had was from a handful of faded leaflets on display in the hotel lobby. I thumbed through scuffed flyers promoting the usual attractions: the National Museum ('opening hours are liable to vary, check before you visit'); St George's Anglican Cathedral and the Promenade Gardens. The one brochure that did seize my attention featured the Kaieteur Falls. With an unbroken drop of 750 feet, it was described as 'one of the most magnificent waterfalls in the world'. It sounded impressive, but its location in the bush was remote, accessible only by light-aircraft.

I was encouraged, however, by Lucas's assertion that the statistics were 'rigorous'. Apart from the computers, which I expected Gordon would advise on, my work seemed pretty straightforward. I'd probably be flying back to England sooner than expected.

I was waiting for Xavier in the hotel foyer when I was handed a note.

Mr Radstock, due to unexpected family business, I am unable to take you to the airport this evening. Festus will arrange a taxi for you. XYZ

I was surprised and annoyed. Xavier was my logistics coordinator, supposedly available at all times. But then a cautionary voice in my head told me to stop behaving like a colonial jerk.

'How do you want me to drive?' the taxi driver asked. 'Fast or slow?'

It was nearly dusk as we headed out of Georgetown and travelled alongside the mile-wide Demerara River.

'Safely,' I replied.

The river, the colour of Assam tea, was flowing swiftly, carrying along tree trunks and branches. Large anvil-shaped clouds were building and sudden gusts of hot wind buffeted the car. Despite the road being scoured by deep ruts and potholes big enough to paddle in, the taxi man drove at breakneck speed.

'I want you to drive slowly,' I shouted.

'This IS slow. It is dangerous to go any slower.'

Apart from a couple of lethargic guards with guns, the airport was empty. The check-in gates were closed and there were no flights listed on the arrival and departure boards. I found a counter marked Enquiries. There was nobody there. Through a window I could see a corpulent man lying in a chair with his feet on a table. I coughed. He didn't move. 'Hello,' I called out. Still no movement. I knocked on the counter and shouted louder. The man shifted in his seat and turned his face towards me. He grunted and moved his head back and forth as if he was trying to focus.

'You have a bad cough,' he said.

'I'm looking for my luggage.'

'Ah. I have a list.' I told him my name and he ran his finger down a sheet of paper. 'Mr Radstock, your bag is at Piarco.'

'Where?'

'Port of Spain.'

'That's Trinidad!' What's it doing there?'

He ignored my question. 'Do you want it? I will send a message.'

'How long will it take?'

'I will get for it you.' He shrugged and shuffled back to his office. Through the door I watched as he took up the phone, sat back in his chair and put his feet on the table. He closed his eyes. I was afraid he was going to fall asleep again. Thankfully, after thirty seconds I could see him speaking.

'Your luggage will be on the next plane.'

'And when is that, next week?' I said sarcastically.

'You are in luck. God willing, it will be here in four hours.'

'It's not listed on the arrivals board.'

The man gave a wry laugh. 'The arrivals board is misleading.'

'What am I supposed to do for the next four hours?'

'You are new to this country, yes? Things happen at a natural pace here. Sit down and take it easy. Breathe the cool night air. Enjoy yourself.'

I bought a bottle of Banks beer from a woman with a cool-box and settled on a bench outside the arrivals building to contemplate the wide amethyst sunset. Listening to the chorus of the night I watched a silent electrical storm illuminate the sky many miles away over the forest.

There was nothing to do but lime.

EIGHT

'I know exactly what Englishmen like.'

It was 6.00 am when my phone rang.

'Good morning, Mr Radstock, how are you today?' It was Roxy. I felt muzzy and numb. I'd returned from the airport at 3.00 am and had very little sleep, being woken frequently by the relentless howls and yelps from what I guessed was a dog's home behind the hotel. The suitcase, when it eventually arrived, wasn't mine. I was increasingly uncomfortable in the unfamiliar heat and longed for clean clothes. I was told, however, my luggage would definitely, it is guaranteed, be delivered to my hotel within the next twenty-four hours.

'I'm tired.' I said to Roxy, yawning.

'This is not a climate for rushing about. You need to relax.' I'd feel a lot more relaxed, I thought, if I stopped getting these early morning calls. 'When do you want me to come and see you?' she said.

'Not today, I have important business to sort out.'

'I will visit you tomorrow. Do you like a morning or evening visit?'

'Evening is best for me,' I said.

'Do you like anything special?'

'You're the expert. I'll take your advice.'

She laughed. 'You like a surprise, I will surprise you.'

'Not too much of a surprise, I'm English you know.'

'I know exactly what Englishmen like.'

'Good, I will see you tomorrow.'

'Have a good day, Mr Radstock.'

Contrary to what Lucas had assured me, the data proved elusive. Xavier took me to a dilapidated two-storey building that once housed the Department for Statistics. The front door was locked. A sun-bleached notice tacked to the wall stated the office was closed, and information was available from the relevant individual government departments.

It was difficult to find anybody to talk to. With little success, we went from one department to another, there being no central government complex, with the ministries dotted around town.

'Tell me about the Minister,' I said to Xavier as we travelled across the city.

He was silent for a moment, and then glanced at me. 'You must be very careful of Dr Professor Lucas.'

'It's unusual to call yourself both Doctor and Professor.'

'Professor is his forename.'

'That's his birth name?'

'Some parents give their children aspirational names. The technical term is nominative determinism – if you call your son Judge, Prince or even President it is thought they are pre-destined to be high achievers.'

'Interesting idea.'

'It worked for Lucas. He's not a medical doctor. He started his career in the police. He was a champion boxer and due to represent Guyana in the 1982 Commonwealth Games but had to withdraw because of a hernia.'

'After that he changed plans and quickly moved up the ranks of the civil service. As soon as he became a minister he awarded himself the title of Doctor.'

'Why not,' I laughed. I remembered Lucas's huge pugilist's fists. I wouldn't like to be on the receiving end of them, I thought.

Xavier said that while most people ignored their ancestry and thought of themselves as Guyanese, Lucas liked to emphasise his roots. It gave him a moral authority, especially with the Asians, who had come here of their own free will, the fools.

'Do not underestimate him,' Xavier said seriously. 'He is prone to outbursts of extreme violence. He has an entourage of bodyguards – we call them the Tonton Macoute.'

'Like Papa Doc Duvalier's thugs?' I vaguely remembered an Alan Whicker TV programme about the Tonton Macoute, a murderous private army in Haiti, and their rule of fear.

'Exactly.'

'I see.'

'And never question his qualifications. He has a terrible temper.'

'I have no intention of upsetting him,' I said.

We visited the Ministry for Youth Culture, the Ministry for Agriculture, the Ministry for Foreign Trade and the Ministry for Amerindian Affairs. It was always the same. I would be shown into a forsaken room lined with bookcases, but containing no books, and asked to wait. I would hear the scraping of chairs and a low murmur of voices in a nearby office and then be informed the data was too old to be of use, or was currently being updated and was not yet available for release, or the statistician was on extended sick leave.

NINE

I thought she was going to blow me a kiss.

So far the hotel restaurant had been empty, but tonight there was an excitable party of eight at the table next to me. They were in convivial spirits, drinking Moët & Chandon, laughing loudly, and talking about a night-trip they were due to make up-river to watch caimans. With little silver hammers they were cracking what looked like giant lobster claws.

A woman, in her early 30s, wearing a striking traffic-light red trouser suit and lipstick to match stood up to make a toast. She had a North American accent. She caught my eye and smiled and then held up her champagne flute and – for a moment I thought she was going to blow me a kiss – mouthed 'Cheers'. I felt self-conscious eating by myself but raised my glass in acknowledgement. With her immaculately styled ash blonde hair and her confident smile she was disturbingly beautiful. I wished I could have joined her and her cheerful party.

The heat of the night was oppressive. A black insect the size of a chipolata dive-bombed the chandelier and crash-landed onto my table. To my horror I saw it was a giant cockroach. I had never realised cockroaches could fly as well as scuttle.

Back in my room, I telephoned Aurora. I hated long distance calls; all the time I was aware of the meter ticking and the cost mounting. There was too much pressure to say something significant. I wanted to tell Aurora about the exotic and unfamiliar world I had entered. But I knew I would waste these precious moments asking what the time was in the U.K. and enquiring about the weather.

The call went straight to answer-phone. I sat on my king-sized bed and felt as lonely as a lighthouse-keeper, far away from the one I loved.

I lay under the fan, trying to catch a whisper of a draught, and began to read Under the Volcano. It was set in Central America so I hoped it might give me some insight into Guyana. I'd heard somewhere it was the 11th best English Language book ever – but after twenty pages I found the endless descriptions of drinking a staggering quantity of alcohol were making me thirsty. I turned on the television instead.

I was watching an episode of Friends, the one where Rachel realises Ross is a tiresome jerk, when the phone rang. I thought it was Aurora.

'Hello, darling,' I said.

'Are you alright?' Came Gordon's voice.

'Ah! Yes!'

'Don't take this the wrong way,' said Gordon, 'but you sounded a bit over-familiar. Not the sort of telephone manner we expect from our field workers. We like our researchers to sound more assertive, and be respected.'

'Sorry, I was expecting a call from my milliner,' I lied. I wasn't sure what DoDO's policy was on paying for expensive long distance call-collect calls from loved ones.

'Really? Well, I'm glad I've got through to you. I'm using our special line. Anyway, I'm pleased you're having a good time. I thought you would. You ought to be paying us! I'm delighted to hear about the parrots. Do they have a small yellow patch on their head? If so they are yellow crowned parrots. It's a pity you won't see any macaws, they're only in the jungle. Look, Felix, I haven't got much time. Do you mind if we focus on work for just a minute?'

'Certainly, there've been some problems...'

'We only have challenges in our department. How's the car?'

'What car?'

'What car!? The Land Rover Discovery.'

'Very comfortable.' It was the one thing in this bewildering country I felt I could rely on.

'Well, keep an eye on it – it's worth a life-time's wages.'

'Xavier looks after it.'

'Good man. Now, you'll be pleased to hear I've arranged for our contact in Corriverton, Ellis Deane, to show you round. She's been there three years and has a good knowledge of the area.'

'Corriverton?'

'It's on the border with Suriname.'

'Suriname?'

'Yes, Suriname, used to be Dutch Guiana. Corriverton is an interesting frontier town and will be an excellent opportunity for you to observe the grey economy in the raw.'

'Are you asking me to leave Georgetown and go to Corriverton?'

'Shoot down there in the Discovery. Your logistics man will know the way. You might see some interesting parakeets. Did you know there are twenty-eight species of parrot in Guyana? Of course you do, you're the expert.'

I was beginning to regret mentioning the damned parrots. 'Corriverton must be at least a day's journey away,' I said.

'So?'

'Dr Professor Lucas said I wasn't to travel to the interior.'

'Is that what he's calling himself these days? Does he still wear that tribal kit? The last time I heard he was just plain 'professor'.'

'He's not a proper doctor,' I said.

'Anyway, Corriverton is on the coast, it's not in the interior.'

'Are you sure?'

'Look Felix, it's not as if I'm asking you to smoke hallucinogenic frog turds with Yanomani headshrinkers,' Gordon chuckled.

'By the way,' I said, 'My suitcase hasn't kept up with me.'

'Where is it?'

'At Piarco.'

'I wouldn't hold your breath. At least it's not still at Heathrow. I hope you packed a tie in your hand-luggage.'

'So what should I tell Lucas?'

'Don't say anything.'

'I've heard rumours...'

'We've all heard rumours – politicians thrive on rumours. It's part of the culture. Ignore it. Lucas is a pussycat.'

I felt uneasy about this. 'Will Ellis know where to get some stats?'

'Certainly.'

'If Georgetown's anything to go by, it's not that easy.'

'I understand, Felix. Working in an unfamiliar country can be very frustrating but you need to be flexible. If you can't get figures, use observational techniques. Unpack the evidence, sniff around a bit, shine a light into the shadows, that sort of thing.'

I had absolutely no idea what he was on about.

'Oh, by the way, I'd like you to check out Ellis.'

'What do you mean?'

'Assess Ellis's state of mind.'

'Like how?'

'Ellis's predecessor had a breakdown. Corriverton is a tricky posting. Too much sun, too much rum. Or it could have been the long term effect of the anti-malarials. They can put the brain through the wringer a bit. Anyway, rumour has it Ellis is going the same way. Ask Ellis a few questions and check the score on the crazyometer. You know the routine: the day of week, who's Prime Minister? How many wives did Henry VIII have? Why is a carrot like a potato? Just a quick report. We like to know what's going on with our staff. We don't like them to go troppo crazy and end up in the snake pit.'

Was Gordon serious? 'But this is nothing to do with the labour market. I'm not trained for this sort of thing.'

'I'm not asking much, a page or so. Put it on the invoice.'

'Gordon, while I've got you, there's a number of other things I need to talk about.'

'Yes, go on ...'

The light in the room flickered and the connection faded. By the time the hotel generator had kicked-in the line was dead.

I was too wired to sleep. I decided to take a stroll to clear my head.

I left the hotel compound and walked along a deserted, traffic-free road. I wondered where everybody was. It was no cooler outside – the air felt thick with humidity. Perhaps, at the sea-wall the heat would be less intense. I ambled past a house where people were talking in low tones on a veranda. A woman was swinging languidly in a hammock, her hand gently brushing the floor. The homely aroma of spicy jerk chicken hung in the air. A large bat – or moth – zipped past. Guided by the pewter light of a bright moon and the occasional street lamp, I wandered in the direction of what I guessed might be the ocean. A half-asleep watchman sat on a chair by a closed gate. The wide streets, with buildings set back from the road, felt safe. I remembered Gordon had warned me not to go out at night. 'It's a lawless place, Georgetown. You'll be shot and thrown into a ditch.' What did he know? That might happen in Langley, but not here. That was the problem with Gordon, deskbound and overly anxious. He needed to get out more.

I passed a row of dusty shops no bigger than cupboards. On the door of a travel agent, among the special offers of flights to Florida and Canada, a poster advertised excursions by light aircraft to the Kaieteur Falls. Although tricky to get to, this spectacular cascade looked beguiling, as did the lush rainforest with its fabulously coloured macaws and gorgeous glittering butterflies. Unfortunately the Falls were in Lucas's exclusion zone – a trip there would be out of the question.

After twenty minutes I felt a touch of breeze on my face and could make out the shadow of the sea-wall. As I got closer I saw the silhouettes of figures walking on the rampart. I climbed the bank and in front of me was a shell-grey ocean, glittering with hundreds of flickering lights. Groups of people were putting little boats into the water with flowers or nightlights on them. The calm sea was shimmering with innumerable little rafts, made out of paper plates or polystyrene food boxes. Some of the vessels contained what looked like cakes or samosas. There was a smell of sandalwood joss sticks.

I sat on a bench and took in the scene. Behind me the land was perhaps fifteen feet lower than the level of the ocean. There were people, families, promenading along the broken concrete footpath catching the night-time sea breeze. Next to me a woman, wearing a gold-edged turquoise sari, and her little boy, were sharing a picnic. They looked at me with curiosity. The woman stood to take a photograph of her son. I pointed at her camera and indicated I could take a picture of both of them.

I asked what was going on.

'It is full moon, this is our festival of lights.'

'It's very beautiful.'

'Please, you must have some food. This is a time for sharing.'

Although I wasn't hungry I accepted a samosa. It was warm and tasted of potato and cumin. Apart from the Toblerone, it was the best thing I'd eaten since I'd left England.

I promised myself on another evening I'd find a little bar blaring out roots reggae, and lime. I'd come all this way, it would be stupid not to. But it was already late and I had a busy day ahead.

I stared at the night sky. The stars appeared different, as if somebody had messed them up. The moon was also strangely altered. Was this the same moon I looked at in England? At first I couldn't work out the difference, but then I realised the moon was on its side.

Watching this festival in the warmth of the night, gazing over the shimmering ocean, with the smell of the sea, my sweet Aurora felt so far away.

TEN

A message from Roxxy.

Back at the hotel a piece of paper torn from a note-book had been pushed under my door.

I thought you were expecting me. I will phone to re-arrange. Roxxy x.

ELEVEN

God will punish the children for the sins of their fathers.

The car door closed with a satisfying clunk. Inside the air conditioning was blowing cold – the interior of the vehicle was spotless and smelled of pine deodorant. I settled back into the cream-coloured leather seats. I could live in one of these, I thought.

Although my briefing papers were yet to arrive, I was eager to get on with my work. Xavier had arranged visits to a number of educational establishments. My first stop was the Princess Elizabeth Technical College.

Xavier told me about Guyana's history as he drove me there.

'We've got a rich gene pool in Guyana. We're at a confluence of cultures - races have been mixing for centuries. We're one of the most diverse societies in the world.'

'You obviously haven't been to Brixton recently.'

Xavier didn't seem to get my joke and ignored my comment.

He continued: 'In the seventeenth century the white man came with slaves from Africa.'

'Not a good start.' I felt uneasy talking about slavery. What can you do? An apology seems superficial. The damage done is so deep, and the shame of the perpetrators beyond understanding. 'I'm sorry for what my forebears did,' I said meekly.

'Yeah, well, it's history now,' said Xavier.

'But it continues to haunt us all. The horror is so bad it's hard to comprehend.' Ideally, I'd like to acknowledge, apologise and move on. But it's not as simple as that.

'That's what they did in those days.' Xavier didn't seem that bothered. 'It's up to us to free our minds. Think about the future, that's more important.'

'But the white man benefited from it.'

'Yes, he did. In fact, yes, you do. "I am a jealous God," ' Xavier recited in deep voice, ' "God will punish the children for the sins of their fathers".'

'I think God already has,' I said.

'Yeah, well, maybe one day all God's children will sit down at the table of brotherhood.'

I wanted to change the subject so I told Xavier about my visit to the sea-wall. Xavier was alarmed when I said I'd walked there. 'It is very dangerous to walk in the city at night-time,' he said. I told him I felt safe, there were many families around. 'Families, yes,' he said, 'but no lone white men.' He said people disappear; there are packs of wild dogs. He warned that small-holders graze their cattle on the verges at night time. 'The cattle have big horns.' I told him that I didn't see any cattle. I was beginning to think this was a plot put about by taxi drivers to scare people.

'There was a festival,' I said. 'There were lots of votive lights on paper boats.'

'The Hindus like their festivals,' said Xavier.

There was a packet of Bristol cigarettes in the glove compartment. I picked it up and inspected it. The box was white with a red and gold motif. On closer examination I could see it was the crest of the City of Bristol.

'I didn't know you smoked these,' I said to Xavier.

'I don't. It's not my brand.'

'Bristol – that's where I come from.'

Xavier turned and looked at me. 'What? You come from the cigarette factory?'

'No, Bristol, it's a town in England.'

'I thought Bristol was the name of a cigarette. I never knew it was a place.'

'That's where I live. Bristol is famous for its cigarettes.' I didn't like to mention that it was also known for its involvement in the slave trade. 'Look,' I said, pointing to the packet, 'it says 'Made under licence from W.D. & H.O. Wills, Bristol. UK".'

'So where is this Bristol?'

'A hundred miles west of London.'

'I've always thought that Bristol cigarettes were Guyanese. Their slogan is "Bristol – our OWN taste",' he recited just like an ad. 'Everybody smokes them.'

'Well, they're English.'

Xavier was silent. He stared straight ahead. I could sense he was annoyed by this.

We were now on the outskirts of Georgetown in a suburb of new bungalows with red tin roofs. We drove by a neat, white-painted church and then a Hindu temple with an alarming statue of a giant spitting cobra at its entrance.

'Tell me more about the history of Guyana?' I asked.

'In 1823 there were rebellions and many people were killed. The slaves had heard, mistakenly, it turned out, that the British government had outlawed slavery and they were free. The slave masters were having none of it. Two hundred and fifty enslaved men and women were executed and their heads set on spikes all around Georgetown.'

'That's appalling,' I said.

'Slavery was abolished ten years later in 1833. At that time it is said that there were 85,000 slaves in the country. Plantation owners were given compensation – not a dollar, nor an apology, was given to the freed slaves. And the plantation system carried on. The estate owners hired indentured labourers from India. The only difference was that they came of their own will. But once here, the Asian Indians still had few, or no, rights. Eventually, the plantation system fell apart and my ancestors got together and bought their own land.'

In the Principal's dusty room tables were piled high with folders of yellowing papers. On the wall behind a large desk was a faded picture of Queen Elizabeth wearing a crown and coronation robes. She looked barely old enough to go out on her own, let alone rule an empire.

The Principal, a slight man wearing a thin beige suit, welcomed me with the usual pleasantries. Did I have a good journey? Where was I staying? Yes, he knew of the Stabroek Lodge, it had a very good restaurant, but he'd never eaten there himself.

Speaking with a sad air of defeat he soon got down to more pressing matters. 'This country is in a bad way. We cannot afford to buy text books. The world is changing but our academic books are all out of date. We cannot even photocopy.' A Xerox machine behind the Principal's desk was being used as a plant stand. 'We spent hundreds of dollars on that machine. Within weeks a power-surge made it useless. We train people to mend them but we have no spare parts.'

I asked what careers his students went on to.

He shrugged. 'Most of them leave the country. Our best students move to Canada or the USA. Others go to Africa. The government of Malawi took a whole class of our trainee teachers. Even in Africa our students earn more than here. What future does our country have without qualified teachers?'

I was impressed by the heartfelt way he said this. 'Maybe my report will be of use.' I wanted to suggest something helpful, but didn't know what. I was beginning to realise that these were bigger problems than I was used to. It wasn't just a matter of shifting figures from one column to the next.

The Principal took me on a tour of the college. Housed in a series of low brick buildings, it was clearly under-resourced and largely empty. I peered through a classroom door. The chairs and desks were battered and broken. There appeared to be no students. 'Where is everybody?' I asked.

'Study leave,' the Principal replied. 'We do not have the resources to open every day.'

We peered into a room with waist-high sockets around the walls but with no computers attached.

'I'm sure the computers will arrive soon,' I added, hoping to cheer him up.

He gave a deep sigh. 'You really think so?'

'Certainly.' Why was I saying this?

'And who do you think will get these computers?'

'They are for schools,' I guessed.

The Principal laughed sarcastically. 'For schools! Those computers will never go to schools. They will be sold on the black market. Or they will sit on some official's desk in the Ministry. Until,' he raised his mottled hands in the air, 'they blow up!'

My head was buzzing, the heat was getting to me. 'I'll do my best to help you,' was all that I could come up with.

The Principal gave a slow smile. 'Well done Mr Radstock. You go ahead and do your best. If you really want to help, go back to England. Go back to England and tell the people to buy our sugar and rice.'

'I'm sorry I can't do more.'

'Save your sympathy for your ailing monarchy.'

Later that afternoon, as we drove through the centre of Georgetown, I told Xavier about our planned visit to Corriverton. He appeared surprised.

'Nobody said anything about leaving Georgetown. I will need to check with the Minister,' he said.

I didn't like the idea of Xavier talking to the Minister about my movements. 'I was told that you would be at my disposal.'

'Mr Radstock, I am at nobody's 'disposal'. The colonial days are long gone.'

I could feel myself blushing. 'Xavier, I didn't mean it like that. I was told that you would be working for me as my logistics co-ordinator.'

'We are working together,' said Xavier. 'Personally, I see this as more of a partnership.' He chuckled to himself. 'You and I are like Butch Cassidy and the Sundance Kid.'

'That doesn't end well,' I said. 'Starsky and Hutch would be better.'

'Yes, Starsky and Hutch. You can be the blonde one.'

'Of course,' I laughed, and so did he. 'But there are things that I need to do. With your help, of course,' I added quickly.

Xavier wound down his window at Georgetown's only set of traffic lights to speak to the passenger of a car that had pulled up alongside.

They both talked in a thick creole accent that I could barely understand. Xavier leant out of the vehicle and high-fived the man. We drove on.

'And, Mr Radstock, there are things that I also have to do. I have a number of evening engagements.'

'I appreciate that, but I only have a limited amount of time here.'

'You must relax Mr Radstock. It is too hot to be rushing about.'

'Xavier, I think at the moment, it would be a good idea not to mention to the Minister that we are going to Corriverton. As a economist I like to work undercover. Knowledge of our presence might influence the gathering of raw data.'

Xavier nodded cogently.

Back at the hotel, while the electricity was on, I checked my emails.

Felix. In haste. To confirm, DoDO want you to visit the border town of Corriverton. Briefing paper attached. You must persevere with your search for hard statistics. Glad you are enjoying yourself. Best wishes. Gordon.

PS The computers are part of a development package that DoDO is

providing. I will explain later.
PPS Be discreet in Corriverton, keep a low profile.

My briefing document was also attached to the email. I clicked on the file but was unable to open it. Gordon, the fool, had sent it in an incompatible format.

At least my lost luggage had arrived. My suitcase, however, was in a bad state. It appeared to have been mangled by heavy machinery and was marked with oil stains and rubber skid-marks. Inside, a couple of my shirts looked as if they'd been tried on. One of them, clean when I had packed it, had a brown stain down the front and smelled heavily of perspiration. It had been neatly re-folded.

TWELVE

The Millennium Bug, the revenge of the geeks.

Eventually I got a call through to Gordon.

'What time do you call this?' he said. He sounded breathless. I'd forgotten about the change of time zone.

'Is it late?'

'It's two in the morning.'

'Sorry, I'm surprised you're still at work.'

'Felix, you'll have to make this short. I'm very busy. I'm in the middle of a 24-hour fire-drill.'

'24 hours!'

'We're a big department – it's a full-on role-play scenario. If a Scud missile pops through the window, I want to know which fire extinguisher to use. I've already said more than I should. This is classified information.'

'Don't worry, I won't tell anybody.'

'As we enter the new millennium you can't be too careful.'

'I've got a couple of questions,' I said.

'Have you been to Corriverton yet?'

'That's what I want to talk about. And the contract.'

'I'll do what I can, but if it's anything specific to do with the labour market, I'll be worse than useless. The number crunchers have all been requisitioned by Whitehall to work on the Y2K bug.'

'The what!?' I'd heard squeaks about this before I left England, but hadn't taken it seriously.

'The Millennium Bug, the revenge of the geeks they're calling it. For years people have laughed at their spotty faces and their pebble specs, but now the geeks are in charge. The geeks are going to make us suffer. We're at their mercy, Felix. They've got us by the balls with a bloody great monkey wrench and on the first second of the new millennium they're going to tighten that wrench so hard our nuts will pop. It's global meltdown.'

'That's a bit melodramatic.'

'You mustn't underestimate the danger. Between you and me the government is seriously concerned. The panic could be worse than the bug itself. Richard Madeley on This Morning TV is stirring up the public into a frenzy. He's telling everybody to stockpile ten weeks of food and run to the hills. British Telecom has set aside £500 million on bug fixing. If we don't sort this out the banks are going to crash, shops will run out of food and planes are going to drop out of the sky. It can't get much worse. Russia could hack our systems to death – apparently their computers aren't susceptible. Something to do with the Cyrillic alphabet.'

'The cold war finished eight years ago.'

'It's bloody serious, Felix. We need to get you back from Guyana by the New Year at latest.'

'I can assure you I'll be back way before Christmas.'

'Contrary to popular belief this Y2K thing isn't going to happen all at once.'

'I thought that was the problem.'

'That's what Whitehall initially thought. But the software archaeologists have dug deep and found these bloody nerds have sprinkled their malicious bugs all over the place. It's nerd sabotage, it's I.T. Armageddon. As I understand it, they reckon the bug can hatch anything up to a month before the millennium.'

'I thought it was all to do with the date changing from 99 to 00.'

'That's part of it. Some computers will think we've gone back to 1900. All of a sudden, we've lost a hundred years and Queen Victoria is on the throne. Imagine that!'

'I've always wanted to time travel.'

'It's not funny, Felix, I can assure you. The maximum destruction and collapse of civilisation. Make sure you have your research notes printed out. There's no guarantee that backing up your computer will help.'

'I will, if I can find a printer that's not jammed.'

'People are already beginning to panic-buy. Stockpile cornflakes, that's what I say. I hope you've got plenty of tinned food and bottled water at home. Bloody hell! The red telephone is ringing. That'll be the Minister. Felix, I've got to go. I have important matters to deal with.'

'But I've got some questions.'

'Email them to me.'

'The email isn't working.'

'Good to speak to you, Felix. You're doing a grand job. Remember, cheerfulness in adversity. Oh, and print out everything. And keep what I've told you under your panama. Have a good time in Corriverton.'

'I wasn't able to read the contract.' I was shouting down the phone. 'The hotel's edition of Word is from the Dark Ages.'

'Okay then, I'll fax it to you. It's important that you know what we want.'

'That would be helpful. Before you go I need to ask you about Corriverton...'

'I hear it's an interesting place. You'll like it. Be discreet, though. I'll call you as soon as I can. Look out for macaws. Bye!'

I put the phone down and sat on my bed. What was all that about? I hadn't yet got my head round this Corriverton excursion. Apart from shining lights in curious places, what was I going to do there? The original deal was to gather data in Georgetown. 'Zoom in and zoom out again', Gordon had said. There had never been any mention of Corriverton. And 'Border town'? What did that mean? 'Be discreet'. I thought my job was to ask questions. How was I going to do that and keep a low profile at the same time? And when did I say I was enjoying myself? Where the hell did he get that idea from?

THIRTEEN

I thought I was going a little mad.

Apart from Festus, who was asleep at the reception desk, the hotel seemed empty. Despite the beers, I was feeling too hyper to sleep. I sat for a while and attempted to read Under the Volcano. Occasionally there would be the squeak from a distant corridor but, surrounded by the rich smell of old wood, I tried to enjoy this rare moment of calm. From what I could gather, the book's protagonist – a disgraced minor diplomat, who was divorcing his wife – was on a twenty-four hour bender. You didn't need to be psychic to figure out where this was going. Massive liver failure and death by alcohol poisoning wasn't a subject that I currently wanted to immerse myself in.

Eventually, I fell into a fitful sleep but woke shortly, sweating and nauseous. The constant scream of night-insects and amphibians filled my head. I felt ill in my stomach and was unable to think clearly. I turned on the light and staggered to the bathroom and stared at myself in the mirror. For a moment I thought I was going a little mad. Not infrequently I have acid flash-back dreams where past misdemeanours of love and theft return to terrify me. But this was different. My face was blurred round the edges and seemed to be disappearing into white space before my eyes. Disturbing rustling and clicking noises came from nearby – mosquitoes and bugs bounced off the light bulb.

Never before had I experienced anything like this. It was as if a cog had slipped in my brain, and all my thought processes were unravelling. I was spooling fast forward. There was static fuzz and white noise. I brushed my teeth, hoping to clear the nightmare in my skull. I wondered if my drink had been spiked. Maybe it was the anti-malarials? I wanted to escape to somewhere safe and quiet, away from the appalling heat. Sitting on the bathroom floor with my bare knees touching my chin, I closed my eyes and wrapped my hands over my ears. At least the polished teak floorboards felt cool. What was I doing, across the ocean, far away from the one I loved? All I wanted was to be with Aurora. I wanted to be in her arms and smell her camomile breath and her unperfumed skin. I wanted her to say how much she loved me. Trying to clear my head and think of nothing, I started counting.

After my first encounter with Aurora in the zoo I visited the butterfly house every week. I knew she'd return. It wasn't until April, however, that I saw her next. I invited her to join me for tea and cake in the cafe.

Aurora was an artist and illustrated natural history books. She spoke about her time in Africa. She'd been working in Mali, copying fragile fifteenth-century Songhay manuscripts from the ancient university in Timbuktu. She was fascinated by the blue men of the desert, the Tuareg. Timbuktu was exotic, but a dump. There were no roads – you walked out of the town in the direction you wanted. In the past, travellers who found their way to this Saharan city were well looked after. The Tuareg were a hospitable people – they weren't so good at saying goodbye, however. If guests attempted to leave, they would be executed in the desert, beheaded by a Tuareg sword. The Tuareg wanted the myth of Timbuktu to remain untarnished; they didn't want the reality of a modest, baked-mud shanty town to crack the illusion

I told her about my labour market research and the Radstock Framework©. 'You have to look beyond the figures, to see what they mean. There's always a story hidden in there. There are pictures and rainbows. It's my job to find them.'

'How fascinating,' she said.

We arranged to meet the next week. We spoke in whispers in the hot-house as the butterflies circled our heads and landed on our hands. I asked Aurora if she'd come with me for a walk on the Downs. 'I'd like that,' she said.

We strolled for hours, talking about our dreams and ideas. We walked across the Suspension Bridge and looked down at the river hundreds of feet below; Aurora held my arm tight. She said she was surprised that I, for a non-coffee drinker, was such a positive person. In the pub she sipped Malibu and pineapple juice. The cider was sulphurous but I drank six pints, anyway. We spent the night in her attic-flat; a glorious woozy tangle of tongues, flesh and limbs.

Over the following weeks Aurora and I explored the old docks of Bristol. We rode the harbour ferry with a quart of Thatcher's not-so -discretely wrapped in a brown paper bag, enjoying the oily warmth and vibration of the boat's engine. We admired the boats and imagined where we would sail. I took her to a gallery and we viewed the exhibitions of conceptual art. She hated them.

'How can this be art? They can't draw. There's no skill.'

We stood in front of a photograph of a line of flattened grass in a meadow. There were also some words on the wall about rambling.

'I've never seen anything like that,' I exclaimed.

'No wonder!' Aurora groaned.

'It's avoiding elitism.'

Aurora was charmingly annoyed. 'I trained long and hard to be an artist,' she said.

'The artist is looking for a reaction.'

'He certainly makes me angry.' We both laughed. 'This constant desire to shock is so boring,' Aurora said. 'I prefer Lepidoptera.'

Later, I would watch Aurora draw – I was entranced by the concentration on her face as the delicate lines she drew became pictures, magically revealing the hidden details of familiar objects.

For the first time ever I had found somebody who understood me. I lost my self-consciousness about counting on my fingers. 'It makes sense,' she smiled. Something had happened – I wanted to be with Aurora all the time. I wanted to know all about her. I craved her serene company and wanted to explore her body and taste her skin. We were the same height and a perfect fit. She was beautiful and had become the centre of my life. The world looked new to me. I was weightless. I was flying. I was falling. I was in love with her.

How long I was crouched on the bathroom floor I have no idea. When I came round, I felt light-headed but calmer. I gargled water from a bottle and lurched back to bed for a short and restless sleep.

FOURTEEN

I was now enjoying the journey.

Xavier was keen to leave early in order to arrive in Corriverton before night-fall. It would take a day of rolling along the coast road and we'd have to cross the two-mile-wide Berbice River by ferry. Although the road was as smooth as a dance floor, Xavier said driving in the dark could be dangerous.

I asked the waiter if the kitchen staff could knock up one of their extra-large eggs for me. I was still feeling queasy and needed something to settle my stomach.

'Special treat. I glad you enjoy.'

'Special treat?' I asked.

'Chef not able to get more eggs.'

'Oh?' I'd seen plenty of chickens wandering around Georgetown.

'Stealing from nest of iguana is dangerous.'

'Let's get this straight. You're telling me I've been eating iguana eggs?' I'm not quite sure why, but I found the idea of eating a reptile egg for breakfast slightly unsettling.

'They local delicacy. Most Europeans reluctant to try.'

Suddenly, my stomach pains felt worse.

Before we left the Stabroek Lodge I searched the shelves of the library for books on Guyana. I'd given up reading Under the Volcano, it made me feel lonely and depressed. It was also putting me off alcohol. Alongside heavily soiled nut-busters by the likes of John Grisham, Tom Clancy and James Patterson I found a copy of Ninety-Two Days by Evelyn Waugh. The title didn't exactly grab me, but flicking through the pages I gathered this wasn't some Orwellian dystopian-nightmare-countdown novel, but a diary of a journey made by Waugh through Guyana in the early 1930s. By the look of the accompanying illustrations, not much had changed in sixty-five years. I put the book in my pocket, promising myself that I would return it on my homeward journey.

'There is a fax for you,' said Festus.

He handed me some sheets of paper. The first page was the covering letter stating that this was a contract between DoDO and myself. At last! However, the following six sheets were blank. Festus noticed me staring at the empty pages. 'The fax machine ran out of ink,' he explained matter-of-factly.

'What have you been doing with this car?' I asked Xavier. 'It smells like you've had a bonfire in it.'

The Land Rover had already lost its new smell of plastic and Shake n Vac.

Xavier sniffed and looked at me blankly. 'Wood smoke. It is the smell of Guyana.'

Once away from the centre of Georgetown, we drove past haphazard shanty huts hammered together with planks of wood and tin, some no bigger than garden sheds. Many houses had poles in their yards adorned with ragged flags and bunting. The yards in the suburbs were bigger, with plots of vegetables – I recognised sweetcorn, gourds and string beans. Roadside stalls sold neatly stacked pineapples. Delicate white egrets scavenged among the plastic bags on the rubbish tips.

The coastal plain was cut by drainage ditches. In the marshy fields, bordered by feathery palm trees, rice grew. Large metal tubes, like gigantic discarded tin cans, lay scattered in the paddy fields. 'Archimedes Screw, a pump for water irrigation,' Xavier explained. Humpback cows, some with patterns stencilled on them, wandered freely in the traffic. 'This is the longest straight road in the Caribbean,' said Xavier proudly, as he reached forward and touched the St Christopher pendant. 'Seven miles.'

Despite being one of Guyana's premier routes, the road was mostly a pot-holed single-lane track. An overloaded mini-bus sped past – I couldn't tell whether the passengers were waving, or shouting in desperation.

Xavier was an attentive driver and a knowledgeable travelling companion. He patiently answered my questions about the people, the buildings and the weather.

'Today, basically,' he said, as if he was reciting from a text book, 'the population is forty percent African heritage, forty-five percent Asian heritage, ten percent mixed and a handful of Chinese who came here to open restaurants and sell drugs. The remainder of the people are European.'

'What about the native Indians?' I asked.

'There's very few left.'

'But in Georgetown you showed me their big round hut.'

'Nobody bothers about them.'

'Surely this is their land?'

'They live in the bush.'

'So?' I asked.

'That's miles away. We don't count them.'

'That doesn't seem right.'

'They are left to their own traditional ways.'

'From what I've heard, in Brazil their lands are stolen, the forests cut down and the rivers polluted.'

Xavier was quiet for a moment. 'Perhaps that's something you should investigate.'

A couple of times I asked Xavier about himself, but he was reluctant to talk about his background.

'Zeeland? That's an interesting name,' I said.

'The name was imposed on my family by the Dutch.'

I wasn't sure what Xavier meant. Was he adopted? 'Do you speak Dutch?'

'No, you misunderstand. It was a long time ago. Many generations ago. It is my slave name.'

'Oh!'

'I keep my name out of respect for the suffering of my ancestors.'

'Yes, we shouldn't forget.'

'You white people want to disregard what you did to my African brothers and sisters.'

I wished I hadn't started this conversation. 'No, no, no,' I protested.

'We are proud of our heritage, Mr Radstock. We built this country. We will overcome, but we will never forget. History isn't just a book that can be closed and forgotten. Slavery has left the most terrible legacy that remains deep in our psyche. The past colours the present, memories live on, they don't go away.'

'I know. I struggle to do the right thing – but I'm not sure what the right thing is.'

Xavier gave me a disapproving look that suggested I didn't understand. 'I'm sorry if the facts make you feel uncomfortable, but that's just how it is. Xavier Yolando Zeeland,' he repeated. 'Do you know what Yolando means?'

'I don't think I do.' I didn't like to say that I thought Yolando was a girl's name.

'A seeker of mental, physical and spiritual freedom. He who can't be bound.'

'I like that, that's good.'

We missed the car ferry, which took thirty minutes to cross the Berbice River, and joined a long queue waiting for the next sailing in two hours. Small white and turquoise-blue fishing boats lay on the river bank. I wandered along the quay to a malodorous market and looked at all kinds of ugly wide-mouthed fish.

The light was beginning to dim and by the time we drove onto the ferry there was an orange-tinged sunset. My father once told me that because of the curvature of the earth tropical sunsets are bigger affairs than we get in more temperate climes. He was right; as the heavy sun started its rapid descent the sky and the river were ablaze with a dying amber hue.

I stood on the deck, savouring the cooling breeze. This was an adventure, and for once in my life I thought I could roll with the flow. I was enjoying the journey and had come round to the idea that this was an excellent opportunity, without disobeying Lucas's orders of course, to see more of the country. It was good to be away from Georgetown; I was excited by this massive river, its brown water draining a mysterious land. I'd come this far, so why not? In the absence of hard, quantative data I'd gather what economists call soft information. I hoped Gordon would be okay with that.

A couple of longboats were in the middle of the river, trawling with nets – even in the fading light I could see the catch was disappointing. At most there were half-a-dozen small fishes flapping in their baskets.

Xavier joined me on the deck as we approached a shoreline studded with coconut palms. He noticed me looking at the fishermen. 'It is not good,' he said. 'Chemicals from the mining hundreds of miles up-river have killed many fish.'

'That's a shame, I like fish.'

'You must be extremely careful when eating river fish. Some are very poisonous. One species is particularly dangerous. At first you feel a slight numbness of your lips and tongue – nothing serious. But then breathing becomes difficult and you begin to slobber like a dog. You feel sick and then the diarrhoea starts.'

'Doesn't sound fun.'

'It gets worse.' Xavier appeared to enjoy telling me this. 'The diarrhoea is followed by a catastrophic drop in blood pressure which causes the heart to deflate like a punctured balloon. Death follows instantly. The whole process takes just twenty-four hours – during which time you remain fully conscious until the final cardiac arrest. It is so painful patients have been known to beg their doctor to get it over with and kill them. It is a dreadful thing to witness.'

'It's a dreadful thing to experience, I'd say. Which fish is this?'

'It is difficult to tell. It is best to stay away from river fish altogether.'

'Okay, so fish is off the menu. How about ackee?' Though I wasn't exactly sure what it was, I'd read somewhere that ackee is a staple Caribbean food.

'You also need to beware of ackee. Parts of it are poisonous. If it is not prepared properly you can get vomiting sickness. This can also be fatal, but death takes a little longer, probably a week.'

'So what is there to eat?'

'A toasted cheese sandwich. You cannot go wrong with a toasted cheese sandwich. It's almost the national dish.' Xavier grinned, as if he was enjoying a private joke.

'Toasted cheese sandwich, the national dish? Really?' This didn't sound right to me. I'd already noticed the production of both cheese and bread was not particularly suited to the humid tropical climate.

Xavier laughed. 'After pepperpot.'

'What's that?'

'It is a stew that is constantly kept on the fire and topped up with whatever is at hand.'

'Yeah, I'm sure a toastie would go down well.' I was beginning to regret that I hadn't bought more Toblerone.

It was dark now. Our vehicle splashed through puddles from a rainstorm not long before. At least Xavier knew the route. We drove through villages with names like Leeds, Lancaster, Good Hope, Better Success, Profit and the less hopeful Now or Never.

A black cow loomed out of the darkness and stood in the middle of the road. As we swerved round the ton of meat I found myself thinking that I wasn't yet ready to die.

It was getting on for ten o'clock when, at last, we pulled into Corriverton. Xavier dropped me on the main drag at the Sweet Dreams Guest House. Meanwhile, Xavier said he had a cousin that he would lodge with.

DoDO's representative in Corriverton, Ellis Deane, was due to meet me the next morning at 8.30.

'We have two days in Corriverton,' Xavier announced. 'After that I must get back to Georgetown. I have some important business to attend to.'

My room was furnished with not two, but three king-sized beds. I wondered what lurid goings-on this arrangement catered for? On one of the walls hung a disconcerting painting of a bug-eyed boy with a glutinous tear on his rosy cheek. The concrete floor gave the room an industrial, rather than domestic, ambience. The gloss sea-blue walls were stained by the crusty remains of squashed mosquitoes. When I opened the bathroom door there was a scuttling sound, but by the time the light bulb flickered into action, whatever made the noise had disappeared.

Although the fridge wasn't working, it contained half a dozen bottles of warm Banks Beer that I reckoned would help me through the night. I turned on the television, tucked the edges of the mosquito net under the mattress and crawled into bed. The picture was grainy and the sound distorted. At first, I couldn't make out the language. It wasn't the creole accented Guyanese I was accustomed to. It had a Flemish honkety-plonkety rhythm. There were shaky, low budget adverts promoting market stalls selling meat, vegetables, skin whitening products and, as far as I could gather, the imminent arrival of competitively priced computers.

I shook a Toblerone bar from its case, and slid my finger along the silver paper. I hadn't eaten since breakfast. The chocolate melted slowly in my mouth revealing the grains of soft, chewy nougat. For a moment, lying on my bed, I was transported to my childhood in Somerset, to a frosty Christmas morning, sitting on a rug in front of a log fire, surrounded by hastily torn wrapping paper. In this dismal room, listening to the clatter and whine of the air-con, it felt like the memory of a distant world.

PART TWO

ONE

They'll think you've double-crossed them.

'I'll level with you,' said Ellis. 'You've put me in a bad situation. A right bad situation indeed.'

Following our discussion over breakfast at Renata's I realised I needed to contact Gordon urgently. I wanted to read the details of my contract and find out exactly what I'd signed up for. I felt uneasy. I didn't have a clear picture of the scope and purpose of my work. Maybe I'd misunderstood what I was being asked to do.

Ellis suggested we email from a computer in the Mayor's office which was on the ground floor of Corriverton Cricket Club's pavilion. We left the bordello and walked down the lively Main Street.

'The rumours about computers are nothing to do with me,' I said firmly as we weaved our way along the crowded sidewalk.

'You can't shrug off your responsibilities just like that,' Ellis replied.

'I'm sorry Ellis, but I don't see what I can do.'

'Just by association with you I'm going to be in big trouble. But that's nothing compared to the deep shit you're going to be in.'

'Look, I've…'

'They'll think you've double-crossed them.'

'Why would they think that?'

'Do I have to spell it out? Because they were expecting you to bring computers.'

'But there never were any computers.'

'That's not the point. They'll think you've sold them.'

'But I haven't.'

'I'm telling you. That's what they'll think.'

'But why?'

'It doesn't look good. You roll into town in your swanky car and your Chinese silk tie. What do you expect people to think? Con-artists end up in the river.'

'I'm not wearing a bloody tie!'

'Felix, because of you, there're going to be a lot of angry people in Corriverton. There's a supply chain you've got to think about. And that's just here. Over the river in Suriname they're going to be effing livid.'

'What's Suriname got to do with it?'

'That's where the computers were going!'

'What?'

'People have put down deposits. We're talking several months' wages.'

'That's ridiculous. The computers were never meant for Suriname.'

'So you do know about them.'

'I don't. All I'm saying is, if there were computers, they wouldn't be going to Suriname. But there aren't any, so it doesn't matter.'

'The more I think about this the worse it is. I need to get you out of here.'

I'd never seen a building like it. From a distance, despite its state of dilapidation, the pavilion reminded me of a magnificent, incongruously moored, tea-cutter. With its jaunty clock-tower, finials, flagpoles, florid scrolls and turrets this imposing baroque building could once have been a home fit for a colonial governor. Ellis explained that life revolved around cricket. In England, I'd always thought of cricket as a game for chin-deficient losers with too much time on their hands. In Guyana, there were no theatres and only a few speak-easy cinemas. Cricket was more than a sport, it was the glue of social cohesion.

'Leave this to me,' she said as we walked up the wooden steps. 'And for goodness sake, don't say anything about the hardware.'

Inside, three people were standing in front of a dead screen. One man was irritably pushing the on/off button. 'Bloody 'ting. He no start.'

The power had surged and blown the fuse.

'That was a waste of time,' I said.

'It happens constantly,' said Ellis. 'In this country you learn to be patient. We'll come back later.'

Ellis led the way back to the hotel. We cut across the scorched cricket field and soon found ourselves back on Main Street. The sun was beating down on the top of my head. By now I'd given up any hope of Roxy knocking up a custom-made panama and bought a hat from a roadside stall. It was a wide-brimmed Huckleberry Finn hat with stray pieces of straw hanging from the brim. It looked a bit rustic, but it did the job.

'What do you think?'

Ellis looked at my hat and sniggered. 'That's hardly going to throw them off the scent, if that's what you're thinking.'

'I wasn't.'

'Where's your driver?' Ellis asked.

'Xavier, my logistics coordinator, is staying with his cousin.'

'Who's his cousin?'

'How should I know?'

I realised I had no idea where Xavier was. We hadn't even arranged where to meet, or when.

Ellis raised her hand to her forehead in despair. 'He's probably nipped over the border as well. Don't expect to see your Land Rover Discovery again.'

'Hang on a moment, the Minister said Xavier was a good man. Xavier and I are working together. We're a team.'

'There's good and there's good. Down here in Corriverton the Minister's recommendation is worth jack shit. We're living in a different world from swanky G.T.. Take my word for it, as we speak, your shiny new car is being shipped over the Corentyne to Suriname. It happens all the time.'

'You're freaking me out. How am I going to get back to Georgetown?'

'We'll sort that out later. It might take a few days though.'

'I've got to get back before the computers crash.'

'I thought you said...'

'No, no, no, I'm not talking about the phantom computers, this is the Millennium Bug. I'm not supposed to say this, but the Y2K virus is going to be a lot worse than expected.'

'You lie low in your hotel room. I don't want you attracting any more attention to yourself.'

'I won't wear a tie, I promise.'

'I'll search for Xavier,' said Ellis. 'Don't open the door, don't speak to anyone.'

TWO

The sound of a silencer being screwed onto the barrel of a hand-gun.

There was a voice in my head howling 'get out of here'. What was I, a self-taught number-cruncher from the sleepy West Country, doing, on the other side of the world, on the smuggling super-highway of South America? Was this the time to take that emergency flight out of the country? Why wasn't I staring at spreadsheets in an office of gently humming computers? Christmas was only a month away. I should be buying presents, struggling home to Aurora in the dark after work, wrapped up in a heavy winter coat against the stinging rain. Adge had been right – I shouldn't have come.

Damn Ellis! I wasn't going to be intimidated by... by what? Maybe Gordon was right and Ellis was unhinged. Perhaps these rumours were merely an invention of Ellis's overactive imagination.

For the moment, however, I needed to ignore her paranoid ramblings and concentrate on my task. I was going to adopt a strategy economists call Flexible Thought Planning (FTP) and use observational techniques to gather information – not as robust as hard data, but, for the moment that's all I had to work with.

I took some chocolate from the warm fridge, bent off a slab and sat by the window. Nothing in my life had prepared me for this. Smuggling, guns and a cutlass in the skull were so far removed from my normal experience that none of this seemed real.

So what was happening in this town? From behind the grubby net curtain I watched the activity on the street.

A man carried a clutch of emerald green lizards, the size of small cats, by their tails, slung over his shoulder. I could see a stack of pineapples - more oblong and rugby-ball shaped than the fruits we have in the UK.

Did I see that? It was all so quick. A man bumped into a passer-by and discreetly slipped him a packet. Maybe I imagined it. Maybe he was just another mercury poisoning casualty.

A brown cow, as big as a van, wandered across the busy road, taking its time, oblivious to the traffic weaving around it.

A group of men was sitting outside a grog shop, slapping playing cards onto a table and laughing. One of the liming men glanced up and waved at me. I ducked behind the curtain.

I wasn't sure what I was looking for. Strip away the exoticism of this tropical scene and it was like anywhere else in the world. Young and old, men and women, healthy and sick, doing their best, trying to make the most out of what they had.

Under the hammering mid-day sun the activity on the baked street started to calm down. Apart from the occasional mini-bus the road was now empty. The pariah dogs were asleep in the shade. Even the cows had disappeared. The heat was making me sleepy. I turned the ceiling fan to full rev to keep me awake.

There was a knock. From my chair I could see the shadow of feet through the crack of light at the bottom of the door. If it was a mob coming to lynch me, at least it was a small mob. Maybe it was just one man, an assassin with a firearm. I tip-toed to the door and listened. There was the soft scrape of metal on metal, like the sound of a silencer being screwed onto the barrel of a hand-gun.

There was another knock.

'Mr Radstock. Are you there?'

I stood still and held my breath.

'Mr Radstock, it's me?'

'Who's me?' Damn! I shouldn't have said that.

'Me, Xavier.'

I opened the door an inch, ready to slam it.

Xavier was standing there, dressed in starched white shirt and black trousers. He was holding a water bottle with a metal screw-cap in his hand.

'Xavier!' I exhaled.

'Felix, what is up? You look scared.'

'Where have you been?'

'Staying with my cousin. I told you.'

'Yes, I know. But I was worried.'

'I do not understand.'

'Come in.'

'Nice room. You could fit a family of eight in here.'

I walked over to the window and looked for the Discovery.

'Where's the vehicle?'

'I have some bad news.'

'More bad news?'

'I'm afraid so.'

'What is it?'

'The Land Rover has been stolen.'

'What!'

Xavier held his hand up to his neck. 'Choke and rob,' he coughed. 'I'm sorry, Mr Radcliffe. There were six of them.'

'I don't believe this. How are we ...?'

Xavier pointed to a donkey cart parked across the road. 'See. From now on it's going to be horse and cart for you and me.'

'Gordon will be furious.' I was furious. 'You shouldn't have let it go.'

'I fought them off, but then one of the rude boys, Bang-Bang, pulled a gun.'

'Who's Bang-Bang?'

'Bang-Bang is a well-known murderer. I've seen his picture on a wanted poster.'

'They were probably bluffing.'

'He's not called Bang-Bang for nothing.'

'This place just gets worse and worse.'

'Is the car all you are worried about? Aren't you going to ask about me?' Xavier said with a hurt tone to his voice. 'What about your partner? Starsky and Hutch, remember?'

I felt bad. 'Hey, are you okay?' For someone who had just fought off six gangsters Xavier looked remarkably unruffled.

Xavier said nothing. He turned away and looked out of the window at the donkey cart. 'We're going to have to buy a sack of carrots,' he spluttered. His whole body was quaking. I thought he was crying.

'Great! That's the last bloody thing I need! Where the hell are we going to get carrots?'

'Unfortunately they are out of season.'

'Carrots out of season! That's ridiculous. What are we going to do?'

Xavier looked at me over his shoulder and burst out laughing.

'What?!'

'Your face!' he said. 'You should have seen your face! Priceless.'

'What do you mean, my face?'

Xavier was buckled up in hysterics. 'Felix, I am joking. Look! See!' He pointed down the road in the opposite direction, towards Renata's. 'There.'

Half a dozen boys were standing round the Land Rover, admiring the spotless vehicle.

'Very humorous,' I said flatly. 'Is the car okay?'

'Of course it's okay. It's the best car in Guyana,' Xavier said proudly. 'Those boys are guarding it.'

'This is not a good time for jokes.'

I wanted to change the conversation. I was feeling bad about my lack of concern for Xavier's safety, even if he had made up the whole daft and annoying story.

'How's your cousin?'

'He is very busy. He had to work late last night. The import/ export business is very good.'

'What does he deal in?'

'Electrical goods. He is preparing for an imminent delivery of computers.'

'Ellis says I'm in danger and we need to leave immediately.'

Xavier laughed. 'I understand DoDO is concerned about the veracity of Miss Deane's reports.'

'She does have a vivid imagination,' I said.

'Now, what have you had to eat today? The only danger you are in is from starvation.'

'A couple of pieces of Toblerone.'

'That's hardly a square meal.'

'It goes surprisingly well with beer.'

'Tonight I have organised a special treat for you. You will see Corriverton at its best.'

'Ellis said I should remain behind locked doors.'

Xavier rolled his eyes. 'How are you going to do your research?'

'I'm using high resolution observational techniques.'

'As I understand it, DoDO likes its staff to mingle with the community. Not just peer out of the window.'

'It's not safe for me to go out.'

'I wouldn't take what Miss Deane says too seriously. I have booked a table for both of you at the Riverside Restaurant to eat wild meat.'

'What wild meat?' I wondered exactly how wild this meat might be.

'Bush meat. It depends on what they catch. Unfortunately, the capybara is out of season at the moment.'

'Capybara?'

'The world's biggest rat, a rat the size of your English Labrador.'

'Mmm.'

'It is very good.'

'What a pity I'll never get to know what giant rat tastes like.'

'With a spicy cayenne sauce it is just like guinea pig.' Xavier's eyes lit up. 'Iguana is in season at this time of year, however.'

'Oh good!' I said, not wanting to upset Xavier further.

'And then I have arranged for you and Miss Deane to have a drink with Jim Bucket, the manager of the Corriverton branch of GuyBankCo.'

'Are you sure I'll be safe?'

'Jim trained in the Soviet Union, he is a very interesting man. He will tell you all you need to know about the workings of Corriverton and its...' Xavier did what I thought was a rather poor mimic of my English accent '... labour market.'

'Thank you, that will be useful. Will you be joining us, Xavier?'

'No, I don't drink. I hope you'll excuse me, I have other business to attend to.'

THREE

I hadn't brought my swimming trunks.

'They won't pay a ransom, you know.' Ellis had reluctantly accompanied me to the Riverside Restaurant.

'What?' 'Don't say I didn't warn you. DoDO never pays ransoms.'

'If anything happens to me, it will be my own fault entirely.'

'As a freelancer DoDO will deny your existence. They won't even acknowledge you're working for them. You're on your own, Felix.'

We were sitting at a table by a window overlooking the river. I gulped down a shot of rum in one and gasped as the high-octane alcohol freeze-dried my mouth. 'Whoa, that's good.'

'Eight-year-old rum' said Ellis, 'wait till you try the fifteen-year stuff.'

'We'll keep that for later.'

'You're supposed to savour it, not just knock it back.'

The menu at the Riverside Restaurant listed an extensive selection of bush meat including capybara, iguana, jungle oyster, peccary, tapir, spider monkey and some other animals I'd never heard of.

'Is there a vegetarian option?' I asked.

'There's jungle oyster, but you should never eat it when there's an e in the month,' Ellis replied.

I looked across the estuary. There was a barely visible line of trees on the far bank – at this point the Corentyne River must have been several miles wide. The sun was low in the sky; in twenty minutes it would be dark.

The shoreline was busy with boats coming and going. Some were dangerously over-laden with what looked like fridges, freezers and other white goods.

'You mustn't underestimate the strength of the currents,' Ellis warned. 'Many an unsuspecting person has been swept to a watery death.'

'Thankfully, I haven't brought my swimming trunks.'

'They say there are only a few crocodiles – they call them caiman here – in the estuary.'

'I don't think I'll put that to the test, thank you.'

A urinous smell of cooked kidneys wafted in the air; I couldn't tell if this was coming from the kitchen or the river. 'What do you recommend?' I asked.

Ellis shrugged. 'Wild meat isn't really my thing.'

'Today I saw a guy with some giant lizards. I thought they might be iguanas. They looked surprisingly meaty.'

'Many of these animals are endangered.'

'Maybe I ought to pass on the wild meat then.'

'You'll be okay with iguana, they're fairly common.' Ellis put the menu down. 'I think I'll have a toasted cheese sandwich.'

'Are you sure? I thought you didn't like cheese. Don't you want one of the 'specials'?'

'I had a large lunch.'

A waitress, wearing no shoes, came to take our order.

'What dat ting you want, darlin?'

'Is there any fish?'

'River fish only.'

I remembered what Xavier had said about the river fish. 'What about a vegetarian option?'

She stared at me, trying to figure out what I'd said. 'Vegetarian what?'

'Are there any vegetarian dishes?

'We have spider monkey.'

'I think that's meat.'

'Spider monkey very succulent. Dish of the day. I have it myself for breakfast.'

'That sounds nice, but I'd like the iguana. With rice, please,' I added decisively.

'Iguana very short. The road to Lethem impassable after rainy season. You have spider monkey instead, darlin?'

'I've got my heart set on the iguana.' The thought of spider monkey was too much of a double whammy: spider plus monkey equals no deal.

'I ask cook what else he do.' The woman smiled sweetly and walked slowly away.

'So is that Suriname across the water?' I asked, looking out of the window.

'Yes, it's a strange and unpredictable place.'

'Have you been there?'

'There's not much to see. Although the civil war has ended, armed bandits still control the remoter parts. They're also partial to a bit of kidnapping.'

'Not advisable to visit then?'

'The capital, Paramaribo is like Georgetown with its quaint wooden colonial houses. There's an old fort made entirely of Dutch bricks brought over the ocean in boats as ballast. Otherwise bird watching is about as exciting as it gets.'

'I'll stay in Guyana. It sounds marginally safer.'

'For some people it is!'

Raised voices came from the kitchen and the woman shuffled back.

'Darlin, all we have is spider monkey.'

'Oh?' I said looking at Ellis.

'Can you do a toasted cheese sandwich, love?' Ellis asked.

'Yes, darlin. How many you want?'

'Two please,' I said.

'I'll ask cook.' The woman turned and hobbled away.

'Do you think that's a yes?' I said. 'There doesn't seem to be much on the menu.'

'We'll see.'

'Tell me,' I asked. 'What keeps you in Corriverton?'

Ellis ran her fingers through her short blonde hair. Her jaggedy pixie haircut suited her high cheek-bones. In this heat, with her glowing skin, she looked really rather attractive.

'You know how it is, things drift by. Suddenly I've been here three years and this is where my friends are. I haven't got much to go back to in Sheffield – when I left there were no jobs.'

'It's Tony Blair's Britain now – boom time. The bars are open twenty-four hours and they're building new super casinos.'

'That's a weird form of socialism.'

'It's called New Labour. It's got to be better than seventeen years of Conservative government.'

'I don't think I'll be rushing back.'

She was right. I realised how glad I was to be away from Tony's cronies. I remembered that May night two years before. The euphoria of watching the Tory regime crumble. The elation of seeing Thatcher's smug acolytes crash, one by one, to the ground. We screamed with joy and jumped up and down as Michael Portillo lost his parliamentary seat to some unknown pip-squeak. It was the end of an era; the Tories had been chucked out for ever. The next day, tired but happy, I listened to Blair speak from his heart, in his endearing way, to the nation.

It took a while to realise things weren't quite right, and Blair wasn't what we thought he was. It wasn't long before he was privatising the national utilities and inviting Thatcher to 10 Downing Street for tea, sandwiches and God knows what. Recently, I'd noticed something self-delusional about the man. I feared his stuttering delivery hid something more sinister.

'I'm not sure about Blair,' said Ellis. 'He's too matey with the US. Before you know it, Britain will be fighting America's wars.'

'The government would never agree to that.'

A man with a knife the size of a machete stood at the kitchen door checking us out. He looked more like a pirate than a cook. I nodded in acknowledgement and gave him the best smile I could manage.

'Yeah, man,' he nodded back, and returned to the kitchen, his curiosity satisfied.

The waitress shuffled over with our food. As she hobbled away she put her hand over her mouth as if she was stifling a laugh.

I bit into my toasted cheese sandwich. The bread was dry and the lukewarm processed cheese tasted rubbery and synthetic. I was beginning to think I should have had the spider monkey after all.

'So why am I here?' mused Ellis, staring out of the window into the distance. 'Sometimes I don't know. I suppose I went into international development to make a difference to the world. People need water, food and education. And they need skills to produce something of value to sell on the open market. How complicated can that be? You see, the people in Guyana have a rotten deal. In my own little way I thought I could help make things easier. Teach reading and writing, provide a bit of health education. You know what they say. Give a man roast dinner and feed him for a day; give him a hen and he'll have omelettes for life.' She shrugged. 'It's not much to ask, is it?'

'Sounds straightforward to me.'

'The problem is much of the development money stays in Europe and is spent on huge salaries and generous expense accounts. With due respect, consultants like you don't do so badly out of it.'

'I thought you said I shouldn't count my chickens.'

'Anyhow, sometimes you have to believe in yourself. Believe you can make a difference – however small. Does that make sense?'

I nodded. I had to admire Ellis. She didn't smile much, but I could see she had a good heart.

'I couldn't do it.' I said. 'I'd miss home, I'd miss England: the fold of the landscape, the changing colour of the leaves.'

I remembered Gordon's crazyometer questions. Apart from an overactive imagination and paranoia, seemingly focused entirely on me, Ellis had, so far, appeared remarkably sane.

'Hey, what's the date?' I asked.

'No idea. Why?'

'Just wondered. I've lost track of time since I've been in Guyana.'

'That's what happens. The sun comes up at 6.30 in the morning and goes down at 6.30 in the evening. All the days are the same. There are no proper seasons. We just get wet or dry. Sometimes I yearn for those unremitting dreary English winter days,' she laughed, 'but then I come to my senses.'

'Did you hear the news about the Prime Minster?'

'No.'

'What's his name?'

'What do you mean, what's his name?'

'The Prime Minister's name, I've forgotten it.'

'Felix, are you alright?'

'Yeah, his name's just gone out of my head. What is it?'

'Hinds,' said Ellis.

'Hinds?'

'Sam Hinds, the Prime Minister of Guyana.'

'No, not the Prime Minster of Guyana,' I said.

'What, Tony Blair?'

'That's it, Tony Blair.'

'Felix, are you sure you're feeling okay?'

I held up my empty glass. 'God, that rum was strong.'

I still felt hungry. 'I could eat another one.'

'You should have had the spider monkey. Much more filling.'

'What about you?'

'I'm fine,' Ellis said. 'Have another butty.'

'No, I'd better not.' Even though I felt famished I couldn't face another cardboard and rubber sandwich.

The river appeared even busier. I could just about make out the silhouettes of unlit boats, scores of them, plying their way through the choppy water.

'The coast-guards occasionally patrol, but they are powerless,' Ellis explained. 'There's a squabble with Suriname over the location of the border. Suriname claims it owns the whole river, while Guyana says the border runs along the middle. The smugglers take advantage of this dispute.'

'Well, I suppose you can be grateful for one thing,' said Ellis. 'At least DoDO hasn't sent you up-country to sample psychotropic plants with the Yanomani.' She chuckled. 'Nobody comes back quite the same from the pork-knocker country.'

'What the heck is pork-knocker country?'

'Pork-knockers. It's what the free miners are called. It's something to do with what they eat.'

'Tell me more.'

'Well, a few years ago, up towards the border with Venezuela, there was a gold rush. Every chancer in Guyana, and roundabouts, flocked there to make their fortune. First Nation people as well.'

'Who?'

'The Amerindians.'

'Of course.'

'You don't need much equipment to dig for gold, apart from a wooden sluice box and a shovel. Just shovel the mud out of the river, sift it, separate it out with mercury, and there you are. Some people make good money. But what do you do with your dunza when you're in the middle of nowhere? Most pork-knockers booze and screw their money away. In no time at all shanty towns have sprung up in the forest to cater for local needs. At Sinclairville, right alongside the grass strip runway, there's a line of grog shacks and knocking shops.'

'And an opera house?'

Ellis looked at me as if I was off my cracker.

'Do you want to hear this, or not?'

'In Manaus,' I explained, 'they have an opera house.'

'That was in the days of the rubber stampede, that was a long time ago.'

'Of course,' I said, wishing I'd kept my mouth shut.

'So knocking shops and grog shacks are where the real cash is made. The sad thing is the gold rush wrought havoc on the Amerindians. The land belongs to them, always has done. It's their livelihood. Traditionally, they hunt, they fish, they grow. But nobody respects that. The miners chopped down the trees and poisoned the rivers. The fish died. Tribes fell apart; the women were forced to make a quick buck selling themselves.'

'Sounds like I'm going to have to adjust the framework and beef up the coefficients for personal services.'

'It's an economy as basic as the Garden of Eden. If you're really interested in the labour market, that's where you ought to go.'

'I'm a desk wallah. Once I've done my work here, I'm heading back to Georgetown.'

'My advice is, if they do send you up-country, demand a gun. It's the wild west up there.'

Ellis didn't seem to understand I was going nowhere. 'Firearms aren't part of my statistical tool-kit.'

'Nothing fancy, not a Kalashnikov, just a hand gun. It makes people think twice. Put a bit of hardware on the table and the monkey-suckers understand you mean business.'

Thinking about it, things might have happened a damn sight quicker in Georgetown if I had slammed a shooter on the desk.

'Thanks for the advice, but that's all totally hypothetical.'

'Up-country is a crazy place. They have weird ideas. In comparison, Corriverton looks like a sleepy suburb of Toytown.'

'This time next week I'm going to be on a Virgin Atlantic flight heading home.'

She laughed. 'Freelancer AND dreamer.'

Ellis suddenly stood up. 'I think we ought to move away from the window.'

'Why?'

'The boatmen will think you are spying on them.'

'Jesus! I'm not wearing a tie, neither am I wearing a hat. What else do you want me to do?'

'Go home.'

FOUR

Research. Intelligence. Spying. There's a fine line between them.

The GuyBankCo office, a six-storey steel and smoked glass box, was the one building on Main Street not constructed of wood. A guard, clasping a battered sub-machine gun, ushered us in from the dark and pointed to a lift.

'This is the only lift in Corriverton,' said Ellis. 'Most people don't use it because of power cuts.'

'Let's walk,' I said.

'Be careful what you say to Jim,' Ellis whispered as we climbed the piss-stinking stairs. 'He comes over as friendly and relaxed, but there's another side to him. He's an unreconstructed Marxist/Leninist.'

'What, hardcore, like Che Guevara?'

'Jim thinks Che's a degenerate liberal. Jim misses the Berlin Wall. And whatever you do, don't ask him about money laundering.'

'Why not?'

'Flipping heck, man. I live here. Don't make my life any more difficult than you have already.'

'A Marxist bank manager – this I have to see.'

We walked up six flights of stairs. Jim lived above the 'shop'. He was standing at the door of his apartment. I put out my hand but he grabbed me and gave me a hug instead. He was an enormous man; my arms were wedged to my sides as I was enveloped by his muscular, bear-like frame. He squeezed me so tight I thought I was going to have an asthma attack.

We entered a high-ceilinged penthouse with views across town to the river estuary and the ocean beyond. To the east, over Suriname, a far-away thunderstorm was silently lighting up the clouds.

While Ellis excused herself and went to the bathroom Jim poured me a tumbler of Johnny Walker Red.

'So, Mr Radstock, tell me about your work.'

'I'm doing research, that sort of thing.'

'Research. Intelligence. Spying. There's a fine line between them.'

'My project may sound like Mission Impossible, but I can promise you I'm not a spy.'

'The end of the Cold War put a lot of spies out of business. I hear these out of work James Bonds have moved on to business intelligence and low-grade industrial espionage.'

Did I really look like a spy? I felt quietly flattered by this. 'I'm afraid I have no idea what you are talking about.'

Disappointed, Jim shook his head. 'We need teachers, but all we get are researchers.'

'Yes, I hear there's a shortage of teachers.'

'In this town the kids don't understand the importance of education.' He pointed to the river and the stream of boats scuttling across it in the moonlight. 'But then why should they when they can make good money doing that? When there is a lack of opportunities people turn to other ways of making money. Unfortunately teachers earn so little; less than a taxi driver. Teaching is the most important job in the world, but nobody wants to do it.'

Jim leant forward and in a hushed voice said he was concerned about Ellis's well-being. 'I fear Corriverton has not been a good influence on her. She spends too much time with Renata's pussy cats. She's getting a bad name. She needs to return to England before it is too late.'

'Ellis says Renata's is the only place she feels safe.'

'She needs to get back to her husband.'

'Husband?'

'She doesn't talk about him, but when she's had a few rums she has shown me photographs.'

'Of her husband?'

Jim lowered his voice. 'Naked pictures. Very sexy.'

Naked pictures of who? Ellis? Her husband? Both!? I didn't like to ask.

'Do you have a family Mr Radstock?'

'Not really.'

'What's that mean?'

'I've got a long-term girlfriend, but,' I surprised myself by what I said next, 'it's not really going anywhere.'

'How old are you?'

'Thirty-three.'

'You should be married. You should have children.' Jim punched me on the shoulder. 'You should have grandchildren.'

'Give me a chance.'

'In Guyana most people of your age have grandchildren.'

'You're kidding.'

'I don't understand you British and your stiff lips. Why do you only like prostitutes?'

'We don't.' I said indignantly. 'That's the Spanish.'

'The Spanish?'

'Forty per cent of Spanish men have used the services of a hostess.'

'That's a precise figure. How do you know that?'

'It's my job to know this sort of stuff. World Health Organisation statistics.'

Jim raised an eyebrow in disbelief. 'So, Mr Radstock, tell me about your research?'

'The labour market.'

'Only last week I had a woman from the International Bank investigating exactly the same thing.'

The I.B. had been set up with good intentions, but like everything else good in this world it had been hijacked by the greed-mongers. It was now one of the most heinous organisations imaginable.

'Who was she?' I asked. The I.B. researching the labour market? This was the first I'd heard about it.

'I have an endless carnival of researchers,' said Jim, 'from the World Bank, the IMF or some investment company enquiring about the 'labour force'. They say they want to help us, create jobs, improve our standard of living, but they're just looking for new markets for themselves.'

'My report will be used by the government to inform investment strategy,' I said, trying to hide my irritation at Bucket's assumption.

'Is that what they told you?'

'Not exactly.'

'You and the I.B. woman ought to get together and share notes. You'd like her, Miss Honeyfield is a very foxy lady.'

I wondered if this woman was having any more success than me in acquiring information. 'She's probably studying it from a different angle.'

Jim laughed. 'The labour market is the labour market as far as I'm concerned. Supply and demand. The exploiter and the exploited.'

'It doesn't have to be that way.'

'That's what it's all about. As Marx wrote,' Jim straightened his massive frame, and spoke as if he were addressing his comrades in the Kremlin, 'the history of society is the history of class struggle. Capitalist and proletariat. But now, with globalisation we not only have a downtrodden class, but also downtrodden countries.'

'Oh yes?' I didn't like to say I thought Marxist theory was passé and no longer accepted as credible.

Jim looked towards the window. 'And one day, one day soon, the working people,' his voice got louder and more intense, as if he was addressing the massed ranks of comrades in Red Square, 'will unite rise up and smash the oppressors.' He raised his clenched fist in the air, bowed his head, and was silent for a moment, as he humbly acknowledged the applause of the multitude.

I nodded thoughtfully, saying nothing. I wondered if I should have followed his clenched fist salute, but thought better of it, and quietly cleared my throat.

After a few awkward seconds, Jim shook himself from his reverie and in a quieter voice said, 'I learnt that in Moscow.'

He appeared to have read my thoughts. 'How can something that is right ever become outdated?' he continued.

Ellis returned and gave me a little wave as if to say, I'll leave you to it, and went to study the view.

'What were you doing in Moscow?' I asked.

'I won a bursary. Before perestroika, the Soviet Union would offer university scholarships. I was very lucky. I read economics.'

'It must have been a shock to leave here. How did you cope with the Russian winters?'

'I owe everything to the Russians. They took me from this place and gave me an education. They opened my eyes and showed me a new world.' Jim took a swig of his drink and held up his tumbler. 'I'd never seen snow before. In Guyana, the only ice I'd seen was in a glass.'

'Are you still in contact with Moscow?'

'I keep in touch. They like to know what is going on. Guyana needs all the help it can get. Here, cooperative socialism is what we strive for.'

'Sounds sensible. I've always shopped at the Co-op.'

'The concept is good – the practice often falls short. People get greedy. They like to look after their families. When you have been poor for a long time it is human nature to take a little bit extra, something to see you through the hard times, which you fear are always round the corner.' Jim gestured towards the river. 'It's not exactly a socialist utopia down there. Look, capitalism began on the backs of slave labour and continues on the backs of the poor. Anything that breaks that cycle has got to be a step forward.'

'Ellis says there is a lot of unofficial trading over the border.'

'Miss Deane does not understand how we do things in Guyana.

I call it freight forwarding, uneducated people call it something else. This is a prosperous town.'

'So smuggling is okay, then?'

'We have a freer concept of state control than you are used to. Inland they have gold, here we have another type of gold. We call it the informal economy. These people are entrepreneurs. I don't ask questions – I'm just a bean counter, it's none of my business.'

'Really?' As a bank manager I thought, maybe, it was his business.

Jim turned and stared angrily at me. 'Are you accusing me of money laundering?'

'No, no, no. I'm just interested in how things work. I'll mention this freight forwarding in my report.'

'You are sailing in dangerous waters. I would strongly advise against that.'

'I'll be discreet.'

'You need to be careful in this town – everybody needs to be careful. Are you sure you don't work for the CIA?'

'I've already told you, I'm working for DoDO.'

'Some other enforcement agency then?'

'I'm English!'

'Of course you are. Fair play, jolly good show and all that. And I bet they're paying you more than a bag of candy.'

'It's not much. And I haven't been paid yet.'

'We are a very small country. There is so much potential in Guyana but we are divided. We call ourselves the country of six nations. Unfortunately, the African Guyanese and the Indian Guyanese never work together. Very different cultures. We should be standing together, shoulder to shoulder, fighting the imperialist running dogs. But you know this already.'

'Yeah, well,' I said. 'The English didn't handle the early days too well,'

'What are you saying?'

'I'm not proud of our history.'

'Don't give me all that slave baloney.'

'I'm sorry about it.'

'It was a product of the times. We must look ahead. We need to be united by our class struggle. As Marcus Garvey said, 'We must emancipate ourselves from mental slavery.'

'I'll drink to that,' I said raising my glass.

'Now, that lady from the International Bank, she was intriguing. She said she was a futurologist. I've never met a white sister like her.' Jim gestured as if he was holding a couple of coconuts to his chest. 'Man, together we emptied a whole bottle of Johnny Walker before we hit the Greenheart Hotel. Though I think she was more interested in knowing about gold than the labour market. Are you interested in gold, Mr Radstock?'

'Mining is part of the labour market isn't it?'

'Hah!' Jim nodded his head slowly, looking at me as if I'd fallen into a trap. 'Did you know Corriverton is famous for its nightlife?'

'I've not heard that.'

'You need to visit. For your survey, of course. Tonight I will take you to the best nightclub in the Caribbean. The view is very scenic and it is handy for the river.'

FIVE

Ellis was in no hurry to leave.

Jim was greeted warmly by a couple of dudes liming outside the Greenheart Hotel. 'Off-duty police,' he explained. 'The hotel is popular for its half-hour short stay option.'

Ellis and I were ushered into a large, low room with a bank of speakers along one wall and a bar opposite. At the far end a door led to a terrace overlooking the Corentyne.

Despite Xavier's earlier reassurances, I felt nervous. I could feel eyes staring at me from the darkness. We were the only non blacks in the room. I glanced at my watch. It was already one o'clock.

This was a rougher, more sexually-charged beat than I was used to. There was more bass, and more distortion – in this heat and dark the music was intoxicating, throbbing with the deep rhythms of life. I'd never experienced anything like it. A sultry woman perched at the bar gave me an I'm-available-for-money look – I returned her stare and smiled. For a moment I felt I was falling under the spell of this beguiling country. If only I could forget Aurora for a moment, just one moment, and really enjoy myself.

'Don't stand too near the speakers.' Ellis shouted in my ear. 'The bass relaxes the sphincter muscles – people shit themselves.'

I laughed. 'Some folks really know how to have a good time.'

'And don't go near the balcony.'

'Jim has already warned me about the delights of the balcony.'

'It's a long drop to the river.'

'I told you, I'm not expecting to have a swim.'

'People might have other ideas.'

Jim handed me a rum cocktail. 'I have been told you are quite a celebrity in Corriverton, Mr Radstock.'

'What do you mean?'

'Why didn't you tell me about the computers?'

'Oh God!' I groaned.

'My friend said everybody is waiting for them.'

'Jim, I'm sorry to disappoint you, but there are no computers.'

'Is that so? There could be serious repercussions.'

'Why does everybody think I've got something to do with this?'

Jim didn't seem to hear what I said. 'Don't worry, stay with me and you will be safe.'

'And when I'm not with you? What then?'

'In Corriverton you are my guest. Elsewhere, I cannot be responsible for your well-being.'

Jim stood directly in front of me and put his hands on my shoulders. I felt as if he was staring into my soul. 'I am beginning to think,' he said 'that perhaps the labour market is a euphemism for something else.'

I felt uncomfortable locked in to his gaze. 'I've told you,' I said, 'I'm not a spook. It's straightforward. As you say, it's just supply and demand.'

'I think there is more to your mission than you are telling me.'

'I don't know what you mean.' I wondered if Jim was alluding to my operation to check out Ellis on the crazyometer .

'Maybe your boss hasn't been entirely straight with you.'

A new DJ had taken over the decks and the floor was filling up. Couples were bumping and grinding – the men were riding their girls like they were in a rodeo, bucking back and forth, holding their arms in the air.

'C'mon let's dance,' said Ellis.

'I don't know.' I felt intimidated by the cool, effortlessly gyrating dudes.

'Relax. It's called Dancehall. Enjoy it.'

I was glad to get away from Jim for a moment. The cocktails and the humidity had loosened me up and I was soon jiving with the best of them. Ellis turned out to be a hot little mover. Hips grinding, this was dirty, sexy stuff. During the day I had found myself looking at her. I'd tried hard to ignore the fact that she was an attractive woman. Although dressed in khaki shorts, desert boots and socks, there was something alluring about her energy. As the evening went on and the pace slowed we hung onto each other. Her breath smelled of the Caribbean: rum and coconut. I could feel the soft contours of her body pressed against me. I had to fight to keep my natural urges under control.

As we left, Jim opened his arms and pulled me towards his massive frame.

'Comrade, we say goodbye, Moscow style.'

'Thanks for your help and advice.'

He whispered in my ear. 'Do you have any glamour photographs?'

'Not like Ellis. My girlfriend doesn't do that sort of thing.'

'You and Ellis make a sweet couple.'

'No, no, no. We're just colleagues.'

Jim looked at his watch. It was three o clock. 'The night is still young.'

'I've got to get some sleep. I leave for Georgetown tomorrow.'

Jim nodded. 'For your own well-being that is a good plan.'

'I promise I'll be discreet.'

I had no idea where I was.

'I'd better see you home,' said Ellis.

'See ME home! What about you?'

'I live near the Sweet Dreams.'

'Are you sure? Why don't we get a taxi?'

'It's no distance to walk.'

'We're not going alongside the river, are we?' I asked.

'Are you worried about the caimans?'

'I thought you said there weren't any caimans,' I shuddered at the thought of these giant reptiles lurking on the water's edge, ready to snap their jaws round a leg.

'You're safe with me,' Ellis said, putting her arm in mine.

I felt uneasy about walking. 'I don't know. I thought this was a lawless town.'

'I'm okay,' said Ellis, 'It's only you they're after.'

'Yeah, well, Xavier said I was perfectly safe.'

'Xavier doesn't live here.'

'You're just paranoid.'

We both laughed. Apart from the occasional cow munching in the darkness, the streets were quiet. It had been an enjoyable night. The threats of violence had come to nothing, I hadn't had an unexpected swim and, indeed, I was getting into this liming business.

For a moment I thought about Aurora and wished I was strolling with her through the hot night.

I imagined her, sitting astride me, lifting up her T-shirt, pulling her shoulders back as she undid her bra. I wanted to lose myself in unthinking abandon. When I returned to Bristol I swore things would be different and I would try harder.

I wasn't ready to crash and Ellis seemed to be in no hurry to leave.

'Want to come up?' I asked.

'Why not?'

We walked past the out-of-order johnny machine. 'There's a local shortage,' said Ellis. 'Everybody is waiting for a new consignment. Pull out and pray, that's the last thing this country needs.'

I fumbled for the key and cautiously opened the door. I could hear animals skittering in the dark. 'Welcome to the bug house!'

'You've got enough places to kip, then,' she said.

'Yeah, plenty of choice,' I said. 'Let's see what's in the mini-bar.'

Ellis lay on the middle bed, splayed-out under the ceiling fan. 'That's better,' she said, enjoying the down-draft.

I opened a warm bottle of Banks for each of us and then settled by the window.

We rested on our separate beds and were silent for a while. So far I'd failed miserably with Gordon's questions. I turned and looked at Ellis. She was lying on her back with the top buttons of her blouse undone, her bra supporting a generous cleavage.

Ellis sat up. 'Do you mind?' she said lighting a roll-up.

'You shouldn't be smoking.'

'I only do it because I'm lonely.'

'Okay,' I said, 'so how many wives did King Henry the Eighth have?'

'Felix, you're babbling. Have you got amnesia again?'

'It's a crossword clue I was doing earlier.'

'Is this a trick question?'

'No, tell me.'

'Every school-brat knows the answer to that.'

'Yeah?'

'Annulled, beheaded, died, annulled, beheaded, survived.'

'I've never heard that version before.'

'Technically, they weren't divorced.'

'So how many wives is that?'

'What the flipping heck is up with you? Work it out yourself, you lazy bastard.'

A lizard scurried up the wall by the bathroom door. To my surprise, I didn't mind this animal creeping around my room. I must be getting used to this country, I thought.

'Jim said you had a husband.'

'Yeah?'

'He said you showed him photographs.'

'Did he?'

'Sexy photos.'

'Give over! That wasn't my husband, they were pictures from a magazine. I think it was Robbie Williams or some other toss-pot like that.'

'So tell me about your husband.'

'His name is Roger. Roger, over and out I used to call him.' She smiled. 'It was a long time ago.'

'Yeah?'

'That was one of the reasons I came here. To get away from all that.'

'From all what?'

'The never ending greyness. The everyday dullness and predictability of life when you have little money. We met too early. I had to leave. At least here, life is colourful. And I never know what's going to happen.'

'I'm thinking of getting married,' I said.

'Good for you,' she said, raising her drink.

I leant over and we clinked bottles. 'Maybe,' I said.

It was quiet, apart from the comforting hum and click of the ceiling fan. In the street outside, a barking dog was answered by distant howls from across town.

Ellis lay on her bed and blew smoke into the air. 'So, is that it then?' she said.

'I can't remember any of the other crossword questions.'

'I wasn't meaning that.' She raised herself on one elbow and gave me a mischievous smile. 'Me here, you over there.'

'It's too hot,' I said.

'Come on pretty boy, this heat makes everybody horny.'

'Yeah, well, I just thought...'

'Jesus! What's up with you? Every man in this town seems to want to fuck me. Then you come along, the only half decent guy I've met in months, and you go all coy. What's so different about you?'

'Maybe you shouldn't hang round Renata's so much. It gives people the wrong idea.'

'What do you know what I do?'

'Look, we both work for DoDO. I'm trying to keep things on a professional level.'

'Sod that! You said you didn't work for DoDO.'

'You know what I mean.'

'I don't. We've got a bond. We've got to stick together. Com'on Felix, be honest with yourself, you want it. We both want it.'

I looked at her lying on the bed. She was right. Why not?

'It's just...' I was trying to push thoughts of Aurora out of my head.

'I get it. You're not into women...'

'Of course I'm into women.'

'Doesn't seem like it to me. All that hugging with Jim. You like a bear, eh.'

'For Christ sake!'

'I'm going home.'

'Ellis!'

'I thought you were okay. But I should have known. You're just another DoDO battyboy.'

'I told you, I don't work for DoDO.'

SIX

The bush is a terrible place.

The drive back from Corriverton was even more alarming than our outward journey. We'd started early, at 6.30 am, as I'd told Xavier I wanted to get to Georgetown before dark.

For the first few miles, I hid under a tarp on the back seat of the Discovery. I could hear Xavier chuckling to himself. He still hadn't got over his joke about the stolen vehicle. 'You should have seen your face! Oh man!' he said as he slapped the steering wheel.

After half an hour Xavier assured me we were far enough away from Corriverton to be safe, so I moved to the front seat. In places the road surface had been washed away. Pedestrians didn't seem to understand the basics of highway safety. Although it was a busy road, several times people stepped in front of our speeding vehicle, seemingly oblivious to the danger. As we drove through one hamlet, a row of children stood on the verge and hurled stones at us. Had they heard about me as well? Was I some sort of national hate figure? Xavier stamped on the brakes, jumped out of the car and rushed after them. 'I know you,' he shouted, 'I will tell your parents. They will tan your hides.'

'How was your meal last night?' Xavier asked.

'Good.'

'What did you have?'

'There wasn't much choice.'

'Didn't you have the bush meat?'

'You know what? I don't think you ought to be eating those animals. Many of them are endangered.'

Xavier ignored what I said and asked, 'And Jim? How did you get on with Jim?'

'Interesting guy.'

'Don't believe a word he says, he's been brainwashed by the People's Army.'

We passed a wooden sign, 'Goldie's Beach Shack 5 kms'.

'What's that?' I said.

'The coast is mostly mangrove swamp, but near here there's a sandy beach.'

I told Xavier I'd like a closer look. At Village Number 63 – after Whim, they'd run out of inspiration for names – we swung off the main road and bumped along a dirt track flanked by listing shacks and banana trees. Followed by children shouting 'school pen, school pen,' we climbed the dyke and looked at the ocean. The small strip of sand was white and the water coffee brown.

I asked Xavier where the beach shack was. He shrugged and said Goldie was probably only here for the Easter celebrations. I pointed out there wasn't even a shack. Xavier didn't seem interested. 'Castles in the sand,' he muttered. 'Castles in the sand.'

The shoreline was littered with driftwood, plastic bottles and polystyrene clods. The bloated carcass of a large dog was being washed in and out of the sea by the gently lapping waves. It wasn't how I'd imagined a Caribbean beach.

'Is this high tide?' I asked.

'This is low tide. High tide is later this afternoon.'

I stood for a moment enjoying the breeze of the great sea. Two black frigate-birds, angular-winged and fork-tailed, hung in the sky like paper kites on a string. I breathed deeply and tried to relax.

'Is this what you wanted to look at?' asked Xavier.

'Does anybody ever swim here?'

'Swim in a latrine? Why would anybody do that?'

We resumed our journey. Xavier pointed to the left, towards the low hills on the horizon away to the south-west.

'Ah man, you wouldn't believe the world ends over there, just ten miles away.' One of Xavier's favourite topics of conversation was the one time he went into the bush. 'You must not use the term jungle. It has colonial connotations: in Guyana, bush is the proper word.'

'Okay.' I'd never thought of it like that before.

'I travelled up-river with an Englishman. Once we got to the rapids we had to leave the canoes and walk. The bush is a terrible place. There are man-eating tigers.'

'Tigers?'

'Big black bush tigers – very dangerous.'

'I didn't know there were tigers in South America.'

'In Asia, they say if you come across a tiger in the jungle you should show your throat as a sign of supplication. Never do that with a Guyanese tiger. It enrages them even more. The tiger will interpret this as a sign of weakness and rip your gullet out in seconds.'

'I think it would take great sang-froid to show your throat to a tiger.'

'There is no escape. If you see a tiger you face certain death.'

Xavier continued his litany of bush horrors: piranhas would strip the flesh off your hand if you trailed it in the river; electric eels could generate enough heart-stopping voltage to jump-start a truck; indestructible soldier ants ate everything in their path; carnivorous plants screamed when you cut them down.

'Did you meet any First Nation people?' I asked, remembering the term Ellis had used.

'Who?'

The new terminology was lost on Xavier. 'Amerindians.'

I was interested to observe Xavier's response. He was becoming strangely agitated. His jaw was clenched and his knuckles were tight as he squeezed the steering wheel. 'Today, the Amerindians are mostly welcoming and speak good English. In the past they were said to be a fearsome and cruel people. In Suriname the Amerindians helped the runaway slaves set up their own village communities, but in Guyana they took great delight tracking them down. They showed no mercy and would cut off the hands of their victims as proof of capture. You don't forget brutality like that.'

'Yeah, but that was 150 years ago.'

'The Amerindian population is growing. They still dwell in the bush, but unlike everybody else, they don't want to leave the country. Where would they go?' Xavier turned and looked at me with a hint of alarm in his eyes. 'Some say they have secret powers.'

'People don't believe that these days, do they?'

'Although many are Christian they also practice their ancient tribal magic. Shamans play a big part in everyday life. They bequeath charms and officiate at births, deaths and tribal events. There's a tale about a tribe living by the Kaieteur Falls going through perilous times. They'd had a number of serious hunting accidents and, to make matters worse, their land was being encroached on by raiders from the north. The shaman said they should make a human sacrifice. So, to appease the Gods a young man was pushed over the edge.'

'Yeah?'

'For a moment, it is said, he swept and soared like a swallow.'

'Amazing.'

'But then gravity asserted itself and he crashed to his death on the rocks below.'

'Were the Gods appeased?'

Xavier was silent for a moment. 'No, but it gave the tribe something to talk about – it took their minds off their difficulties for a while.'

'Their secret powers sound a bit dodgy.'

We both laughed.

'What work do the Amerindians do?'

'Mostly subsistence farming and fishing – some mine as well.'

'Do you think there are any stats?'

'I doubt it. Why would there be?'

So that was another cavernous hole in my report. 'The bush is an all-enveloping experience,' Xavier continued. 'The humid heat, the burning light, the raw colours, the smell of growth and decay. For the more perceptive, this assault on the mind can prove to be too much. It is a terrible place where the senses can be overpowered. Never again, Mr Radstock, am I going into the bush. Never again.'

The road back to Georgetown took us through miles of sugar plantations. Canes like giant bamboos lined the road. Every few hundred yards the greenness was intersected by irrigation canals with empty black metal barges moored along their banks. At one point I spotted a mess of factory sheds, steel pipes and chimneys. 'What's that?' I asked.

'A sugar mill.'

'We need to investigate.'

'You must be quick. We don't want to miss the ferry again,' Xavier warned.

'This is empirical research. I need to get in there and check it out.'

At last I was going to see the labour market in action. I imagined powerful machinery mangling the raw green cane. The extracted juice would be boiled over massive fires, the air sweet with molasses. And then, at the end of the process, the finest Demerara sugar – Guyana gold; crystallised sunshine! - would be lovingly packed into sacks destined for consumption at breakfast tables around the world. I loved seeing what went on in factories, how things were made, watching skilled craftsmen, studying complex mechanisms. I'd always been fascinated by observing people at work. This was the reason – apart from the generous training grant – I had originally become interested in the labour market.

But as we parked at the front of a barn-like shed, the factory appeared empty.

'Where is everybody?' I asked.

'Breakfast?'

'Sound the horn.'

After a couple of minutes a side-door opened and a security guard dressed in khaki, with gun in holster, peered out and stared at us.

'Good morning!' I shouted.

The man ambled over.

'Good morning,' I repeated. We shook hands. I noticed that he was missing two fingers on his left hand.

'I'd like to speak to your Head of Human Resources.'

'Wha' ya say ?'

'Head of Human Resources. The man in charge of recruitment.'

'Wha' ya want?'

'I'm from England. Employed by the Department of Development Overseas on a labour market survey.'

The man laughed. 'Labour market survey! They sure hot topic. Wha' ya say ya name again?'

'Felix Radstock. Where is everybody?'

'We closed. End of season. Wrong time a year.'

'Can I have a look around?'

'Harvest not 'appen til April. Come back May. Plenty people then.'

'I won't be around in May.'

'Where ya say ya come from?'

'The UK. DoDO.'

'I busy.'

Although the guard turned to leave, I sensed he wouldn't take much persuading. Bored people always like to talk about their work.

'Just a quick look.'

He stopped and not so discreetly rubbed his thumb across his fingers making the international sign for baksheesh.

'You make contribution?' he shrugged.

I handed him a $10 note. He glanced at it, unimpressed, and put it in his trouser pocket.

I pointed to his missing fingers. 'Piranha bite?' I asked.

He smiled. 'All you foreigners tink dat. It accident in field. Many cane cutters lose fingers. Cutlass plenty sharp. Two month later, I get sweet revenge.' The man laughed, showing gold teeth. 'That taught him a be more careful. Him now a called 'One Hand'.'

The vast space, three stories high, was lit by shafts of white light shining through cracks in the wooden slats. A sweet smell that reminded me of fairground toffee apples hung in the air. The factory was a forlorn sight. Giant cogs, conveyor belts, guillotines and heavy hammers lay still and silent. As my eyes adjusted to the light I could see that the floor was alive with hundreds of mice. With mounting horror I could imagine the rodents swarming up my legs. I wanted to tuck my chinos into my socks; I wanted to get out of the building.

The guard noticed my alarm. 'Factory cat he plenty lazy.'

'And fat, I expect.'

'When machinery work you no hear the squeal of a pig.'

The place was a nightmare. It wasn't just mice scuttling around in this crapulous demi-world; high above, a rat the size of a dog jumped across the rafters.

'I think I've seen enough,' I said, moving towards the entrance.

'You must have tour.'

'No, I get the picture.'

'English visitor must have ten dollar visit.'

Glancing at my watch I gave Xavier a knowing look. 'We need to catch the New Amsterdam ferry.'

Xavier gave a reassuring smile. 'It's alright, we've made good time.'

'I must be back in Georgetown by this evening. I've got some important calls to make to England.'

'We'll be back by sundown, I assure you,' Xavier smirked. I swear he was up to his old tricks again.

Xavier and the security guard seemed unfazed by the waves of mice which thankfully parted as we walked towards them. The handrails were tacky to the touch and a syrupy stickiness permeated the building. We walked along rickety gangplanks and peered into giant cauldrons and massive spin-driers.

'So, tell me about the process?'

The guard explained that the cane was harvested in April and May and brought to the mill by barge along the canals. The canals were used both for irrigation and transport.

'Who cuts the cane?'

'It done by hired labour.'

'This was once an important industry,' Xavier chipped in, 'but as you can see the machinery is old and the farming techniques are wasteful.'

'The youth, they all wanna be cricket man or Puff Daddy,' said the guard.

Xavier continued. 'They fire the fields before they cut the cane. It is hard, hot, dirty and dangerous. The unions demand better wages. But the bosses say they can't afford it. Nowadays people don't like to work in the cane field. Who can blame them? Some years the cane is left in the fields to rot.'

'That's crazy.'

'The importance of the sugar industry to our country's development, now and in the foreseeable future, cannot be over-emphasised.' Xavier spoke as if he was reciting from a pre-prepared speech. 'Yet, Guyana cannot compete with the global market. We sell raw sugar to Europe through the EU Sugar Protocol. But they pay bottom dollar and insist on doing their own refining. Refining is where the money is made. How long we can sustain these losses I don't know.'

I was surprised and impressed by Xavier's insightful analysis. He was obviously a quick learner. Xavier's time with me would not be wasted.

'I understand the people of England know the name Demerara,' said Xavier. 'But the sugar that is sold under that brand comes from Mauritius.' He punched his palm with his fist. 'These pirates rip off our name and trade on our good reputation.'

Glad to be out in the fresh air again, away from the rodents and the sticky heat, I brushed myself down – I was covered in dust and fluff. Miraculously, Xavier's clothes were spotless.

'Thank you for your time.' I said to the guard.

'Say hello to the woman,' he replied.

'What woman?'

'From International Bank. She here last week. She not afraid of mouse!'

Could this woman be the same heavy drinker that had so impressed Jim Bucket?

'Xavier, I must say you're picking up this labour market jargon pretty quickly. I'm sure you could get a better job than just driving.' Xavier glanced at me, clearly annoyed. For a moment he was quiet but then in a low voice whispered: 'Please Mr Radstock, do not disrespect me.'

'I'm not disrespecting you.'

'Well, you are.'

'I'm sorry. I'm just trying to be helpful.'

'Thank you,' he said, as he stared straight ahead and put his foot on the accelerator.

As we neared New Amsterdam, Xavier became concerned about the car engine.

'Hear that?' he asked, his head cocked. 'A knocking sound.'

I couldn't notice any difference. Because of the rough terrain there were many knocking sounds.

Although we were several miles inland I could still discern the sea-wall in the distance. At one stage the dyke appeared to be topped by something white and moving – like melting sugar-ice dripping off a cake. I couldn't make it out.

'What's that?'

'It's the water coming over the levee.'

I felt a surge of panic. I'd never fancied the idea of death by drowning. How long would it be before this tsunami hit us?

'Xavier, shouldn't we do something? Like get the hell out of here.'

'It's high tide. It happens all the time. Much of the coastal plain is below sea level.'

What was wrong with the Dutch? Why didn't they build their settlements on hills like everyone else?

Xavier continued, 'A little flooding – you learn to accept it.'

'Are you sure we're safe? Don't you worry about it?'

'God moves in mysterious ways. One day that sea is going to come over the wall with a vengeance and reclaim the land. And there will be nothing we can do about it.'

'Xavier, I admire your pragmatism.'

'It is my faith. You can't fight God. You can't fight an ocean. Guyana is constantly under threat from forces beyond our control. With global warming, your global warming, much of this country will disappear.'

'I don't think I'm going to sleep well knowing that.'

'You get used to it.'

It had been a long journey – we'd been driving since first light and it was now getting dark. When we got back to Georgetown I was looking forward to reacquainting myself with the cool cotton sheets of the Stabroek Lodge. I'd talk to Aurora on the phone and tell her about my adventures, though I reckoned it would be best if I didn't mention Ellis. I also needed to speak to Gordon about the contract. So far progress had not been as good as I had hoped – I was hardly off the starting blocks. I decided if Gordon asked difficult questions I'd obfuscate, and if that didn't work I'd put the phone down, and hope he thought it was another power cut.

Xavier was tired. There was much clashing of gears and high revving. 'This is not good,' Xavier said.

SEVEN

A voluptuous woman at my doorway.

We lurched into the courtyard of the Stabroek Lodge and parked next to the three Toyota Land Cruisers.

'Welcome back, Mr Radstock,' said Festus. 'Did you have a good trip?' The racket of the evening chorus of tree frogs, and whatever other creatures made those grating, squeaking noises, was revving up to full throttle.

'It was interesting to see the macro-economy of another region of Guyana.' I didn't like to mention the death threats or that I'd had to leave Corriverton hidden under a blanket. 'I'm glad to be back though.' At least, in Georgetown, I felt safe from machete attack – or an impromptu defenestration and swim in the river.

'Have you heard the news from England?'

'What news?'

'The Prime Minister's wife...' for a moment I wondered if I was the person now being tested '... is pregnant.'

'Goodness me!'

'It is said that she conceived when she was staying at one of the Queen's houses in the countryside. The Guyana News speculates that your Duke of Edinburgh may be the father.' Your Duke of Edinburgh! I'd never before thought of him as being anything to do with me. Besides, the thought of the Duke of Edinburgh rogering Cherie Blair wasn't an image I particularly wanted in my head at that moment.

'I have some messages for you,' Festus turned and took a couple of papers from a pigeon-hole. I could hear a lively party in the adjoining bar – the tour group I guessed. Perhaps, later on, I could introduce myself to the woman in the red suit and buy her a rum punch.

'Ah yes. Roxy,' Festus winked at me, 'has been trying to contact you.'

'Good, I want to speak to her,' I said, eyeing up the scruffy country-boy hat that was resting on my luggage.

'Also, Mr Gordon from DoDO has phoned several times.'

'Thank heavens.'

'He said he is working at crisis level but he will call you again soon.'

'Have I got the same room?' I asked.

'Certainly, sir.'

I felt like I was coming home; I could feel myself relaxing, looking forward to sleeping in a room that didn't feel like a dormitory and, in the morning, eating a full buffet breakfast. Though, this time, probably without the giant egg.

'Oh!' said Festus, 'Wait a minute, please.' Flicking through the ledger he shook his head. 'I'm sorry Mr Radstock, there has been an administrative error. Let me speak to the manager. I'm sure we can sort it out.'

I sat down. I felt deadbeat. All I wanted was a shower and a change into fresh clothes.

Festus returned. 'It seems we have no reservation for you.'

'You must have. I booked before I left.'

'Of course.'

There was shouting and laughter from the adjoining lounge, the door opened and a man staggered out of the room. He was already fumbling with his zip in readiness for a piss. He gave me a bewildered look. I pointed, 'Toilet over there.'

Festus continued, 'My apologies, we have let your room to somebody else.'

'That's a bloody nuisance.'

'It is not a problem, Mr Radstock, we have a sister hotel, the Silent Night Guesthouse. I will book you a bed there.'

I was too tired to argue. At least I could hang onto Ninety-Two Days.

'It is in the centre of town. The guesthouse is conveniently located for all the local amenities and is very comfortable. It has the added benefit of a pavement bar – I'm sure you will like it. Your friend Roxy is a regular visitor.'

'Is she? That would be useful.'

'She can help you relax.'

'I certainly need to get my hat sorted out.'

'Roxy has many satisfied customers.'

The Silent Night Guesthouse was bang in the centre of Georgetown, on the noisiest street in the city. Motor bikes careened up and down; jalopies stuttered and backfired. The pavement bar was busy with a raucous mix of men having after-work drinks and hardcore limers. I was taken up a concrete staircase to my accommodation. There was a double bed and a wash basin. I pulled back the curtain for some fresh air, but there was no window, merely a blank wall. Neither was there air-con or a fan. I could feel my chest tighten at the thought of spending a night in this claustrophobic tomb.

'I'd like to see some other rooms.'

'This is the only one we have.'

Over the last few days I'd had little sleep and was too exhausted to quibble. 'Okay, I'll take it'

'Is there anything else I can get you?'

'A window would be good.'

He laughed. 'It is best to book in advance if you want a view.'

At least with no window I wouldn't be bothered by mosquitoes.

'There is a shower down the hall. You can have all the water you want at no extra charge.'

'Festus said it was convenient for the local amenities. What are they?

'Ah!' The man thought for a moment. 'Yes, everything is within walking distance.'

'What is?'

'The amenities.'

I was too tired to pursue this further.

I found it difficult sleeping on the thin foam mattress in my stale, airless room. Even with no window, the hubbub of the street drinkers below permeated the walls of my little black hole. I began reading the Evelyn Waugh book I had borrowed from the Stabroek Lodge. Ninety-Two Days didn't start well. In the preface, a sanguine Waugh asks who in their right mind would buy, and read, a travel book of no scientific value about a place they have no intention of visiting? Quite so. I looked at the author's picture – dressed in khaki navel-hugging shorts, Waugh had a bad-tempered mouth, and the smoothness of features that is prescient of middle-age rotundity. It appears that he was on the run from a broken marriage so he took a slow boat to the Caribbean. But why Guyana? Because he knew so little about it. That was sixty five years ago. Little had changed: Guyana is still an abused and neglected corner of the South American continent.

Eventually, I drifted off and dreamt of the sea flooding over the dyke. A malevolent and unstoppable wall of water, higher than a two-storey building, was surging over the sea-wall and bulldozing its way through the town. Although the giant wave appeared to lumber slowly across the landscape, cars driving at full throttle endeavouring to escape were no match for its velocity. Houses were pushed over, and crumpled like toys.

I yelled for help, and then I was under water thrashing around in the darkness like a doll in a washing machine. I couldn't breathe; I was fighting through the debris to get to the surface. I awoke in a sweat. Putting on the light I noticed the wall next to me was smeared with blood and my left hand was grazed and bleeding. I crawled out of bed and opened the door hoping to get a fresh breeze and some oxygen into my unventilated cell. But the night air was as still as stone.

I fell asleep again and imagined I saw the silhouette of a voluptuous woman at my doorway. She entered my room and whispered in my ear. 'I need to take some measurements.' Her hands were soft and caressing. 'Do you normally measure with your mouth?' I gasped. 'You have a big head,' she murmured.

I woke again, hobbled to the door, and closed it.

EIGHT

'Do you have a gun?

Breakfast of bone-dry toast and bitter guava jam was served on a veranda overlooking the street. Despite the previous night's claustrophobic cell and vivid dreams I was feeling pleasantly relaxed – as if a build-up of tension had been released. Across the road was one of the few buildings in Georgetown not made of wood. A once stylish two-storey art-deco block, its sweeping concrete lines were stained and its shutters broken. The sidewalk was busy with people walking purposefully to work or school. From a wooden donkey cart a woman was selling fruit – elongated pineapples, finger bananas, large red apples and spiky tropical produce I didn't recognise.

I phoned Aurora. An unfamiliar voice, a male voice, answered the phone.

'Aurora?' I asked.

'Hang on, just a mo.' I could hear him shout 'Aurora, there's some bloke on the phone for you.'

'Hello?' came Aurora's voice.

'Who was that?' I asked.

'Oh hi, Felix. How's it going?'

'Hi,' I said, 'Who was that?'

'The builder.'

'Why's a builder answering your phone?'

'I asked him to. I was in the bathroom.'

This sounded a bit too chummy for me. 'What have you got a builder for?'

'You know, he's putting up some shelves.'

'I was going to do that.'

'I thought I'd get it done while you're away. It was going to be a surprise.'

'Right.' I didn't want to talk about DIY. 'How are you?' I asked.

'Yes, good. And you?'

'I'm back in Georgetown.'

'I didn't know you were travelling around.'

'I'm not supposed to be. But I'm back in the capital city now. They've got parrots in the trees.' Over the line I could hear banging and then the scream of an electric drill.

'I can't hear you, Felix. What did you say they've got in the trees?'

'PARROTS.' Why did I always say this!? 'They've got parrots in the trees. Green parrots.' The drilling was even louder. 'Can you ask the builder to stop drilling?' I shouted.

'What?'

'Stop the fucking drill!'

'I can't hear a word you're saying. Felix, you'll have to call back later.'

'It'll be a while. I'm going up-country, I'll be out of reach.'

'Sorry, I can't hear you, Felix,' she said. The line went dead.

I wished I hadn't bothered. I didn't even have a chance to ask about the weather. I wondered if Aurora understood how much I loved her. But now I felt depressed and disorientated. And I specially didn't like the idea of some builder putting up shelves and eating my chocolate Hobnobs. I hoped that was all he was doing.

I needed to concentrate on something else. Next on my list was to phone Gordon and get hold of the contract. I felt disinclined, however, to give Gordon a detailed update on my progress. The visit to Corriverton had not been a success. I hadn't been able to gather any official statistics, while my empirical research was still thin. With his twisted slant on things, I didn't think that Jim Bucket was a credible source. And despite my interrogation, I reckoned Ellis hardly registered a score on the crazyometer. In fact, she was probably the sanest person I'd met so far.

As I was drinking my coffee I was brought an envelope containing a printed email from Gordon:

Felix

We keep missing each other. I would like you to make a minor detour to Linden and visit Al Int. I want to know about their future plans for expansion. I will explain when we talk next. Yrs. Gordon.

PS Have you seen any green and red parrots yet?

Where, exactly, was Linden? Of course I knew of Al Int, Aluminium International, a global player in mineral extraction, but I wasn't aware of any mining activities in the vicinity of Georgetown. Linden? Hadn't Ellis mentioned a quiet little mining town called Linden? I needed to speak to Gordon immediately.

To my surprise, an hour later, I got straight through to him, and, for once, the line was free from static hisses and interruptions.

'I thought I was just zooming in and zooming out,' I said.

I'd since had a brief look at a map and seen that Linden was a couple of hundred miles inland. There was a road going directly there, but I had no idea what condition it was in.

'It's there in the contract,' Gordon replied in his annoying plummy voice.

'I haven't seen the bloody contract yet.'

'Don't get stroppy with me, laddie.'

Patronising bastard. 'It's just that I...' I could feel myself losing it. '... haven't read the contract.'

'Well, you ought to. This comes under 'other duties commensurate with the project'.'

'That could be anything.'

'Look, it's not a big ask. If you can't get any stats from Al Int, I'd like your general impressions. Find out extraction details about the bauxite. How are they doing? Who are their customers? What are the projections? There are rumours about 'rare metals'. You know what 'rare metals' are, don't you?'

'Of course. There's a growing demand for them for mobile phones and other I.T. applications.'

'Sniff about a bit. Draw some maps. Be discreet though, these mining companies can be sensitive about sharing this sort of information.' Gordon paused: I could hear him clear his throat. 'By the way, are you tooled up?'

'My software is back in England.'

'Do you have a gun?'

'A gun! Why would I want a gun?'

'Quite right. In the circumstances it's best not to. Firearms only tend to escalate matters.'

'Why would I need a gun?' I repeated.

'You won't. I was just interested.'

'Economists work with social models and data. We don't use guns. I'm not Indiana Jones, you know. '

'Of course you're not. Archaeology is totally different. Forget I said that.'

'Dr Professor Lucas has banned me from going into the interior.'

'Don't start all that again. Linden is hardly the interior.'

'It's inland. It's not like Corriverton, on the coast.'

'That's why we've supplied you with a logistics coordinator.'

'Lucas expressly forbade...'

'Lucas doesn't need to know. Anyway, how's the report shaping up? Is a pattern falling into place?'

'Well, no, I've not been feeling too well.'

'Oh?'

'The other night I blacked out. It's knocked my confidence.'

'It's probably the anti-malarials kicking in. Some over-sensitive people find Mefloquine causes feelings of persecution and paranoia.'

'I thought you said it would help me sleep.'

'You've just got to ride it. Everybody hits that dark spot sometime during their trip. You'll feel better in a couple of days. The suicidal feelings will pass, though you might experience some hair loss.'

'What!'

'Not clumps.'

'That's okay then.'

'Just a slight thinning. Some find it advantageous in the sticky tropical climate.'

'I think I'd prefer to keep the full thatch.'

'So, as I was saying, it would be useful if you could give me some headline figures of your work so far.'

'I've got a range of data,' I lied. 'I just need to verify and collate.'

'I'd like something now, some ball-park numbers.'

'I'll get a summary to you soon.'

'I need to report to the M & E jedis[2], they're asking questions.'

'Can you send the contract again?'

'I'll get my secretary to look it out straightaway. Oh, and by the way, you'll be pleased to hear we're tightening the garrote on these Y2K blighters. I think they might start squeaking fairly soon. So we need to sort out your return air travel pronto. Anyway, let's have some headlines, please?'

'Let me think. The really interesting findings are ...'

Click. I put down the hand-piece on the receiver.

Xavier was drinking an espresso at the pavement bar. As ever, he was smartly dressed in an immaculate white shirt, ironed grey flannel trousers and shiny loafers. I wondered if, now I was back in G.T., I

2 Monitoring and Evaluation Team

ought to be wearing a tie – I had a nice little orange silk number that would go well with my chinos and linen jacket.

When I told Xavier that we were travelling to Linden he became unexpectedly agitated. He said he was concerned about the Discovery and had planned later in the day to take it to the garage for a check-up.

'I'm sure it'll be fine,' I said.

'It's new, it may need some re-tuning to suit the tropical climate.'

We met again at noon.

'There has been a change of plan,' said Xavier.

'But I thought we had agreed we are going to Linden.'

'We are. Bring your luggage down, I will get the vehicle.'

I paid my hotel bill which was more expensive than I had anticipated. I was charged $30 for 'miscellaneous services' but was reluctant to query this.

I met Xavier on the sidewalk outside the hotel. 'Unfortunately, the Land Rover is no longer available,' he said. 'I've taken it to the garage for repairs.'

'You're kidding me?' I felt strangely disturbed by this news. The Land Rover was my one source of stability during this trip. When the going got tough, I was reassured by the thought that I could cocoon myself in its cool, comfortable interior and view this alien world through the safety of its thick windows.

'It has major carburettor problems,' Xavier replied.

Two youths sped past on a motorcycle. 'Yo! Xavier!' they both shouted and laughed. Xavier ignored them.

'How quickly can it be mended?'

'It depends how long it takes to get the parts from England.'

'So how long?'

'Weeks... months, maybe.'

'This is a disaster,' I said. 'What are we going to do?'

Xavier pointed across the road. 'This will be our transport for the next few days.'

'What?' All I could see was a Toyota flat-bed that appeared to have been rescued from a scrap heap.

'There.'

'That pickup truck? Ha, ha, very funny, Xavier, you've played this prank before.'

'I'm not kidding.'

I looked up and down the road trying to see the Discovery. But there was no sign. 'It was funny the first time, but your joke is getting tiresome.'

'I promise the car is in the garage.'

'Yeah, right.'

'This is our transport, it really is.'

'But we can't travel in that.'

'Why not?'

I walked over to inspect the vehicle. It was a piece of shit. The windscreen was cracked, the tyres mismatched and several of the body panels were painted different colours. A dusty one-eyed teddy-bear was strapped to the radiator grill.

'I can't be seen in that.'

'It is very reliable.'

'It's a clown's car.'

'It is not.' Xavier sounded indignant. 'My brother used it for his wedding.'

'How long ago was that? It's a wreck. It's a bent bucket on wheels.'

'Mr Radstock, at my own personal expense I'm lending this to you. This is my truck. See, there is my St Christopher.' Sure enough, hanging from the rear-view mirror, along with various kitsch Catholic mini-icons, rosary beads, whistles and a lighter, was Xavier's precious medallion.

'Xavier I appreciate your kindness...' Why did I always end up apologising '... but do you really think we will get to Linden in this?'

'The road to Linden is the best in the country.'

'You said that about the rutted track to Corriverton.'

'The Linden road is new. It is metalled and perfectly straight for hundreds of miles. It is probably the best road in South America. Maybe the world. One day it will connect Georgetown with Manaus. It will be an important labour market generator. It will open up the riches of the Amazon basin to our country.'

'Okay, so the road is good, but what about your truck? Will it be able to cope? It will be hotter inland. Does this vehicle have air-con?'

'You can wind down the windows.'

'It'll be like sitting in a microwave.'

'Don't wear your tie then.'

'I haven't worn my tie since Corriverton.'

Xavier looked at me. 'Ah yes' he said. For a moment he stared at my hat and then grinned. 'Nice coolie hat, they'll like that in Linden.'

'There's no seat belts,' I said.

'You insult my driving.'

'Xavier, I appreciate the loan, but I don't think DoDO would be happy for me to be seen in this. As you said we need to make a good impression.'

'That was in Georgetown. In Linden they don't like a show-off.'

'People will get the wrong idea.'

'Wrong idea!' Xavier glared at me. 'Oh, I get it!'

'What!?'

'The white massa likes to be driven by a smartly dressed black man.'

'That is NOT what I said.'

'Massa and servant all over again.'

'You're putting words into my mouth.'

'We'd agreed we were partners.'

'DoDO likes its researchers to be respected,' I said slowly but firmly.

'And if you are spotted in my truck you won't be respected. Is that it?'

'Xavier, that is bullshit and you know it.'

'Your report will be all the better if you are driven around in my pick-up.'

'And how do you work that out?'

'The best research is done by people who are not socially removed from the objects of their study.'

'Yeah? Well, I'd dispute that. When people realise they are being observed, artificiality can set in. Research shows there can be an up to thirty percent rise in standard deviation.'

'When the people see you in your big fancy car, with all your airs and graces, they give fancy answers. If you are a passenger in my car everybody will think you are one of them. Travel with me in my truck and your research will be all the better. You will get a true picture of Guyana.'

I could see I wasn't going to win this. 'I suppose you may have a point.'

'Starsky and Hutch then?' Xavier said, holding out his hand.

'Yeah, Starsky and Hutch,' I agreed, as we bumped fists.

Xavier grinned. 'Remind me again, which one am I?'

NINE

If it's got a mouth, it's going to bite you.

We left Georgetown and drove along a muddy track that ran parallel to the banks of the Demerara. A sign read 'Starve the rats – burn your rubbish'. After half an hour we turned onto the new road to Linden. It was indeed, as Xavier had promised, a very fine asphalt black-top, uniquely smooth for Guyana and empty of traffic. The long straight highway disappeared into a dancing mirage. After ten miles the road left the dead-flat coastal plain and climbed onto an undulating upland, perhaps 300 metres high, of brilliant white sand. It was as if these were dunes from a long-lost coastline. The temperature had now risen; the air was hot and still, and the sky cloudless.

Xavier steered with one hand, the other dangling out of the window. So long as we didn't go over 45 miles an hour the ride was not uncomfortable.

'This is the only road in Guyana,' said Xavier, 'where it is possible to break the 70 mph speed limit.' In this vehicle, I thought that would be highly unlikely.

Unfortunately, the smooth surface was broken frequently by a series of small holes in the middle of the road. 'There were cats-eyes,' Xavier explained, 'but they were dug up and sold.'

Faded skid marks pointed to an overturned truck that had long ago veered into the bush. 'With no traffic this is a dangerous road,' Xavier explained, 'drivers fall asleep at the wheel.'

The land supported a scrubby vegetation of prickly gorse-type shrubs, not dissimilar to those found on English heath-land. The sparse trees had straggly lines of moss drooping from their boughs. There were an alarming number of pumpkin-sized wasps' nests hanging from the branches. A pair of grimy vultures tugged at the roadside corpse of what might have been a dog. It was a hostile landscape, but at least we were no longer under threat of drowning in floodwater.

I was interested to observe that Xavier didn't like being in the countryside. The sight of the wasps' nests set Xavier off on another excitable rant about the interior. 'Man, those wasps are evil. Go within fifty feet of their nests and they attack like killer darts. The pain is excruciating. Have you ever had your hand slammed in a car door? I'd rather that than be stung by one of those vicious creatures. Mr Radstock, the bush is an evil, evil, place. It is the land where God did not finish creation, and all the reject animals were sent.'

This landscape didn't look like the tropical rainforest that I'd been anticipating. Vast sections, as far as the eye could see, had been logged-out, leaving only the occasional stump and dry undergrowth.

Xavier explained we weren't yet in the true rainforest, the wood here was called purple heart. When felled, it has a reddish-blue tinge to it. There was also iron wood, a timber as hard as granite.

'There's a tree by a road junction in Linden that nobody has ever been able to cut-down. Razor-sharp axes bounce off it like rubber balls. Chain saws overheat and grind to a halt in minutes. Slash and burn is the traditional culture round here,' said Xavier. 'Which is all right when it's done by small-holders. But when the multi-nationals start practising it, the land doesn't have time to recover. This land is on life-support and the prognosis is not good.'

It wasn't just the insects that made him uncomfortable. 'Xavier, I'm beginning to get the measure of you. I've noticed that you're a bit of a soft-handed city boy.'

Xavier nodded. 'My brothers are averse to agricultural work. We have a temperament more suited to an office environment. Working on the land, we leave the coolies to do that.'

'Fair enough.'

'People who work on the land get nothing for their labours. It's the middle men who make the profit. Do you think that the farmer and miner are rich? They get very little for back-breaking toil. International companies pay bottom dollar for our sugar, diamonds, gold and aluminium and then process our raw materials elsewhere to sell at maximum price. The last thing I want to do is be in the fields. My people have had enough of that work.'

'But surely that was a long time ago?'

'It's a hurt that runs deep.'

'Sure, but we nearly all come from a labouring past.' I remembered visiting my great-grandfather's home deep in the Somerset Levels. It was in a remote and terrible place. The weather was harsh, the cider apples sour, the land barren and liable to flooding. 'Two generations ago my family were tied labourers living in a damp brick house on the banks of the River Parrett. They were at the mercy and whim of the landowners.'

'It's not the same. Your family were free to leave. They weren't chained up at night. Your grandmother wasn't flogged and raped by the landowner.'

'In medieval times the Lord of the Manor would have first dibs on the village maidens,' I said. 'What I'm saying is, I hardly ever think of my forefathers. It certainly didn't affect my career choice.'

'You're not working in the fields now, are you?' said Xavier.

'Very few people work on farms. I know the stats. In the UK less than one percent of the population is employed in agriculture and related services.'

Xavier sighed. 'You don't understand do you? There's a lot of healing to be done. It starts with honesty.'

Xavier told me more about the Amerindians. They drank a home brewed drink called Cassiri, made of chewed cassava root spat into a bowl and left to ferment in its own juices supplemented by human spit. Down in one, whether you liked it or not. It was like swallowing a glass of snot. It didn't sound like one of the world's greatest cocktails.

We pulled up for a piss stop. Since we'd left Georgetown we'd passed through no settlement and seen no houses. A vast black bird glided silently overhead. In the distance I could see thin brown fumes from charcoal burning.

'You must never relieve yourself directly into the river,' Xavier shouted over his shoulder. 'There is a tiny fish, the toothpick fish, that will swim up your stream of urine and enter into your dick. It has little spikes like a fish-hook, and will stay in your piss channel. It is so painful people have screamed to have their penis macheted off.'

'Really? Have you actually seen this fish?'

'I read about it in a book.'

It sounded like fiction to me, but I thought I'd heed this advice, nevertheless. 'Thanks for the warning!'

Xavier grunted, and out of the corner of my eye I could see him make a great display as if he was stuffing something the size of a fire-hose back into his trousers.

'And don't stand still on the forest floor, you must always keep moving. The bullet ants have a bite out of all proportion to their size. It's as if you have been shot, but the pain lasts for twenty-four hours. Just remember, in the bush, if it has a mouth, it's going to bite you.'

Every half an hour or so a truck laden with timber thundered by in the opposite direction, going to the coast. The air became increasingly humid. The asphalt surface had come to an end and we were now driving along a hard-packed red laterite road. The truck was rattling so much I was getting triple vision.

I thought about Lucas. Where were the statistics he had promised? They must be out there somewhere. An early flight home seemed increasingly unlikely.

And what about the mystery woman from the I.B.? Who was she?

Maybe she could advise? How could I get in contact with her? Should I warn Gordon about the activities of the I.B.? Perhaps not.

It was late afternoon when I spotted a single shaft of white smoke cutting the solid blue sky like an exclamation mark.

'The aluminium works,' Xavier announced. 'In twenty minutes we will be in Linden.'

TEN

I was their last hope.

Like Georgetown, Linden was another spacious settlement laid out in a grid with clapboard houses in green plots set back from the road. From a distance it had a sleepy back-of-beyond look. But closer inspection revealed something less attractive. The hot air was gritty and tasted acrid; every surface was covered in a fine white powder. The dust from the bauxite mine was on tin roofs, cars, plants, and, no doubt, in the inhabitants' lungs and stomachs.

Xavier had booked me into the Rendezvous Guest House, an unpretentious establishment that had seen busier times.

'I'd like a room with a window, please.' I said when I checked in. I didn't want to leave things to chance.

'Certainly, sir. Overlooking the road or the courtyard?'

'Courtyard, please.'

Xavier had gone to stay with a family member so in the evening I sat by myself in the incongruously named Tudor Bar, a large echoing hall painted in black and white. With a range of ineptly stuffed animal heads hanging on the wall, the place had the melancholy ambience of a colonial hunting lodge. Apart from a dusty caiman suspended from the ceiling, the animals were not easy to identify. Several of the heads could well have been domestic cats, while something that resembled a giant otter was labelled 'Water Dog'.

Later, after a toasted cheese sandwich, I was given a candle in case the generator failed.

Back in my room, the unearthly din from the tree frogs – amplified by the confines of the courtyard – was burrowing its way into my brain. I leant out of the window and clapped my hands in a futile attempt to silence them. When I turned off my bedside light I realised I had no matches.

'Did you have a good luncheon?' Xavier asked.

I'd noticed that nobody in Guyana used the term breakfast. Guyanese also greet you in the evening by saying 'Good night'.

'I was offered a meat casserole, but it was too early in the morning.'

'Ah, pepperpot. Very good. Next time you must eat it.'

'I tried it. It was too rich.' The jet-black meat had a pungent odour that reminded me of when my grandmother used to boil bones for the dog. 'It was a bit too gamey.'

'Some people call it the hundred-year-old stew.'

'Hundred-year-old rat for breakfast!' I laughed.

'You insult our national dish,' Xavier said indignantly.

'I thought toasted cheese sandwich was the national dish.'

'Pepperpot is much better than your fish and chips.'

'Xavier, stop being so sensitive. I'm sure it's very good. But I prefer toast and marmalade for breakfast, thank you very much.'

'For my people it is comforting to know that food is always available.'

Before I'd left Georgetown, I'd been able to phone Aluminium International to arrange a visit to the works. At first, the woman I spoke to was hesitant, as the mine was in 'shut-down mode' but when I explained about DoDO she became more enthusiastic. She would organise a tour of the site for me and a meeting with the Senior Management Team.

The bauxite works consisted of enormous air-hangar-sized wooden sheds and multi-storey silos presided over by a massive chimney. Although the chimney continued to guff out its dusty effluent, apart from security guards at the gate, the factory appeared to be devoid of workers. I wondered why Gordon was so interested in this forlorn place.

I was greeted by a weary guide who explained that these days there really wasn't much to see. He drove me round the site in a beat-up Jeep across a white moonscape, broken by startling sky-blue lakes. There were a number of open cast mines, not particularly deep – perhaps fifty feet or so. Rusting conveyor belts on stilts criss-crossed the land. A row of massive yellow tipper-trucks with wheels higher than a man stood idle outside the crushing sheds. As we drove we threw up a cloud of dust – I could taste the bitter ore in my mouth.

I had to pump my escort for figures, which I jotted down. Linden, a company town, was built entirely around the bauxite mine. It was now Guyana's second largest urban settlement. The mine had been established at the beginning of the twentieth century. In those days it had been a small affair – the bauxite was dug by shovels and transported by mules. Over the years, production increased and machinery was installed for crushing, sorting and drying. By the 1950s hundreds of people were employed, including a large foreign workforce. The company was nationalised in the 1970s and had struggled to maintain profitability. The mine was subsequently leased to Al Int.

'I understand you have a meeting with the managers. They will tell you about the current situation.'

Sitting round the table were eight men, all middle-aged and grim-faced. I guessed I'd arrived at a bad time.

I was shown to my seat. The wood-panelled room felt as if it had been stripped of all its fittings – apart from the table and chairs there was no other furniture. Even the walls were bare.

'Thank you for coming to see us,' said a dour man.

'Have I visited at a difficult moment?' I had to shout over the rattle and whine of an air-con unit.

'No. It is most opportune.'

'Yes?'

The man handed me some sheets illustrated with graphs and

bar charts and told me about the mine's per capita output and their excellent health and safety record. His colleagues nodded gloomily. 'But we are going through a time of great change. This is a good mine. The bauxite is of high quality and the workforce dedicated. But there is less demand and world prices have dropped.

'As you know, the mine is for sale. Al Int has taken what it wants, and is going to leave us with very little. Linden will be a ghost town inhabited by sixty thousand people.' He stared at me, giving me a despondent look. 'Nobody wants to buy the mine. We need the Department of Development Overseas to help. We need you to help.'

The same had happened with the coal mines in England ten years before. The quality of the coal was good, but the global market had changed. Margaret Thatcher exacerbated the hurt by sending police on horseback, like conquering vandals, to break up the demonstrations. It was a medieval rout – tight-knit mining communities had their souls ripped out.

I looked at the bewildered faces round the table. They gazed back at me with pleading eyes. All I could do was listen and nod. I was their last hope. A labour market researcher from England their last hope. How desperate was that?

I asked for maps, which I was readily given, and bluffed a few questions about the quality of the ore, future capacity, facilities for transport and so on. Sure, I'd highlight this in my report; DoDO might take notice. But once again the people of Guyana had been well and truly shafted.

'I'll do what I can,' I said. I wondered why Gordon had sent me here. Did he know the mine was up for sale? What information was he after? I hated myself at that moment.

ELEVEN

Felix Radstock: British Business Guru.

The interior of the pick-up was steely hot.

'Here, sit on this.' Xavier handed me a hessian sack. 'It'll save you grilling your backside.'

Xavier said he had a surprise for me.

'I don't like surprises.' I had an uneasy feeling that Xavier had secured some capybara meat for supper.

'Everybody likes surprises.'

'This whole country is a surprise.' I was beginning to long for the predictable. 'After a while you can tire of surprises.'

'Well, you're going to like this one.'

'It's not another of your jokes, is it?' After my sobering visit to Al Int I wasn't feeling in a particularly humorous mood.

'What jokes?'

'Like you being mugged and the car stolen.'

Xavier chuckled. 'Oh man, you should have seen your face.'

'I'm glad it amused you.'

As we bumped along rutted roads I began to fear for the longevity of the vehicle. Much more of this and the chassis would suffer irrevocable metal fatigue. We lurched past a row of buckled tin-roofed shops selling household goods, ironmongery and 'Box Chicken – new improved box'.

'What's Box Chicken?' I asked.

'You hungry?'

'I'm curious as to what it is.' As well as longing for the humdrum I realised I had also gone off my food. In the last twenty-four hours all I had eaten was a toasted cheese sandwich and a couple of segments of Toblerone.

'Exactly what it says. Chicken in a box.'

'Oh right, Kentucky Fried Chicken ... that sort of thing. Not capybara, then.' I looked at Xavier, trying to gauge his reaction.

'No, that would be 'Box Rodent'.'

An air of anxiety hung over Linden. There were many empty business premises and abandoned shanties. You can't just leave a place this size to fade back into the bush. At Courts Furniture Store youths were liming on the sofas and three-piece display suites outside on the sidewalk. One day, I feared, these people would decide they had had enough and rise up.

We drove past a circus tent. 'The evangelicals are in town,' Xavier explained. 'They are like vultures, they move in when they sense something is dying.'

'So if we're not going to the guest-house, where are we heading?'

'I thought you'd like to meet the community researchers.'

'Community researchers? Who are they?'

'They are keen to speak to you.'

'What? Now?' I was tired. 'Can't we do this another time?'

'They're a group of volunteers. They are very enthusiastic. They undertake community projects – they investigate and analyse local issues and so on.'

'Xavier, I really haven't got time for amateurs.' Community researchers were the last people I wanted to meet. They might ask some cogent questions.

'They'll have information you can use in your report.'

'I doubt it. The Radstock Framework© is multi-dimensional. They won't understand the model, it's software defined – explaining it is complicated.'

'Maybe you could tell me about it sometime?'

'You wouldn't be interested.' I wanted to change the subject.

We pulled up at a wooden building on stilts with a shallow tin roof. Eager faces were looking at us from a window on the first floor.

'Now aren't you glad you're not travelling in the Discovery?' said Xavier.

'Not particularly.'

Xavier stuck his neck forward and peered at the windscreen. 'Man, this glass is filthy. I don't know how I could see through it.' Xavier handed me a dirty rag. 'I'll squirt, you wipe.'

'Let's do that later. They're all watching.'

Xavier waved at the smiling spectators.

'They won't mind.'

'It would be rude to keep my audience waiting.'

'Okay. Later then.'

I got out of the truck and closed the door.

'Don't slam it!' Xavier shouted.

On a notice board, by the entrance door, was a poster with my picture on it. Underneath it said:

British Business Guru

Felix Radstock

Here tonight – One night only

Someone had scrawled across my portrait in black felt tip: 'Sold Out.'

'Piggin' hell? Where did that come from?'

'I knew you'd be pleased.'

'Pleased!' I wanted to run. 'British Business Guru! How long have I got with them?'

'An hour or two. They've got all evening.'

'An hour or two! I don't have anything prepared.'

'They are very keen to hear from a business guru.'

'I bet they are.' It was a shame they weren't going to.

Walking up the stairs to the entrance Xavier started to snigger. 'Oh man, something has happened here!'

'What?'

'That is really, really funny.'

'What!?' By now Xavier was bent over double with hysterics.

'Look at your ass.'

I contorted myself so that I could glimpse the back of my chinos.

'Oh shit!' I muttered under my breath.

Dye from the hessian sack had transferred red and black print onto my trousers. 'GuySuCo' – in reverse – was emblazoned in three-inch high letters across my backside. I tried to rub off the ink, but it was already imprinted hard and fast.

It took a while for Xavier to be able to speak. 'You can't leave, they've seen you,' he said wiping tears of hilarity from his eyes.

'Is this your idea of a joke? I'm getting sick of your jokes.'

'No, Mr Radstock, this is an accident, I promise.'

'You're trying to humiliate me aren't you? What have you got against me? I'll look like an idiot.'

Xavier shrugged. 'Keep your back to the wall. Nobody will see.'

'Of course they'll see.'

'It happens all the time.'

'Well I haven't noticed it. This wouldn't have happened if we were travelling in the Discovery.'

Xavier shook his head. 'You just can't let it go, can you?'

I sidled into a classroom furnished with long wooden tables, their dented surfaces worn smooth with age. There was a grating of benches as everybody stood up. Twenty pairs of sharp and enquiring eyes stared at me.

The spokesperson for the research team, a dreadlocked man with what looked like a spliff sticking out of his breast pocket, introduced himself as Crunchie. He welcomed me and said the researchers had a number of 'crucial questions' they were eager to discuss.

I introduced myself and said that I was undertaking a study of the labour market. A general murmur of approval echoed around the room. I emphasised that I didn't want to baffle them with jargon and complex theoretical constructs. I made some general observations that the ideal economy was one where supply matched demand, and that there were challenges for Guyana in today's global market. Heads nodded slowly in acknowledgement. Choosing my words carefully, I explained that a healthy economy needs a good education system, a functional health service and a plentiful supply of jobs. I didn't like to mention Linden was about to lose all these.

Eager to play for time I opened-up the session for questions. A forest of hands shot into the air.

I was asked if I saw a contradiction between the concept of free market forces and the trade quotas that were invariably foisted upon Guyana.

Someone else questioned the recent assertion of the UK's Chancellor of the Exchequer that the government had defeated the economic cycle of boom and bust. 'Surely this is a force of nature that cannot be broken. Do you think, Sir, this belief will come back to bite you on the ass?' The group laughed wildly, banging the table and stamping their feet on the bare floorboards so much so that a thin cloud of dust hung in the air. They seemed remarkably well informed, at times quoting directly from the New Statesman and The Economist.

But what they really wanted to talk about was the sale of the mine.

'My children were born in the Al Int hospital, they were taught in the Al Int school and now work in the Al Int factory,' one man said. It was a cosy arrangement that suited everybody. Until, that is, Aluminium International decided to quit. 'What will happen to this town when the bauxite works close?'

I assured them that there were many companies across the world that would be interested in such a successful operation.

When I turned to write my contact address on the blackboard there was a roar of laughter.

'Sir, you sponsored by GuySuCo?'

'As you can see I was sitting on some sacks.'

My new-found friends found this hilarious. 'He like a stick of rock. Cut him open and he got GuySuCo running all the way through him.'

'No disrespect to our honourable visitor,' Crunchie barked. 'He travel long way to talk to us.'

A man, tall and dignified, stood up. 'The future is out of our hands.' There was a respectful silence as he spoke. 'Something has to change, we need a new deal. We want our pride back.'

They seemed resigned to the situation. 'We have big gardens and can grow our food,' said one of the older men. He gave a weak laugh. 'But that is all.'

Thankfully, we had no time to discuss the Radstock Framework©. Their craving for knowledge was heart-breaking and they were as charming and enthusiastic a group as you could wish for. Their positivity was being stretched to the brink. How much economic collapse can a community endure before it lashes out? I wondered, as I left, why these people weren't doing the work I had been commissioned to undertake. And at least they didn't ask about the imminent arrival of computers.

TWELVE

'They have voodoo in their blood.'

On our return journey from Linden Xavier resumed his rant about the awfulness of the bush. It wasn't just the hostile environment of the interior that he didn't like; he seemed uneasy about the Amerindians and their customs.

'Tribes used to mark their territory with shrunken heads,' he said.

'You're kidding!'

'Shrunken heads the size of an orange. They peel the flesh from the skull and stick it on a post. It dries into a perfect miniature head, teeth and all.'

'The teeth would be out of proportion.'

'They shrink the teeth as well.'

'How do they do that?'

'I don't know.' Xavier hesitated. 'Voodoo?'

'They don't shrink heads these days, do they?' I asked.

Xavier gave a nervous laugh.

Usually, Xavier was reluctant to talk about himself, but on this long drive, at the wheel of his own truck, with the straight and empty road disappearing into the dancing heat, he seemed more relaxed and open to questions.

'Xavier, how come you haven't got a wife? A handsome man like you should be a grandfather by now?'

'Maybe I am!'

'So do you have any children?'

Xavier sighed. 'I have a daughter in England. She lives in south London. A place with a funny name. Toot...toot...Tooting!' he laughed.

'What's she doing there?'

'She's a very clever girl. She's training to be an accountant.'

'When did you last see her?'

'Four, five years ago,' he said sadly. 'I miss her dreadfully. I am saving to visit her. Hopefully, I will go to London next year.'

'Do you have a wife?'

'I have responsibilities enough without a wife.'

'Yeah?'

'My mother died five years ago, I have a sixty-year-old father and a kid sister to look after.'

We were now back on the asphalt road and I could talk without my teeth rattling and my voice being distorted by the vibration.

'So tell me, Xavier, what did you do after you left school?'

'After high school I went to the University of Toronto.'

'Toronto?' I hadn't noticed a Toronto on the map of Guyana.

'Toronto...' Xavier said slowly, as if he was speaking to an idiot, '... Canada.'

At times I found Xavier difficult to read and couldn't tell whether he was joking or not. 'You never told me this.'

'You never asked.'

'What did you study?'

'Economics – that's why I was assigned to you.'

'That wasn't explained.'

'I have a doctorate.'

'In what?'

"A comparative study of employment in emerging economies."

'Wow! That could be useful.' I was feeling bad about this. Why had I underestimated Xavier's education? There was so much about him I didn't know.

'It hasn't done me much good, has it?' said Xavier.

'Why don't you call yourself doctor? Dr Zeeland! It sounds impressive.'

'My employers won't allow me.'

'Why not?'

'Perhaps Dr Professor Lucas feels threatened.'

'He's not even a real doctor. Maybe that's the problem.'

'You assumed I was merely your driver.'

'No, no, no, it's just that I didn't understand what logistics coordinator meant.'

'Don't worry, you aid people all make the same assumption. You forget to ask the locals.' The frustration in Xavier's words was palpable. 'What do we know, huh?'

'Xavier, I didn't realise. I'm sorry.'

'What do we know about our own country?' he said sarcastically.

'I've valued your contribution. I found your comments about sugar production very interesting.'

'If you want any help, just ask.'

For a moment our truck rocked as a timber transporter overtook. I looked up at the massive trunks of greenwood, stripped of bark, like some vast, brutalised skeleton.

'Why haven't you joined the brain drain like everybody else?' I asked. 'I don't understand - what are you doing here?'

'Guyana is my country. I live here with my family. I love my country, it is my home, it is my birthplace. I am at peace here.'

'Yes, but everybody leaves.'

'People have no loyalty. If all the educated people leave how are things going to get better? What future will our children have? Besides, somebody's got to stay and do the jobs.' He laughed and shook his head. 'Somebody has to drive the visiting aid workers.'

'Oh man!' I felt like a high-grade prick. Why did I underestimate people all the time? I needed to watch out for signs of that European superiority complex.

'Don't worry, you're not the first.'

Even with both windows wound down the mid-day heat was ferocious. The landscape was changing. We'd come over the ridge and stretched below us was the treeless coastal plain covered by many miles of cane fields laid out in a grid.

'Okay then, in your capacity as Dr Zeeland, what's the probability of me getting raw statistics in this country?'

'Statistically speaking, zilch.'

We both laughed.

'Xavier, from now on I will call you Doctor.'

'I think it is best you don't.'

It was Friday afternoon and I was thinking about what I'd do over the weekend. I wanted to wash the sour taste of Linden out of my mouth. I was intrigued by the Kaieteur Falls. Evelyn Waugh, a man not known for his enthusiasms, had written that the Falls were one of the greatest, most inaccessible, least advertised natural wonders of the world. They could be worth checking out.

'How do you fancy a little sight-seeing trip?' I asked.

Xavier shrugged.

'I think we should go to the Kaieteur Falls. Having come this far it would be a wasted opportunity not to.'

Xavier didn't share my enthusiasm. 'I have to inform you, Felix, that you are not allowed to travel to the Kaieteur Falls.'

'I'm sorry to hear that. Why not?'

'You told me, the Minister said you were to remain in Georgetown.'

'I don't think Lucas fully understands my brief.'

'You have already broken the rules. You have broken the rules twice.'

'I don't see the problem, I'm sure my curfew doesn't extend to the weekend. It won't be part of the job. I can't come halfway round the world and not visit such a natural wonder.'

'I have to remain in Georgetown to oversee the repair of the Discovery.'

'But you said the parts wouldn't be arriving for weeks, maybe months.'

'I have to guard the vehicle from looters. It is vulnerable. People will see that the car is not in use. They will try to steal its CD player or its wheels.'

We were now in the outskirts of Georgetown and stuck in a slow-moving jam of taxis, flat-bed trucks and hand-carts. Xavier's manner had changed. During our journey we'd been getting on well. But now, as we inched through town, he seemed less relaxed.

'But it's your job to accompany me on my research,' I said. 'You're not just my driver, you know.'

'Yes, research in G.T.. It is not within my remit to travel inland. I have already overstepped the mark and put my employment at risk.'

'I appreciate you accompanying me to Linden. I'm sure I can arrange for DoDO to pay expenses on top of your wages.'

'I prefer to remain in G.T.'

'You'd like the Kaieteur Falls.'

'You and I, we like different things.'

'I've read it's very beautiful.'

Xavier shrugged. 'Maybe, if you think a lot of water is beautiful.'

'It's more than a lot of water! The change would do you good.'

'I don't like the bush,' Xavier said firmly. 'There will be creatures.'

'What sort of creatures?'

'Tigers. All sorts. I like to live in a town. I like paved roads and concrete and houses.' He glanced down at his spotless shoes. 'I like to stroll on a sidewalk, and not feel the dirt under my feel. I don't like to get muddy.'

'Xavier, you're a big wuss.'

'Where would I stay?'

'With me at the lodge.'

'With you!'

'Yeah, what's wrong with that?

'DoDO won't allow.'

'Why not?'

'They don't. They'd expect me to sleep in the servant's quarters.'

I hadn't thought of it like that before. I'd assumed Xavier was using the opportunity of our journeys to visit relatives. I didn't understand that he wasn't allowed to stay with me. 'Haven't you got a cousin there?'

'I don't know anybody at the Kaieteur Falls. Very few people live there. And the lodge is not big.'

I remembered what Xavier had said about the Amerindians. Suddenly, I understood Xavier's reluctance.

'Is it the Indians?'

'Indians? What Indians?'

'The Amerindians. You don't like them, do you?'

'I've got nothing against them.'

'You're scared of them.'

'I am not!' he protested.

I could sense I'd hit a nerve. Xavier was silent for a moment. 'Some people say they have secret powers,' he said hesitantly.

'What sort of secret powers?'

'People say they have voodoo in their blood. My cousin told me about benab he had visited. The Amerindians had a glass bottle with an evil spirit in it. I don't know where it came from or how the spirit got in there. All they would say is "very bad ting happen if you open bottle". Xavier gave a shudder. 'They were truly frightened of it.'

'That's nonsense. You don't need to be afraid of that.'

'There are phantoms in the bush. There are elves that walk backwards and river porpoises that impregnate young girls.'

'You don't believe all those stories, do you?'

'You shouldn't meddle in things you don't understand. You must be careful.'

'What a load of rubbish.'

'You Brits have your superstitions – you make a wish when you blow out a candle; you touch wood to stop bad happening; you don't walk under scaffolding.'

'That's different,' I said, but I could see what he meant.

'Not to an Amerindian.'

The Friday afternoon traffic had come to a halt due to a herd of cows blocking the road. We stopped opposite the Mighty Tadpole International Car Wash - a man with a sponge and a bucket of ditch water. Next door was a garment workshop with racks of clothes hanging from the ceiling. Three men were bent over their pedal-operated Singer sewing machines.

'You are putting me in a difficult position,' said Xavier. 'Dr Professor Lucas is a powerful man. I could lose my job. Or worse.'

'As you said, you're not just a logistics coordinator. You and I are a team. We should do things together.'

'If you carry on like this there will be no logistics to coordinate.'

'I promise nothing will happen to you,' I said.

'Dr Professor Lucas is a ruthless man. He is very clever. People are scared of the Minister.'

'That's a bluff. Gordon said he's a pussycat.'

'People disappear. They say he keeps the heads of his old enemies in his deep-freeze.'

'That's just tittle-tattle to intimidate people.' Xavier seemed genuinely nervous. 'Look, I have absolutely no intention of upsetting him. Nobody would need to know about our little adventure.'

I couldn't get the picture of the Kaieteur Falls out of my mind. I reckoned if old sour-face Waugh could be so captivated by its scale, and the majesty of its setting, it must be pretty good. I tried another tack.

'Do you know what?' The more I thought about it, the more I liked the idea. 'While we're at the Falls, perhaps we could make a quick visit to those pork-knockers?'

'Dr Lucas would definitely not allow that. Besides, they are several days' trek away.'

'That's a pity.' I'd continue this conversation later.

THIRTEEN

Time to soak up some Caribbean atmosphere.

At least, this time, I had a room at the Stabroek Lodge. I was disappointed, however, to find the American woman and her coterie had moved on. Gone, I guessed, on their wildlife safari up-country. So, after a cheerless supper of chicken, rice and peas, I took a walk to explore the town some more. Maybe, this time, I'd stumble across a sticky-floored reggae bar and soak up some real Caribbean atmosphere?

I left the hotel compound and went in the opposite direction to my previous stroll to the sea. I followed the wide road and then turned off in search of the town centre. I'd read in a leaflet that the cathedral was the biggest wooden building in the world – I was interested to see that.

Here, the streets were narrower and the houses smaller. Some of them were mere shacks on stilts. Razor wire, on top of wooden fences, glinted in the moonlight. I listened to the sound of the city. Someone was playing 'No Woman, No Cry', children were laughing, a door slammed and then there was a shout. I continued heading in what I thought was the direction of the town centre, though I was becoming less confident that I knew where I was. The drainage ditches were stagnant, the black water boiling with mosquito larvae. A pack of hyena-type dogs pushed past – thankfully they ignored me. I walked by boarded-up shops and empty market stalls. A sign read 'We buy second-hand suitcases. All conditions considered'. A group of youths was hanging out by a makeshift pavement bar. Silently, they watched. I was beginning to question the wisdom of this walk. I felt annoyed with myself for being so paranoid – I was in an unfamiliar place, that was all.

And then, the streets widened, I saw the famous market clock and recognised where I was. There were cars and taxis gliding past and a few shops, lit by harsh neon lights, were open.

I was about to leave the reggae for another night when I heard the thump of a sound system coming from a nearby shebeen. The doorway was guarded by a couple of bouncers who nodded and greeted me with a 'goodnight'. Rather than walking down into some dingy smoke-filled dive, I was ushered upstairs to a large, brightly lit room with half a dozen pool tables, and a central bar buzzing with men and women of all ages and colours. I stood at the bar and shouted for a draught beer and then settled at a table by a window overlooking the market, which was still busy even at this time of night. I didn't know what to make of the place. I was a little disappointed that nobody tried to sell me weed, nobody paid me any attention. From my window-seat I watched people in the square below gather around an acrobat and his sidekick. After several false starts, the performer took a running jump and dived through a small flaming, wooden hoop. It was basic entertainment, even so the crowd whooped and yelled in appreciation.

A sleek white Land Rover sped through the square, horn blaring. I thought Xavier said there was only one Discovery in Guyana? The driver, with Rastafarian dreads, his chin held up high in an imperious manner, looked familiar. For the moment, I couldn't place him, but I was sure I'd seen him before.

PART THREE

ONE

Ninety seconds until our certain death.

Da Silva ambled round the Cessna. He walked with the gait of a man more at home on a horse than the controls of a light-aircraft. He kicked the threadbare tyres and held up a litre bottle of Eldorado Rum to the light to gauge its contents. 'Pre-flight check. All A-Okay.'

I'd never thought baggy harem pants twinned with an embroidered brocade waistcoat and a sweat stained confederate hat, was a classic look for an airline pilot, but somehow Captain Da Silva managed to pull it off. He was also wearing a holster with a revolver in it.

'What's that for?' I said, pointing to the gun.

'Bandido,' he smiled. 'Stops my passengers from getting clever ideas.'

The plane was smaller and less sturdy than I had expected. It was a left hand drive; I sat in the front while Xavier squeezed into the cramped seat at the back. Strangely, apart from a few extra dials and switches, the cockpit reminded me of a Hillman Hunter, the family car we had in the 1970s. The tiny cabin was grillingly hot and stank of fags, booze and flatulence.

'Who do you work for?' Da Silva asked. 'Overseas aid?'

'International development, that sort of thing.'

'You guys sure know how to bend an elbow.' Da Silva mimed knocking back a drink.

'Not me, I'm here to work.'

'That's what they all say.'

'No. Really.'

'Yeah, they all say that as well.'

As we taxied along the runway I looked around and was alarmed to see a jumbo jet waiting behind us. Surely the slipstream would blow us out of the sky as it overtook us? Da Silva didn't seem bothered. We bumped along and lurched into the air. Da Silva had given me headphones and a mouth piece, but neither seemed to work so we communicated by shouting and pointing. I was pressed into my seat by the sharp ascent.

Our plane shook like a washing machine and rolled sideways as the jet roared overhead. Da Silva raised an extended finger. 'Give us space, muthersucker.'

As we circled above Georgetown Da Silva leant over and yelled in my ear. There was a howling gale in the cabin as the sliding windows didn't fit too well.

'So where do you want to go?' He had the breath of a dog that had eaten too much tinned meat.

'Kaieteur Falls.'

'Really?'

'I thought that's what we'd arranged.'

'People change their mind. We've got enough gas to nip over the border and do some business. Guyana's a small country. If you know where they are, there are corridors that are off radar.' He pointed to his left. 'Suriname over there, straight ahead Brazil, to the right Venezuela.'

'Thanks, but I'm sticking to Kaieteur Falls.'

Da Silva tapped his watch and pointed in a south-westerly direction. 'Two hours,' he mouthed.

Below us, as we rattled across the sky, was the coastal plain fringed by muddy beaches and a dirty brown sea. With its canals and irrigation ditches the land looked neat and tidy – it could have been the Somerset Levels around Weston super Mare.

Da Silva lit an evil-smelling cheroot and then attached a bungee clip from the door handle to the joy stick. 'Hands free,' he shouted, giving me the thumbs-up. He pulled his bottle of rum from the side pocket in the door, unscrewed the cap, took a couple of glugs and passed it over.

'In-flight refreshment!' he yelled. I looked behind me at Xavier hunched on the back seat.

'Alright Starsky?' I shouted. Xavier stared blankly. He appeared to have gone into mental lock-down. I felt bad that I'd dragged him onto this expedition.

'Your friend needs a shot,' said Da Silva. 'There's nothing like a hit of Five Year rum to steady flying nerves.'

'He doesn't drink.'

We were now leaving the coast. The enormous green canopy of the rainforest stretched as far as the eye could see – a vast emerald ocean broken only by the occasional rocky outcrop.

'Hidden under those millions of trees is great mineral wealth,' Da Silva said. He reclined in his seat and pulled his hat over his eyes. 'I'm going to have a few minutes sleep – wake me if anything happens.'

'Happens!? Like what?' I felt uneasy about this.

'We lose altitude. A mountain gets in the way.'

'What mountain?'

'Only kidding. We'd run out of gas well before we hit the Pakaraima Mountains.'

'What about other aircraft? Or turbulence?' The more I thought about it, the more I wanted my pilot to be awake. 'Don't you need to steer or something?'

'Auto pilot does that,' he said pointing at the bungee clip. 'I could have a heart attack and you wouldn't even notice.'

'What about these?' I said, pointing to the dials. 'Don't you need to check them?'

'I have, and they're fine.'

'Keep checking.'

'Is that what you do when you're driving your car? No. You look at your fuel gauge, you check the warning lights and that's it. Usted Culo.'

'What about the bandidos?'

'You're not a bandido. And him,' he gestured towards Xavier, 'he needs his diaper changing.'

'But…'

'The skills of a pilot are overrated. Driving the streets of Georgetown is far more demanding. Flying a plane is pau comido, a piece of cake. There's nothing up here. It gets boring. Often I read a book – sometimes I climb over the seat and crash out in the back.'

Was this guy for real?

'The only thing I have to look out for is debris on the landing strip. The Indians like to stack their firewood on it. At Pirara some idiota built a hut bang in the middle of the runway. That had to go pretty quick. Do not worry my friend. We fly at ten thousand feet. We will have plenty of time to sort things out before we hit the ground. See…'

Da Silva reached forward to the dashboard and turned the ignition key. The engine fell silent.

'What the bloody hell are you doing?'

'Look,' he raised his hands, 'we are still flying.'

All I could hear was the whistling of the air.

'Turn the effing thing on again.'

Although we weren't plummeting in a dead spin to the ground, we were, nevertheless, gliding earthwards at a higher velocity than I felt comfortable with.

'We have, perhaps, two minutes,' Da Silva said, 'before we need to worry.'

'Okay, I believe you. Please, turn the engine on.'

Da Silva's hand lingered over the key for an unnecessarily long time before he twisted it. The starter motor made a whirring noise, clicked and then … and then nothing.

'The battery is low. You two might have to get out and push.'

'Ha, bloody ha. That is not funny.'

'I'll try again.'

'Can you try again, quickly. Please.' The dials on the dashboard had gone crazy – the altimeter was spinning like a roulette wheel. The features of the rainforest were now becoming distinct. We had ninety seconds until our certain death.

He turned the key. I heard a whirring and a click.

He looked at me and shook his head. 'Less choke. Third time lucky, eh?'

'Oh, for fuck's sake!' I wanted to punch this drunken idiot. I wanted to slap his daft face.

I experienced the purest form of fear I have ever known. Oh Aurora! I thought of her, being told about my heroic death in the rainforest. How I had bravely fought with the pilot to stop the plane from crashing. I could see her lovely face crumpling with tears. I wanted to be there to comfort her.

What a pointless way to die. I wasn't ready for this. I could make out individual trees. I could see branches. Leaves. 'Jesus!'

Da Silva tried the ignition again. The engine wheezed and this time groaned into action.

'Hold on,' he shouted as he pulled the control column towards him. 'We need to gain height.'

Da Silva was laughing. 'See. No problem. So long as you are in the air you are safe. It is hitting the dirt that you have to worry about.'

'You stupid bastard,' I said under my breath.

I turned to Xavier. He'd gone into catatonic shock. He had his arms round his long legs which were pulled up to his chest, his eyes were shut and his complexion had turned, I swear this is the truth, to the colour of grey putty.

Once we'd climbed back to ten thousand feet Da Silva said, his hand hovering over the ignition key, 'Now, mi amigo, if you'll excuse me, I'm going to have my nap.'

So long as he didn't turn the engine off, I couldn't give a damn. Da Silva was soon fast asleep, snoring and twitching like a dog chasing rabbits.

For a moment I longed for the safety of England and the quiet satisfaction of sitting at a desk watching a clock tick. After what felt like an eternity, but was in fact only ten minutes, Da Silva shook himself awake.

'Anything happen?' he asked.

'All quiet. There were no mountains to crash into.'

'See, you hardly need me.'

'Maybe, but there is the little matter of landing.'

Da Silva checked the skyline, glanced at the rear-view mirror, scanned the dials and then opened a book of crosswords.

Below, a winding ribbon of silver twisted through the wilderness.

Towards the horizon mist appeared to come from a slit in the earth.

'Fifteen minutes and we'll be at our destination. Are you sure you don't want to go somewhere else?'

'Absolutely certain.'

'Do you want to view the Falls? I can fly in close. It's like being in a car wash.'

Xavier was still in bad way, curled up in a fetal position, whimpering.

'I think we'd better just land.'

We swooped low over the tree tops and touched down on a landing field that had been hewn out of the forest. Thankfully no unthinking local had built a hut in the middle of the runway. The ground was sodden, water shooting high into the air as we lurched across the rough surface. We taxied and parked alongside three identical, shiny and expensive looking Cessnas.

Xavier climbed down from the plane, said nothing, and walked like a zombie towards a shed on the edge of the airstrip.

'Where are you going?' I asked.

Xavier shrugged his shoulders: he didn't even turn round.

'I'll see you later,' I said. I thought he might appreciate some quality time by himself.

TWO

I felt like a god overseeing his world.

My hand trembled ever so slightly as I signed the register of The Eldorado International Guest House. Still suffering from the trauma induced by Da Silva's aeronautical stunts I had momentarily lost all sense of identity, time and space and, for a second, had to think who I was.

Built on stilts, the guest house was adjacent to the runway and provided basic accommodation for travellers visiting the waterfall. There was a spacious eating and drinking area, alongside an open-plan lounge which at night was used for hanging hammocks. There were two private bedrooms at the back, with neither air-con nor hot water, one of which I reserved for myself. I wasn't sure where Xavier had stumbled off to.

After a couple of beers to quell the after-shock of the flight I set off to the Falls.

Despite Waugh's enthusiasm, I wasn't expecting much as I followed a path through the bush to a viewing point. Waterfalls have always disappointed me. As a kid, I remember being dragged through a damp valley on Exmoor to view some wretched stream dribbling over a rock-face. I really couldn't see what all the fuss was about. The awe was underwhelming – there is only so much fun you can have playing pooh-sticks.

Of course, I've never seen Niagara or Victoria. Rather like the lure of watching wild Atlantic surf breaking on a beach, I'm told there's something deeply primeval and hypnotic about those epic natural wonders.

I walked gingerly across a bare, flat rock as big as a tennis court, towards a low rumble like the sound of a distant motorway. Crickets and lizards skittered away in front of me. For a moment I stopped to admire a tiny golden frog, the size of a thumbnail, clinging with its suckered hands to the fleshy leaf of a bromeliad.

There were no ticket booths, no guidebook sellers – I was bracing myself for annoying touts, but there weren't even any of these. I was entirely alone.

Inching towards the edge I looked down into a vast chasm.

Below lay an enchanted valley – I half expected to see Gandalf or Frodo waving at me from a ledge. The drop of the brown water tipping over the cliff and falling for hundreds of feet had a dizzying, mesmerizing effect. A fine spray caused a rainbow. Way below, above the forest canopy, green parrots were gliding in the mist. To get a better view I lay on a smooth, warm crag that stuck out like a finger into the gorge. Through the rock I could sense the thrumming power of the falling water. I felt like a god overseeing his world.

It took a while to comprehend the scale of this untamed landscape. The width of the waterfall wasn't enormous – perhaps three hundred metres across – but it had a beguiling elegance about it. The water poured over the crescent edge and turned into curtains of white spume. The depth of the drop was breathtaking. I focused on a log tipping into the abyss, following its descent, as if hanging in space, weightless, for what seemed like minutes. Shoals of swifts skilfully dodged the water and swooped into a cave behind the cascade.

A flock of macaws, scarlet, yellow and horizon-blue, as vivid as a living rainbow, flew across the valley. I was astounded at their beauty.

Something had changed. I didn't know what it was, maybe fear-induced hormones had kicked in from the flight, but an unexpected calm swept over me. I began to wish that I was able to see more of this fascinating country. I realised I was enjoying myself. Everything about the rain forest was extreme: the heat, the moisture, the pure colour. The bush was teeming with energy; I was alive and in the moment, connected to a greater universe. I felt like a tiny living speck in a giant and joyous ant heap.

Surely, even Xavier would be impressed? I wished Aurora could be with me to share the experience. She'd quietly stare at all this, taking it all in, mindful of the details. Then, in her sketch book, she'd capture minutiae that I'd not noticed: the shades; the textures of the leaves; the light on delicate ferns, the contours of the glistening rocks.

This was a moment that would be hot-wired into my brain and remain with me for as long as I lived. And yet words would never suffice. Later, I would try to explain this blissful episode, but in the end, shrug and smile stupidly and mutter 'it was awesome; you've got to see it for yourself.'

As I walked back to the lodge I thought about all the labour market opportunities. If only they could build a paved runway to accommodate larger planes. And eco-friendly tourist lodges. Also a viewing platform with a restaurant, and high-powered boats roaring below, alongside white-water rafting in the rapids downstream. Kaieteur Falls could be a world-class tourist destination. And this whole, enchanting paradise would be lost.

THREE

Introducing Ms Tallulah Honeyfield.

I could hear distant music. As I got nearer to the guest house I could see a party was in full swing. A woman, wearing a bright amber dress, danced provocatively on a table, while singing into a beer bottle. There were whoops and cries from her audience as she whined and gyrated. 'Hit me baby one more time,' they all chanted.

'Here he is,' the cavorting dancer shouted as I climbed the steps. 'Our shadow. The wanderer!' She was the curvaceous woman with the immaculate hair from the tour group that had stayed at the Stabroek Lodge. Though her hair was not so perfect now. I liked this tousled look better: less New York grand dame, more rough and ready jungle Jane.

'Come and join us, buddy,' said a well-built man with an unkempt Fidel Castro beard. 'The name's O'Connor, Stilton O'Connor.' He pushed a glass of what smelled like rum into my hand. Wearing madras shorts and a grubby Grateful Dead skulls and roses singlet, he was running with sweat and had the hairiest shoulders I'd ever seen. 'The sun has been a bastard today. You don't want to get dehydrated.'

'Stilton? How do you spell that?' I said, thinking that I'd misheard.
'The usual way. S.T.I.L.T.O.N.'
'Oh, right.'
'By six twenty it'll be dark. The generator's sporadic.'
I raised my glass. 'Keep the fluids flowing,' I said. 'Cheers.'
'Have you seen the Falls yet?' Stilton asked.
'Yes, impressive.'
'Longest single drop of water in the world.'
'So I understand.'

'You could fit the Empire State Building in that hole and still have room for the Statue of Liberty on top. The power of nature is something to behold. You see something like that and you've got to believe in God, right?'

The woman in the amber dress came over and introduced herself as Ms Honeyfield. 'But you can call me Tallulah,' she said. 'You were in Georgetown weren't you?'

'Yes, at the Stabroek Lodge. I think I saw you.'

'Seems like everywhere we go, you're there.' She smiled and held my gaze as if she was trying to tell me something. 'Are you stalking us?'

'I thought you were following me,' I said.

'I saw you eating alone. You should have introduced yourself.'

'So how's the trip going?' I asked. Her dress was dangerously low cut and I was aware of her well-defined cleavage.

'We've done all we can. We need to beat it out of here, pronto.'

'I'm getting to like the place,' I said.

'I'm doing my best to keep up team morale. It's taken a dive over the last few days. The bush does strange things to your head: you start to hear unnatural noises and glimpse jungle mirages. We trekked into the interior, it was tougher than I expected. I picked up some seriously weird vibes...'

There was a shout as a man fell backwards in his chair and tipped onto the floor. He lay, apparently unhurt, laughing until he had tears in his eyes.

'Get up, you arsehole,' Tallulah yelled. 'You're making a bad impression on our English visitor.'

'Don't mind me,' I said.

'I do mind you. God, they embarrass me. I don't want people to get the wrong idea.'

Tallulah stared at me, with her mouth slightly open – no lipstick this time. She had perfectly white, perfectly-proportioned teeth. I'd never seen teeth like them.

'I love your old-time accent,' she said. 'It's so adorable. You sound like that character in Jewel in the Crown. Do you get that programme in England?'

I felt flattered. Not so much by the 'old time' but I always thought that Charles Dance, with his polished voice and urbane charm, was rather handsome. 'It's an English production,' I said.

'Really?' she said as if she didn't believe me.

Over in the corner, Da Silva was seated next to a young woman, an Amerindian, I guessed – the first I'd seen on my journey to Guyana. Her hair, the colour of dark chocolate, was cut in a bob and she was wearing denim hot-pants and a pink Hello Kitty T-shirt. Da Silva had his arm round her shoulders – she was sitting stiffly, staring straight ahead.

'Did you see the cock of the rock?' asked Tallulah.

'The what? I don't know. What is it?'

'It's a rare bird.'

'I must have missed it.'

'We'll have to put that right.' I wasn't certain but I thought there was a hint of innuendo in her voice which I decided to ignore. 'It's got a scarlet head – and has an interesting mating ritual.'

'Like what?'

Tallulah laughed. 'A lot of strutting and posing. "Do you think I'm sexy?" All that machismo bluff.'

'I'll definitely look out for it,' I smiled. 'So, how long are you here for?'

'I was planning to leave today, but the pilot needed to depart a couple of hours before dusk. These retards weren't ready. So I've got an evening to fill.'

'The nightlife here is a bit limited,' I said.

'You have to make your own entertainment.'

'Where's everybody sleeping?' I asked.

'They've brought hammocks. I've got a private room though.'

'Me too.' For a moment I felt guilty. I had no idea where Xavier was going to kip. I'd always assumed that he'd have a cousin nearby. But he was right; apart from the lodge, there was nothing here in the bush.

Da Silva and his companion – she was perhaps twenty years younger than him – were now standing in the middle of the room shuffling to the music. They made an incongruous pair. Still wearing his baggy Sinbad pants, he was tall and generously built; she was bamboo thin - her head only came up to his chest.

While Tallulah went to refill her glass, Stilton told me about their expedition into the bush.

'It was kind of scary,' he said. 'They say that too much time in the jungle either sends you crazy or turns you into a poet.'

'You're not supposed to say jungle,' I said. 'The Guyanese call it bush.'

'That's not my problem, Bud.'

'Jungle has colonial connotations - jungle book, jungle boy, law of the jungle.'

'Well, I don't like bush either. The very word makes me tense. We've got a dynasty of the bastards back home. That drunken clown Bush Junior is standing for president.'

Stilton was obviously so off his head that he was going into free-fall hallucination.

'That's a different bush,' I said.

'Thankfully the fool doesn't stand a chance. Al Gore is going to mop the floor with that jerk-off. The thought of Bush as president gives me the frights. The guy's a fuckhead.'

'Anyway, becoming a poet doesn't sound too bad.'

'Unfortunately, you don't get to choose.'

'Did you come across bandits?' I asked.

Stilton told me the problem was the local head-shrinkers. They listen for footsteps and disappear. You never see them, but you know they're there. They move as silently as a phantom in the night – but you can feel their presence. They communicate by making monkey noises. Sometimes you might catch the glint of an eye. If you linger they pick you off. They brew the strongest poison known to man. He saw an ape die in seconds – it just fell out of the trees. Thump. All it would take was a dart from a blow pipe and you'd be sleeping in a lead hammock for the rest of the journey.

I asked whether they had been attacked. Stilton said they'd been extra cautious. They had heard the drumming though. The drums are the jungle telegraph; it means you've been clocked. Stilton laughed hysterically at this point. They're kinda saying to each other, 'dinner's served'. Stilton stayed with a tribe called the Macawaiwai. Their leader was a spunky little fella, he said. Very smart, he had a sixth sense. It was almost as if he could read your mind. Uninhibited – he asked some intimate questions. He claimed the tribe gave up pot-boiling and head shrinking generations ago. Nevertheless, you couldn't afford to let your guard down.

'Look at this,' said Stilton as he shoved a furry hand in my face.

'Look at what?'

'My finger nails.' Stilton's nails were like long and dirty talons. 'In this goddamn climate nails grow at an alarming rate.'

'Can't you clip them?'

'They grow back in days – hours even. Man, I hate this hellhole. It's turning me into a fucking werewolf.'

'It doesn't sound like you're having much of a holiday,' I said.

'You could say that,' Stilton said, emptying his bottle. He gazed into the distance and gave an uneasy smile. He was all over the place.

'The jungle oysters were good though. Best thing I've eaten in ages.'

Before I had a chance to ask what exactly jungle oysters were, Tallulah rejoined us.

'So tell me,' she asked, 'who's this Roxy?'

'I don't know any Roxy.'

'At the Stabroek, they said you had a girlfriend.'

'Oh Roxy! She's not my girlfriend. She's my milliner.'

'Oh my God! You Brits with your butlers and your milliners. Are you going round the world in eighty days, or something?'

'She's fitting a hat. It was arranged by head office in London.' I was beginning to feel embarrassed. I was coming across as a right idiot.

'They said you had a girlfriend called Roxy. You'd go for long walks and meet her.'

'Who's been talking about me?'

'I asked Festus. I saw you eating alone. I was curious.'

'You asked about me?'

'Festus said you went out at night.'

'Yeah, for a walk.'

Tallulah looked at me in disbelief. 'A walk? By yourself?'

'Yeah, by myself. That's what we English do. We go for walks.'

'Walking in Georgetown. You're crazy.'

'Georgetown is a beautiful city, especially at night.'

'Are you sure you don't meet people?' Tallulah looked at me with narrowed eyes. 'People like Roxy?'

'No!'

'Why don't you just jump into a car? Walking sounds like procrastination to me.'

'Walking provides good thinking time.'

It was getting noisy. The other members of the group were now playing cards. I couldn't see what game it was, but it involved much shouting and chants of 'OFF, OFF, OFF'. Da Silva and his friend were leaving the room. He was holding her by the hand and pulling her along.

'So what about the early morning calls?' Tallulah asked.

This was creepy. 'How do you know this?'

'I know all about you, Felix.' She gave me a long look with her try-me eyes and smiled.

'God, I hope not!'

'Why don't we move somewhere quieter?' said Tallulah 'I've got something in my room that might interest you.'

'Sure.' I was enjoying her company. After all this time away from home it was good to relax.

'Join me in half an hour. Room number two. You can tell me all about your walking.'

FOUR

Xavier's decline.

Xavier entered the lounge and sat in a corner clasping a bottle of beer. I was shocked by his swift decline. Gazing into space, he didn't seem to notice me as I walked up to him.

'Are you okay?' I asked. Xavier turned, stared at me, and said nothing. His usually smooth chin was flecked with bristles of grey. He appeared to have spilt red pomegranate juice down his white shirt and his black Italian loafers were scuffed and covered in mud. 'Some journey,' I said.

'I am not flying with that man again,' Xavier replied through clamped teeth.

'Da Silva's alright, really.'

'He's a suicidal madman. I just saw him with some girl. He's a paedophile.'

'She wasn't that young.'

'I don't like him – with his weird clothes, he looks like some sort of fancy dress cowboy. He doesn't dress like a pilot.'

'Okay, I'll find someone else to take us back.'

'I'm not flying.'

'We'll find someone else,' I repeated.

'Not with him. Not with anybody.'

'You're suffering minor post traumatic shock syndrome – have another drink, give it a couple of hours. You'll feel better soon.'

'I'm not drinking and I'm not flying. Right.' I didn't like to tell him he'd already got a beer in his hand.

'There's a tour party here. Perhaps I could get you a lift with them. They have modern planes. They might have a spare seat.'

'Mr Radstock, I am never flying again.'

'That might be difficult. There's no other way out of here.'

Xavier shrugged and folded his arms. 'Well, if that's the case I'm staying put.'

I tried not to show I was alarmed by this. I was beginning to realise how much I relied on Xavier. 'But...'

'Mr Radstock, my job is to help you with your research and drive you round Georgetown ...'

'Which you have done very well.'

'...I was happy to go to Linden, and I could just about put up with Corriverton and its smugglers, but it is not my job, NOT my job, to do stunts in the sky with a pilot who thinks he's a comedian, or to live in the bush like a buck man. I'm a town dweller – I'm not suited to these...' he waved his hand in the air, '... basic surroundings.'

'Think of this as a holiday. This is beautiful. Look,' I pointed at the tour group, 'people pay good money to stay here.'

'It's not my idea of a holiday. Where are the night clubs? Where's the music? Where are the pretty ladies? There's nothing to do.'

'Can't you just lime?'

'This place is not suited to liming.'

'What about the waterfall?'

'I haven't seen it.'

'You ought to.'

'I can't swim.'

'You don't have to swim in it.' I said. 'You just look at it.'

'If I want to gaze at water, I can stare at the ocean.'

'That's different. The ocean's horizontal – this is vertical. This is falling water.'

'I don't care what angle it is. Things like that just make me want to go to the toilet.'

'What's happened to your sense of adventure?'

Xavier stood up and walked away.

'Xavier!'

'I am not flying in any plane. Understood?'

'Look, who's in charge here?'

'Oh, I see. You're the master, eh?'

'I'm not. We're partners.'

'Doesn't seem like it to me.'

'We've got to sort this out.'

'Yes, boss.' he said sarcastically, and marched out of the room and into the darkness.

'You are so freaking annoying,' I shouted after him. He didn't turn round.

FIVE

Cock of the Rock.

Over the last few weeks I'd developed a routine for entering the bathroom at night-time. I'd make a loud noise as I slowly pushed the door, and then reach out to feel for the light switch. I'd stand in the open doorway and scan for uninvited company. I was getting used to lizards, geckos and frogs, but was still not overly enthusiastic about the giant cockroaches and tarantulas.

This time, as I was having a piss, a vampire bat flew out of the bush toilet. I yelled. For a moment, I thought the animal, probably rabid, had latched onto me. I checked for damage, but couldn't see any sign of teeth marks or broken skin.

Tallulah's room, like mine, was simply furnished. There was a small double bed, a table scorched with cigarette burns and a cracked mirror in a yellow plastic frame hanging on the slatted wooden wall. A haze of insects swarmed round a bare light bulb.

'I heard someone shout,' said Tallulah. 'Was that you?'

'No.'

'I thought I heard a scream. It was terrifying.'

'Oh, that could have been me.'

'God! What happened?'

'I had an unexpected altercation with a bat in the toilet. I fought it off, though.'

Tallulah handed me a beer. 'Make yourself at home.' There was nowhere to sit apart from the bed. We clunked bottles together. Her suitcase was open, showing a wash-bag, neatly folded clothes and lacy black knickers.

I caught a glimpse of myself in the mirror and did a double-take.

I hardly recognised the face staring back at me. I'd lost weight, my jaw looked firmer and my cheekbones were somehow higher and more well-defined. My hair, far from dropping out in clumps, was thicker and blonder than I remembered. My skin was clear and I had a honey coloured tan. For the first time since adolescence I was pleased with what I saw. This climate obviously suited me.

'Tell me,' Tallulah asked, 'what did you think of the Falls?'

'Impressive. It's almost primeval how they get to you.'

'They do get to you,' she sighed. 'They do something to you. Four times the height of Niagara. And there's hardly anyone here to see them.'

'There's something dream-like about them. I could watch them forever.'

'The Amerindians say they have magical powers.'

'So I hear.' I nodded and took a shot of beer. 'Stilton told me you'd been trekking in the woods.'

'We went to visit the Macawaiwai.'

'Stilton said they're scary.'

'Bullshit! They are the sweetest people – gentle, dignified souls.' For a moment Tallulah had a far-away look in her eyes as if she was remembering something highly pleasurable. 'They speak excellent English – much clearer than the creole you hear on the coast.'

'So they're not dangerous?'

'Of course not. They haven't got an aggressive bone in their body. There's this tale about a missionary who, uninvited, moved into an Amerindian village. The Amerindians put up with him for a while, but eventually got tired of his requests to abandon their traditional ways and wear clothing and eat with a knife and folk. So do you know what they did?'

'Added him to the pepperpot and ate him for supper?'

Tallulah didn't laugh. 'Felix, you may have a clever accent, but that doesn't mean you can get away with derogatory statements.'

'It's the British sense of the absurd. I thought you'd like it.'

'Sometimes you Brits are off-beam. Queen Victoria doesn't rule the world anymore, you know.'

I felt like an idiot. 'Sorry, that was unacceptable.'

'What the Amerindians did do was quietly, overnight, abandon their village. The missionary woke up to find everybody had gone. They had melted into the forest. You see the Amerindians didn't want an argument – they didn't like to cause offence. They silently packed up and left.'

'And the missionary, how did he react?'

She laughed. 'Oh, the dickweed chased after them.'

'So, Felix, apart from your mystery walks, what are you doing here?'

'Visiting the Kaieteur Falls.'

'I get that, but what else? With your butler, you look like an explorer in search of the lost city of Eldorado.'

'Butler! Xavier is my logistics coordinator.'

She chuckled. 'That sounds so British!'

'I'm working.'

Tallulah rummaged in her bag and brought out a small decorated enamel box. 'Really? Eldorado, doesn't really exist you know.'

'I'm on a contract.'

'Doing what?'

'It's bit technical.'

'Try me.'

'I'm doing what's called labour market consultancy.'

Tallulah straightened and looked at me in surprise. 'Oh my God!'

'What's wrong with that?'

'Oh my God!' she repeated. 'I should have guessed. So that explains it.'

'Explains what?'

She stood up. 'You are spying on us.'

'Why the hell would I spy on a bunch of tourists?'

'Tourists! You're twisting my melon, right?'

'You're on holiday, aren't you?'

'If I wanted to be a tourist I'd be in Rome or Paris, even London. Not this backwater.'

'I don't get it.'

'Felix, like you, I'm on a job. I'm working.'

'Doing what?'

'Writing a labour force assessment.'

I was having trouble taking this in. 'A labour force assessment of where?'

'Where do you think, dumbnuts?'

'You can't be!'

'Why not?'

'Because that's what I'm doing!'

'Holy piss!' said Tallulah. We looked at each other in astonishment.

'Who are you working for?' I asked.

'Isn't it obvious? I'm leading a survey for the International Bank.'

'No! I can't believe it. The I.B.! So you're the person they keep talking about.'

'Who's talking about what?'

'You're the heavy drinking, hard partying, mouse-loving woman from the I.B..'

'Mouse-loving?'

'Everywhere I've been, they talk about you. Jim Bucket said ...'

'You've met red Jim?' she asked.

'Yes.'

'Did he ask you for dirty pictures?' We both laughed.

'And the GuySuCo sugar factory?' I asked.

'I had to bribe the lazy bastard with $100 to get in there.'

'No wonder he wasn't impressed with my $10.'

'Cheapskate Brit!'

'I can't believe this.'

We were both cracking up. Tallulah shook her head. 'Oh, I get it! So you're the dude with the computers.'

'No! There are no computers.'

'What have you done with them?'

'Don't you start. There never have been any.'

'I'd keep quiet about that, if I was you. Some people could get mighty upset if they knew.'

'I don't know where this rumour about computers has come from,' I said.

'It's a clever strategy. It's generated a lot of interest. There's been a mini economic boom created by the anticipation of their arrival. There's been a surge in the sale of computer peripherals. I'm told there's a national shortage of mouse mats.'

'There's no strategy. These computers have never existed.'

She gave me a wink. 'I think you ought to carry on with that little charade. For your own safety, if nothing else.'

'The I.B.!' I repeated. I could hardly believe this. 'I thought you were a tour party. You seem to be enjoying yourselves.'

'It's tough – there's got to be some payback for working away from home. These policy dorks are all on the spectrum, you have to keep them happy or their brains short-circuit and they go nutso.'

'But there's so many of you.'

'We work as a team.'

'What do you all do?'

Tallulah explained that she was a social development specialist. She managed a unit with ninjas covering gender, policy, planning, infrastructure, water, agriculture and, of course, climate change. There were a couple of trainees as well.

I opened another beer and settled back on the bed.

'So, tell me,' I asked, 'what statistics have you gathered?'

She said the data was a freaking mess. How the government knew what was going on, or could make any decisions, was beyond her. Her first recommendation was going to be that they get a proper fully integrated and computerized Geographical Information System. There were a few off-the-peg GIS programmes she could recommend. The I.B. could provide a low-interest grant for that.

'So what data have you got?' I repeated.

'It's a matter of finding the right people.'

'Like who?'

'Hey, come on,' said Tallulah, 'we don't want to discuss work.'

I didn't want to let this go. 'What figures did you get?'

'We'll talk about that later.'

'Who did you speak to?'

'Leave it, Felix, this is a magical place, let's just enjoy it.'

'You're right, we're lucky to be here. The Falls are amazing and hardly anyone knows about them.' I lifted my bottle in salute. 'And let's keep it that way.'

'So,' asked Tallulah, 'why's it taken so long for you to introduce yourself?'

'I've been frantically busy. It's only now that I've been able to take time off.'

Tallulah looked serious for a moment. She put her hand on my leg and asked, 'Do you trust me?'

I looked at her. If a gorgeous woman asks if you trust her, the likelihood is that you're going to say yes.

'Well...' I was struggling to choose my words carefully. 'Err, well...'

'I'm asking about me, not the I.B., you dummy. Do you trust me?'

'Yeah, I know. Yes.'

'So?'

'Implicitly.' I hardly knew this woman. I was intrigued to know what would happen next.

Tallulah moved closer. 'Okay. Close your eyes and open your

mouth.'

I did as she said. We seemed to be getting to know each other rather quickly. I hadn't even asked if she was married or had a lover. Nor had she asked me. Certainly, she wasn't wearing a wedding ring.

I could feel a small, aspirin-sized pill on my tongue.

'What's that?' I was a little alarmed. I don't usually let strangers administer pharmaceuticals to me.

She also put a pill in her mouth. 'Here's to economic development,' she said as she took a swig of beer.

I raised my glass. 'And closer international relations.'

For a moment I felt anxious – if I'm taking a trip I like to know what sort of journey I'm about to go on. Up, down, along or inside out – in such situations it's good for the psyche to be prepared.

'Don't worry, honey, it's just a Masher. More commonly used as a veterinary drug. The team takes them all the time. You'll enjoy it.'

A veterinary drug? Claxons were ringing. 'Enjoy? In what way?'

'It doesn't do the cows any harm. You'll see.'

'No tell me, I need to know. It's not as if I need to increase my milk yield.'

'Relax Felix. Lie down. Everything is going to be all right.' She patted the pillow. 'We're going on a little happiness trip.'

I remembered Gordon joking about sampling hallucinogenic frog turds. That was far-fetched enough. Never, in my most unbridled dreams, did I think that I'd be dropping a Masher with a social development specialist from the International Bank.

We said nothing for a while, lying on our backs and watching the ceiling fan. A fist-sized animal with many legs scuttled across a rafter.

'What's that?' I said.

'A spider?'

How amazing! I realised I loved spiders. Their legs, their multifarious eyes, the way they scampered – they were as fascinating and as adorable as a box of kittens.

'How long does it take for this stuff to kick in?'

'Not long.'

'I should warn you,' I said, 'I have a high tolerance level to drugs and alcohol. I don't think it's having any effect.'

I turned my head and looked at Tallulah. She was beautiful. I loved her so much. I moved closer. Her skin smelled of cream and warm vanilla.

At that moment the lights went out.

'What the …!' For an instant the black-out spooked me.

'Lie here and enjoy the darkness,' said Tallulah. 'We should be able to hear the howler monkeys.'

There were shouts from the bar. It sounded like furniture was being pushed over and glass smashed.

'I think the team is a little over-tired,' Tallulah said. 'They get boisterous. Ignore them. Listen to the jungle. Can you hear the Falls?'

'I think so.' There was such a wall of noise coming from the bush I couldn't be sure.

'Do you know what?' said Tallulah, inching nearer. 'All that falling water makes me feel horny. Does water do that to you?'

Our arms were touching. We were both damp with sweat. 'Now you mention it, yes, it does.'

Tallulah continued. 'Neuroscientists say that fast-flowing water stimulates the part of the brain that is responsible for sexual desire.'

'That's interesting.'

'That's why they build hotels by waterfalls. Niagara, Viagara. Get it?'

'I thought Viagara was Sanskrit for tiger.'

'It's all inter-related,' she said.

'You seem to know a lot about this.'

'Aquaphilia. Any economist worth their shit knows that. Put people with anxiety and depression near a waterfall and they soon cheer up. It's the same as the fluffy kitten syndrome.'

'I think we should investigate further.' I had to concentrate on each syllable that came out of my mouth. Every word felt transcendentally important. 'This could have immense implications for the labour market.'

'I read some research,' said Tallulah, 'that concluded most hotel beds last for seven years. In hotels by waterfalls they're rattled to pieces in under twelve months. Anyway, you should know all about that with your sexy English voice.'

'Yeah, right.'

'Hey, I thought we agreed not to talk about work.'

'What are we talking about?'

'Shush!' said Tallulah. 'Just enjoy the moment.'

We lay on the bed listening to the cacophony of the bush – like a full orchestra tuning up. I tried to relax but the kinetic energy of the Falls was making me restless.

Suddenly, Tallulah sat up. 'Do you think the Falls are fluorescent at night-time?'

'What do you mean?'

'Like when the sea glows in the dark.'

'That would be awesome. We need to know.'

'Yes, we do,' she said.

'For our research,' I said. The cosmos was expanding directly in front of me. Everything was possible.

'Exactly. This is important. We need to check this out. We could harness the energy.'

'The energy of the waterfalls?'

'No, the energy of the glow.'

'Of course.'

'Why has nobody thought of this before?' said Tallulah. 'The world's power crisis could be solved at a stroke.'

I was sorry to leave the bed. But we'd come back later.

There was chaos as we walked through the bar. 'These fucking hammocks don't work', came a voice from the shadows. 'We've been ripped off yet again.' People were falling over each in the dark trying to tie their hammocks to the wall-posts.

'You've got to hang them higher up so they don't sag onto the ground.'

'How the fuck do you get into these things?'

I saw the outline of a body up-end, spin backwards and crash to the floor.

Everybody was laughing. A warm feeling of goodness was flushing through my brain. God, I loved this place. I loved these people.

Tallulah and I strolled by the soft light of the waning moon. Fireflies were zinging all around us, sparking like roman candles. I wondered about Xavier's tigers and chuckled to myself. We stood and stared. The bush felt so alive – it was pulsing with the energy of unseen wildlife. An animal was crashing about in the forest canopy. For a split second, silhouetted against the night sky, a monkey jumped from one branch to another. I felt at one with everything. My DNA was uncoiling – for a crazy moment I wanted to strip off my shirt and join the ape and swing on creepers through the forest. Tallulah and I hugged. I could feel her breasts pressed against my chest. She kissed the nape of my neck.

'Me Tarzan, you Jane,' I whispered.

Eventually, we came to the clearing and walked over the flat rock. I could feel the force of the water sucking me down.

'Careful, don't go too near the drop,' Tallulah warned.

On all fours we inched our way to the cliff-edge and looked over. The Falls were just as powerful and mesmerizing in the moonlight. The water wasn't phosphorescent, but the cascade was liquid platinum from the light of the moon. It hit an emotional button deep down inside and for several minutes we said nothing. It was like one of those metaphysical moments when you stare at the stars and wonder at the scale and size of the universe. Stretched out on the smooth outcrop, still warm from the day's sun, I felt weirdly moved, connected and energised.

'Think of it,' said Tallulah, 'we're lying next to one of the world's most potent natural aphrodisiacs.'

'I bet people get laid on this rock all the time,' I said.

'At full moon probably.'

'Do you think we're alone?' We were so close I could sense her breath on my neck.

'Just us – and the monkeys.' Before I knew it our tongues were touching.

'Felix, from now on I'm going to call you Merrick.'

'Merrick! I thought I was the good looking one from Jewel in the Crown. Merrick was the racist policeman. The ugly bastard with the scarred face and the glass eye.'

'Sexy voice though. Whisper something in my ear,' she said, as she slid her hand into my trousers.

'Cock - of - the - Rock.'

Oh yeah!

SIX

Where's Tallulah?

I was dimly aware of the sound of a plane taking off from the airstrip. It was dawn and I had a screaming thirst. The Masher was living up to its name – I felt as if my brain had been forced through a sieve and turned into porridge. I looked around and was surprised to find I was alone in my own room. I thought back to the previous night. For a moment the recollection of Tallulah made me smile. It had been fun, but... I don't know... I was feeling a little bit guilty. But then, oh fuck, self-loathing swept over me. How could I have done this? Been unfaithful to my dear, sweet Aurora. What was I thinking? I was in another world; an office romance, it meant nothing. It just happened, right? Put the whole incident in a box and throw it away, throw it over the waterfall.

Tallulah's colleagues were packing their belongings.

'Where's Tallulah?' I asked apprehensively.

'Tallulah?'

'Yeah, Tallulah.' How many Tallulahs were staying at the lodge for goodness sake?

'Oh, Tallulah! Sorry bud, I didn't get what you were saying. You have such a strong accent.'

'Tallulah said she liked my accent.'

'Yeah, well that's Tallulah for you. Queen Bee, she understands buckets of foreign lingo.'

'But I'm speaking English!'

The man rolled his eyes as if I was talking nonsense. 'Here, have a beer,' he said.

'It's too early in the morning.'

'It's good for you. If you sweat in your sleep, you can wake up dangerously dehydrated.'

'So where's Tallulah?'

'You need to get some alcohol in your blood. Protects against malaria. The mosquitoes don't like it, they spit it out.'

'Where's Tallulah?' I asked again.

'What?'

'Tallulah.' I really couldn't see what I was saying wrong.

'She's gone.'

'Gone!? But...'

'Yeah. Tallulah and Stilton caught the early flight.'

'Gone where?'

She might at least have woken me and said goodbye. I don't sleep that heavily.

'Georgetown. She's got a meeting with a statistician. We're going to catch up with her later. And then we jump on the first plane home. I've got some Christmas presents to buy for Junior.'

Statistician? Had she really found a statistician?

'Did she leave a message for me?'

'For you?'

'Yes, me. Felix Radstock.'

'Why would she leave a message for you?'

'I don't know. I just wondered.'

He looked me up and down, and nodded cogently. 'Hah!' he smirked. 'Did she give you a Masher? Tallulah the ball-breaker. It's not a particularly exclusive club you've joined.'

The man shouted to his colleague on the other side of the room stuffing a sleeping bag into a case. 'Hey Caspar, we've got another member of the Tallulah fan club here. Masher casualty!'

Caspar cheered and gave a rodeo yell. 'Yeeharr, ride 'em, cowboy,' he said, raising his fist and slapping his forearm in a lewd gesture.

From the bathroom a disembodied voice cried out, 'Yeah, give her one for me, man.'

I wasn't particularly happy with the details of my night with Tallulah being yelped to the whole wide world and his monkey.

'She's your boss, isn't she?' I asked. I wanted to stop this ribaldry.

'Yeah, but she's not here.'

I was beginning to really dislike this guy. 'What about Da Silva? Where's he?'

'Pardon?'

'Da Silva.'

'Sorry bud. Say again.'

Oh for fuck's sake. 'DA-SIL-VA,' I yelled.

'Oh, Da Silva. He took her.'

'But he's my pilot!'

'He said he'd be back later.'

'Back later! When?'

'What? I'm not getting you. You have to speak slower.'

'WHEN WILL DA SILVA RETURN?'

'You're shouting, man. Masher cold-turkey can get you like that.'

I wanted to grab this idiot by his grimy vest and shake him.

'Are you sure you're not dehydrated?' he said as he popped open another can.

SEVEN

Xavier's revenge.

'I've got good news,' said Xavier. He was wearing a sparkling white shirt and pastel blue safari jacket and appeared to have recovered from the ordeal of the flight. 'I've sorted out my return journey. I've arranged to travel back to G.T. by river.'

'I didn't know there was a boat.' My head still ached and I was confused by Tallulah's sudden departure. Why had she left without saying goodbye? Maybe it was best to let things cool off for a while.

'Not a direct boat. At the rapids passengers have to change pirogue and walk.'

'Walk! Are you all right with that? I thought you didn't like walking. I thought you didn't like the bush.'

Xavier shrugged. 'It's the only way.'

'So, when do we leave?'

'No, it's just me going by boat.'

'Oh?'

'You're flying back with Da Silva.'

'Assuming he returns. So I'll meet you in Georgetown tomorrow.'

'It'll take me longer than a day,' said Xavier.

'How long?' I was surprised how calm my voice sounded.

'River travel is not as quick as flying.'

'So how long?'

'It depends on many things. The weather, the flow of the river, the availability of canoes, inter-tribal warfare. Four, maybe five days, at the least.'

'That's too long.'

'I've sorted it out. Meanwhile, you stay here.'

'I've got things to do in Georgetown.'

Tallulah was only in the country for a couple more days. Besides, the hours were ticking by. Anytime now the Y2K virus could kick in.

'I've set up an excursion for you,' Xavier said.

'I've seen all there is to see.'

'You'll like this. I've arranged for you to go up-river and visit some pork-knockers.'

'That's very good of you, Xavier, but Lucas said I shouldn't visit the interior. You know that.'

'Too late, you're here already.'

'I told you, the weekend doesn't count.'

'I thought you'd be pleased. You said you wanted to see the miners. It's not far.'

'I don't know about this, Xavier. Time is short. I need to get back to Georgetown and track down a statistician. Miss Honeyfield has an appointment to see one.'

'Your trek is all arranged and paid for.'

I looked at Xavier. He was smiling – he was wearing clean clothes and his air of composure had returned. 'Is this a joke?' I asked.

'No!'

'This is a joke, isn't it?'

'I swear it isn't.'

'Very funny. You almost had me there.'

'Mr Radstock, I promise you, I am not joking.'

'Really?'

'I swear on my mother's grave.'

I could see in his eyes this wasn't a trick. 'Huh,' I said.

Xavier stared at the floor, apparently crestfallen. 'I thought you would be pleased.'

'Xavier, I am pleased, thank you, I just need a few moments to adjust to the new plan.' I looked out across the airstrip to the greenness beyond. I started to recall all the dangers Xavier had outlined previously: the throat-ripping tigers, the terrifying toothpick fish, the screaming carnivorous plants.

'You said you wanted to visit the pork-knockers.'

'I do. Thank you for arranging it, but what about equipment? I'll need camping equipment. I'll need a sleeping bag and a tent. And a better hat.'

'I've borrowed a hammock and a mosquito net for you.'

'A hammock?'

'It's about time you had the hammock experience,' Xavier beamed. 'You can't visit Guyana and not sleep in a hammock.'

I didn't like to say it, but sometimes Xavier could be just a little bit over-helpful.

I remembered what Ellis had said about going into the bush. 'I'll need a gun!'

'Zadoc, your guide, will look after you. At night-time, you'll be perfectly safe wrapped in your hammock and mosquito net.'

'I'm still not sure about this.'

I thought about Lucas and his warning that the full sensory experience of the bush could send people crazy.

Xavier smiled. 'It's only a couple of days' trek.'

'A couple of days!'

'A couple of days there. And a couple of days back. By the time you return to G.T., I'll be there. And you never know, by then, the Discovery might be fixed.'

'That's four days. I need to clear this with Gordon.'

'Mr Lewis will be impressed. It'll show you've used your initiative and gone that extra mile.'

Xavier was right. If I didn't get the statistics I could at least undertake first-hand observational reporting.

'What about food?' I asked.

'Bush meat. At last you will have a chance to eat capybara.'

I felt Xavier was watching me closely to gauge my reaction. Why hadn't I kept my big mouth shut?

'Well, thanks,' I said. 'So who's this Zadoc? Is he one of your cousins?'

'I told you I don't have any cousins here.'

'Who is he?'

'I have a bachelor uncle who lives in a village a day's walk away. He will be your guide. He is going to be paid by the day, so I suggest you don't linger too much. Uncle Zadoc is a Rasta man. He is very capable. He has spent his life in the bush and is educated in the ways of the forest. He will show you fascinating things. He will capture and feed you wild meat. He tells me he is a first class cook. If you're lucky you might get iguana stew. Very good for your health, nature's antibiotic.'

'What about the tigers?'

'Uncle Zadoc will be equipped for all eventualities.'

I understood. This wasn't a joke; this was Xavier's revenge.

'You may even be inspired by the landscape to write some poetry,' Xavier added.

Or go mad, I thought.

EIGHT

This vast and hostile land.

Zadoc, like his nephew, was tall, slim and good looking. He had Xavier's air of self-possession and poise. The resemblance ended there, however. Zadoc had smoky-grey dreads hanging half-way down his back and wore a grubby, sweat-stained T-shirt and frayed, cotton trousers cut off at the shin.

'Wa gwan,' he said holding out his right hand, banging his chest with his left.

Xavier had given me a rucksack so heavy it felt as if it was full of rocks. It contained a hammock, a fly sheet, a mosquito net, a water bottle and cooking equipment. Nevertheless, I was aware I was woefully unprepared for my trek.

Zadoc handed me a cutlass. 'You will need.' Despite his ragged clothes and his dreadlocks, he exuded a reassuring air of authority.

I felt the sharpness of the blade with my thumb. I swung it at waist level. It felt surprisingly good in my hand and boosted my confidence.

'Snakes, they bite even after decapitation,' Zadoc warned.

Zadoc was in his late forties, I guessed, and spoke with a deep voice in a slow creole I found difficult to understand. As far as I could gather, in the past, we would have made this journey on horseback but all the horses had since perished. When I asked how they had died, he changed the subject.

Wielding his razor-sharp cutlass, Zadoc led the way. He would make short work of any potential dinner that crossed our path. These days, he told me, very few people used the track and without an experienced guide it was easy to get lost. The terrain was so different from the English countryside where hollow-ways and bridle-paths have been etched into the landscape for centuries. Here, within hours of cutting a pathway through the bush, our trail would become overgrown.

Zadoc pointed to a tall, straight tree the size of an English spruce. 'This, telegraph tree. If lost, hit it. It ring like bell. Sound travel many miles.' He rapped the trunk with the blunt side of his cutlass. The body of the tree amplified the noise producing a deep ligneous boom that echoed through the forest.

The forest was unexpectedly dark; the thick canopy high above excluded much of the light. At ground level it was hot and humid – I was surrounded by the sweet grassy smell of rotting vegetation. The forest floor was covered with dead leaves – my footsteps sounded hollow with the accumulation of humus.

We were soon out of earshot of the Falls. In a clearing, a vivid blue Morpho butterfly, a crown jewel caught in a stray shaft of sunlight, flapped past. By now, I had persuaded myself I was going on an adventure and this would be a memorable life experience. I would establish my own rhythm of walking and immerse myself in the surroundings. Somewhere I'd read that long distance hiking liberates the mind. Trekking through the bush would give me time to think.

There was a deafening wall of noise from insects and birds. Zadoc said the constant heat and din of the bush can have a strange effect on those who are not used to it. He talked about the influence of supernatural and malevolent spirits. 'Beware much bad kenaima,' he said, speeding up his walking pace. Hungry to do harm to the living, the kenaima came in many forms: it could push you over a cliff; it could drown you in a river; it could strangle you in your hammock. He also warned we would be passing through head-hunter territory. Though the Amerindians were friendlier these days, it didn't do to upset them.

Unlike most animals that move through the bush with a stealth-like grace, the howler monkeys made a tremendous noise as they leapt from tree to tree. They taunted us with their sinister deep-throated roar. Occasionally, I would catch a glimpse of their ugly, ghoul-like faces. They made me feel uneasy, bringing with them a premonition of tragedy. I soon began to loathe them.

We climbed upwards through the gloom, in places scrambling over jagged, reddish-brown rocks. Zadoc swung his cutlass, slicing through the undergrowth with strength and expertise. He slipped effortlessly through the forest, while I was caught by trailing vines and lianas. In next to no time he was way ahead. My heart was pumping and I was sodden with sweat. The rucksack was biting into my shoulders. Exhausted, dizzy and out of breath, I had difficulty keeping him in sight – I didn't know how long I could maintain this pace.

I remembered what Xavier had said about 'tigers' and felt less sceptical about their existence.

I climbed a craggy outcrop, in places scrabbling on my hands and knees and slipping in the scree. After a while I was above the forest canopy.

Zadoc was sitting on a rock, backlit by an opalescent sky, contemplating the view. 'Behold, God's mighty universe.'

I'd never seen such an infinite and untouched landscape. I'd never realised the vastness of the world. Spread below us, the emerald forest stretched away into the blueness and a distant blur of mountains.

The air was thick with fiery heat. As I drank heavily from my flask, Zadoc waved his hand. 'Plenty slow, plenty slow.'

Viewed from an aircraft the rainforest is somehow diminished. But sitting here amongst the trees, in the throbbing humidity, surrounded by the roar of jungle life, the sense of such space, of such immensity, was overpowering.

'In the beginning, God created heaven and earth,' Zadoc pronounced. Sitting there, leaning on his cutlass handle, he looked like an Old Testament prophet.

But what really unnerved me was that I didn't have a map.

Throughout my life I'd been able to consult maps and travel with the image of the topography in my head. In Guyana, the only chart I'd seen was on a wall in the Ministry of Employment and even then the detail was sketchy. It showed rivers and a few landing strips, but in places it said 'unexplored'. Even a hand-drawn sketch would have been helpful. There was a big white space in my brain where a plan should have been. I realised how much I relied on my guide. It was just me and Zadoc. Nobody else. What if Zadoc were to have an accident? What if I were to have an accident? What about the malevolent spirits?

We sat silently for perhaps ten minutes taking in the view. On the horizon was a vague smudge of mountains. Yet as I stared at this green blanket I could make out faint brown blemishes in the far distance.

Zadoc guessed what I was looking at. 'Negative vibration,' he said. 'Babylon man, he cross border, steal wood and scar sacred landscape. Only the Lord can halt them. It is a crime against nature. God's Eden is desecrated.'

I walked away for a pee. As I strolled back I noticed several brimstone-yellow butterflies gathering round the puddle of urine that was left on the rocky ground. Soon scores of these yellow butterflies were clouding around us. Totally enthralled, I watched them, lace thin, waltzing in the air, like forest confetti.

'They like the piss of an English man,' laughed Zadoc. 'To them, your piss is like the juice of the grape. Me piss is too strong. Me piss like a lion.'

For a moment my mind drifted back to those early days with Aurora in Bristol Zoo. Once, when we were in the tropical house, I thought I'd see if I could hand-feed a butterfly. Apart from Aurora, there was nobody about. I stood motionless with my hand outstretched. It took perhaps five minutes for one of those beautiful creatures to take any interest. But I had the time, and it was warm. The butterfly was weightless – I could barely feel the tickle of its feet.

Its filigree-thin proboscis sucked at tiny beads of sweat in the palm of my hand. With its brilliant, electric-blue wings finely edged in jet black, it was the most beguiling creature I'd ever seen. I realised I was holding my breath. Aurora was watching me. 'Look at this...' As soon as I spoke the butterfly flew away.

But then my mind jumped to a picture of the voluptuous Tallulah spread out on a rock by the Falls. Perhaps the Masher wasn't such a clever idea after all.

The sun was pounding down, and although I was glad of a break I was eager to get back into the shade of the forest. Zadoc pointed at gathering clouds in the distance.

'We go. A storm a-comin.'

For how long we walked I have no idea. The heat was ruthless. The constant chirp and rattle of insects was worming its way into my brain. In the Mediterranean I'd heard cicadas make their harsh stone-on-metal scraping, but this was decibels louder, like the feverish danger buzz you hear in your skull before you faint. I thought about the head-shrinkers ready to pick us off. I saw glints in the darkness, I imagined blowpipes taking aim.

At last we came to a river bank. The vegetation on the ground had thickened; Zadoc hacked a path through creepers and vicious spiny plants to a creek. A couple of toucans flew by. I recognised them from old Guinness adverts – they were, with their yellow beaks the same size as their bodies and their rapidly flapping wings, possibly the most ridiculous birds I'd ever seen. I loved them.

'It is safe to camp here. If you go down river you make mighty noise. Caiman not like surprise.'

'Caiman?'

'They hide in the day. At night river full of them. You shine torch, you see their red eye.'

'Are they dangerous?'

'They attack in self-defence. But not always. It best keep away, you understand. If they attack, you force their jaws together. Their jaw-opening muscles mighty weak.'

'Thanks, that's useful to know.'

The earth appeared to be shifting under my feet. The ground was heaving with ants, millipedes, beetles, arachnids and other evil insects.

'Keep moving,' said Zadoc. 'Put your rucksack on a branch and hang up your hammock.'

I was surprised to see Zadoc blowing up an inflatable pillow. I looked in my rucksack to see if I had one.

'Where's my pillow?'

'Hammock better without. Hammock nature's bed. It adjust to natural body shape.'

'Why have you got one, then?'

'Me have bad neck.'

After we'd set up camp I was expecting Zadoc to explore the bush and hunt for our supper. We'd only brought a few biscuits and energy bars for our journey.

'Lime time,' he said as he lay in his hammock and lit a spliff the size of a Havana cigar. 'Felix, would you like to join me in this blessed communion?'

'Not when I'm at work, thank you,' I said curtly. I was having enough trouble coping with reality – extra weirdness could well drive me over the edge.

Zadoc said nothing for a while. He lay back, sucking and blowing. His hammock almost disappeared, surrounded by billows of smoke.

'And lo, God said thou shall devour the 'erb of the field,' he proclaimed. He was silent for a moment and then said, 'The 'erb is our holy sacrament. It will sting the hearts of those who promote and perform evil.' I didn't fully understand this, though I felt it could be a barb aimed at me.

'So how come smoking weed is part of your religion?' I asked.

'It is written in the good book,' he said as he blew a perfect smoke ring. 'Ganja will heal the wounds of the nation.'

'I must have missed that bit in Sunday School. They don't smoke weed in the Church of England – well, not officially.'

'The Bible says 'thou shall eat the 'erb of the field'. Genesis 3.18."

'How do you know the herb in question is cannabis? It could be sage or thyme, or oregano even.'

'Have you tried smoking those?' he chuckled.

'No. And another thing, you said "EAT the herb of the field" – not roll it up and smoke it.'

'It is more spiritually effective to smoke it.'

'Is that in the Bible as well?'

'The Bible is open to interpretation. You have to clear your mind of prejudice and let the Almighty speak to you. You know what I'm saying?'

'So the Almighty said, "Go out and smoke ganja".'

'Precisely, my friend.'

Eventually, Zadoc climbed out of his hammock and began to slowly and unsteadily gather wood and other combustibles to light a fire. At one stage he froze and let out a low moan.

'What's up?'

'Curupira,' he said pointing at the forest floor.

'Curupira? What's that?'

'Bush elves. Their feet point backwards.'

'How can you tell?'

'You must never follow them. They lead people into the bush and get them lost.'

I looked at the ground. The footprints didn't seem to be pointing backwards. Zadoc was staring at tracks that were obviously our own.

'We must be vigilant. The devil walketh about seeking whom he may devour. We must protect ourselves. I must smoke more 'erb.'

'Is that going to help?'

'The holy sacrament, it guide and protect. It keep evil spirits at bay.'

After half an hour, Zadoc had gathered enough materials to build a fire. The wood was reluctant to light until Zadoc pulled from his bag a half-litre bottle and threw the contents, which smelled like petrol, onto the kindling. The results were dramatic and did the trick.

While Zadoc boiled water and prepared our supper, I continued to lie in my hammock trying to adjust to the heat and get my head together. I thought about the smell of Tallulah's hair. I'd given up falling in love a long time ago. But I couldn't stop thinking about her.

The dark came even quicker in the bush – it was like a candle being blown out. With the lush smell of the forest, the sticky heat, the chirps and screechings of the night and the billows of marijuana smoke, I'd never been in such an extreme environment. At least in daylight I could see all the dreadful insects and arachnids. But, with the intense blackness, I felt on the verge of panic. Despite Zadoc's assertion regarding the protective powers of ganja, I had the horrible thought that a giant spider was waiting to truss me up in my hammock and suck me dry of blood, leaving my body an empty husk. I pushed my mosquito net aside in an attempt to breathe fresh air but was immediately set upon by a swarm of miniscule biting machines.

Zadoc was becoming incomprehensible, and although it was only seven o'clock, there was nothing else to do but try to sleep. Zadoc lay buck-naked in his hammock, impervious to vampires and mosquitoes. He told me, however, to pull the netting tight and away from my skin so bats didn't drain my blood.

I drifted off, but was woken by a curious noise. I was conscious of movement in the dark and the rustle of leaves on the forest floor. I held my breath and remained motionless. I could feel a presence. A man-eating tiger? A malevolent spirit? Hands about to tighten around my throat? Whatever it was, I could sense it was getting nearer. My cutlass was out of reach, by the fire. Should I make a noise and scare the intruder away? I remained dead still, lying on my back looking up at the forest canopy.

Zadoc should have been awake and on guard, I thought angrily. That was what he was paid for. Sleeping on duty was a punishable offence. That was my problem, I was just too trusting. After a day in his company I'd sensed he wasn't as reliable as Xavier had claimed, and his air of authority was merely arrogance. I would make sure he was sacked for gross misconduct. But what would be the good of that? It would be too late; with my tongue swollen or gullet torn out I wouldn't be alive to tell the tale. I should have paid attention to Ellis and brought a gun.

The presence was moving round the camp fire. I listened. A log burst, sending sparks into the air. After a while there was silence; the marauding spirit seemed to have moved on. I nerved myself and peeked over the side of my hammock. Zadoc was standing, naked, stock-still by the red embers of the fire. He was gripping his cutlass.

'Did you hear that?' I whispered.

He stared at me and said nothing.

'Did you hear it?' I repeated.

'Yes. Me heard,' he whispered dryly.

'What was it?'

'Kenaima. It has departed. Go back to sleep.'

Perhaps there was something to this kenaima business after all.

The next thing I knew was it was light. Dawn must have broken only recently for the forest was quiet and the temperature not too enervating. I shook my clothes and checked my boots for scorpions and spiders.

I was surprised to notice Zadoc had already kicked out the fire. His hammock was missing, as was his backpack which contained our food. It took me a while to realise the significance of this. He had gone. He had left me.

Maybe Zadoc knew he was in danger of being sacked. Or was he merely pissed off with me and had, like the polite Amerindians when confronted with the pushy missionary, gently faded into the bush?

As if in protest at the quiet, the howler monkeys started their terrifying, otherworldly growl. I had no idea where I was, or where I was going. I had no idea how to survive in this vast and hostile land. I stood, welded to the spot, not knowing what to do.

NINE

Suspiciously like Cup-a-Soup.

I felt so tiny and powerless in this immense green universe. I scanned the forest for a telegraph tree, but all the trunks appeared the same. As my fear mounted, I heard, in the direction of the creek, the slashing of vegetation.

'Good morning.' It was Zadoc. He was bare-chested and his dreads were tied round his head like a turban.

'Where have you been?'

'Doing me business. Using bush toilet.'

'I thought you'd left me.'

'You sleep like a child, me no wanna disturb.'

I was beginning to lose my trust in Zadoc's navigational skills. The high tropical sun made it difficult to gauge the direction in which we were travelling. Nevertheless, I felt we were taking an unnecessarily oblique route. I had a suspicion we were going round in circles – in several places I swear we crossed our own tracks. When I pointed this out, he said this was the work of the Curupira and we should move on swiftly.

Occasionally, a natural clearing had been created by a mahogany or greenheart tree, several hundred feet high, which had tumbled to the ground and crushed everything beneath it. Here, in the coruscating sunlight, floated blue, yellow and green butterflies.

The forest floor, deep with brown leaves and rotting wood, was boiling with life. Bright yellow millipedes went determinedly on their way, soldier ants devoured everything in their path. The reek and roaring clamour of the forest was terrific. What sounded like boiling kettles, chainsaws and, I swear this is true, the braking of a

London underground train echoed around us. Monkeys, wailing like banshees, crashed through the canopy; vipers slithered by, flicking their venomous tongues. Generally, I like birds, but these were taunting us with their constant shrieks. I wanted to shoot them. I felt I was on the verge of jungle fever.

By mid-day you could hack the poisonous heat with a knife. I could scarcely move – every heavy footstep felt like my last.

Zadoc looked at me. 'We rest for couple of hours.'

'Where do we sit?' I said, looking at the writhing forest floor.

'We use our hammocks.'

Zadoc helped me unpack my bag and, while I stood by listlessly, slung my hammock between two trees. I could hardly climb into it I was so exhausted.

After a feverish nap and a dry energy-bar we continued on our way.

'You okay?' Zadoc asked, concerned

'This is nothing compared with England,' I said. I didn't want to lose face. 'I'd like to see you trying to survive on Dartmoor or the Peak District. I'd give you half a day.'

'You must have mighty fierce tigers in England.'

'We do. The Beast of Bodmin Moor. Hang onto your throat, dude.'

Zadoc rolled his eyes in mock horror. 'So, you wanna lead the way, man?'

'You carry on. I think it would save time, wouldn't it?'

The change happened unexpectedly. One minute we were in the gloom of the bush, protected from the hard sun by a green canopy several hundred feet above us, the next we were in white tropical sunshine and I had to shield my eyes from the bright light.

'Babylon thief!' cried Zadoc.

A brutalised landscape stretched before us – the ground was littered by sun-bleached logs and branches. Ragged stumps of trees reminded me of pictures I had seen of the pulverized terrain of the battlefields of the Somme.

I was dazed by the savagery inflicted on this pure land. Black plastic bags, torn and frayed, clung to the undergrowth. Why was it left like this? The disdain for nature, the lack of care. Who were the people who had done this?

Never had I felt so uncomfortable. A white owl, the size of an eagle, sat on a broken tree. It turned its head to stare mockingly, flapped its wings and languidly flew away. The air was heavy and windless, the heat appalling. I felt as if my brain was boiling – for all I knew steam could have been coming out of my ears. My arms and legs were lacerated and my knees denuded of skin; every inch of my sweating body was itching from insect bites. Not just from mosquitoes but from a whole menagerie of the little bastards. There were bites on bites – my skin was multi-dimensionally swollen, it looked like a relief map of a place called nightmare. Particularly troublesome were pin-prick-small black insects that gave searing stings out of all proportion to their size. When I took off my walking boots and socks I noticed a wet fungal infection growing between my toes. My eyes were stinging and puffed up, even my tongue was swollen and felt too big for my mouth. I wouldn't be surprised if I was suffering from scurvy from our limited and, frankly, inedible diet.

Evidence of Zadoc's hunting skills was sorely missing. What had happened to the luscious iguana stew and succulent capybara steaks I had been promised?

Sitting by a slow-burning fire, Zadoc explained that as a Rastafarian he was not a flesh eater.

"The LORD gave man dominion over animals.' Man's role was not to eat animals but care for them,' he explained. 'Me only eat yard-food, you understand.'

So instead, he heated a pan of water on the fire and mixed it with a dried powder that looked suspiciously like Cup-a-Soup.

I scrambled across ravines and gulches whose banks were lubricated with slippery clay that clung to my clothes and stained my hands. I heard the buzz of a million flies, and then, soon after, smelled the thick stench of putrefying meat. Dead monkey, Zadoc said. I took a drink and tried, to no avail, to spit out the vile stink. We quickened our pace.

There were the paw marks in the mud of a big cat – its deep, sharp claws clearly identifiable. At any moment a tiger could jump out of the undergrowth and leap on my back. I wouldn't even have time to show it my throat. Several times I fell on rocks, or slipped onto needle sharp plants. I was lucky I hadn't broken a limb, which, in this humid climate, would certainly have become infected, if not gangrenous. I have no doubt Zadoc would have been all too ready to amputate the festering member with a swift chop of his cutlass.

And then, amongst the clamour of the jungle, I heard another unfamiliar noise. At first I couldn't be certain, but it sounded like distant drums. By the look on Zadoc's face, he had heard it as well.

'What's that?' I asked.

Zadoc's furrowed brow showed he was worried.

'The drums of the Macawaiwai. They know we here. From now on we must be extra vigilant.'

I thought I was being vigilant already. I scanned the greenery even more intensely for watching eyes.

The drum beat continued for another half an hour or so, and then stopped. Or maybe I wasn't hearing the noise any more as it blended into the din of the forest.

For the first time in my life, I felt homesick. I had an overwhelming longing to be in England, even though I knew it would be damp and cold and grey and dark at four-thirty in the afternoon. I wanted to be with Aurora walking the wet shiny streets of Bristol. I now understood why Xavier had such a loathing of this malevolent landscape.

I studied my swollen and bloodied arms and legs. I felt as if I was operating in an underwater world; there was a faint and insistent hum in my brain. At least I was too tired to scratch with my disturbingly long nails.

And as for the pork-knockers, I'd forgotten why I was so interested to see them in the first place. A while back it had seemed like a good idea. Why not? I wondered how Xavier was getting on with his journey to Georgetown. Surely it couldn't be as bad as this? I swore to myself, on no account would I ever return to such an inhospitable and alien environment. I'd never thought of myself as a Buddhist, but I was beginning to believe in the concept of reincarnation. I must have done something very wicked in a previous life to deserve this. The trek to Buena Vista was the worst two days of my life.

TEN

A tiny, dismembered head.

Zadoc came to a halt. He stood stock-still, his whole frame rigid. He put his finger to his lips, gesturing for me to be quiet, and then waved his hand as a warning. 'Not too close,' he mouthed.

'What's that?' I said. I was becoming irritated by Zadoc's ganja-fuelled fear of kenaima and wood elves.

Zadoc pointed down the trail to a stake in the ground decorated with black and yellow zigzag markings.

'Heck post. To protect against evil spirits.'

On the stake was a tiny, dismembered head about the size of a grapefruit. Even from this distance I could see it was the head of a girl, her hair matted and dirty, but still clearly blonde.

'Bloody hell!'

'This very bad,' said Zadoc, nodding slowly and seriously.

'A shrunken head. Who would do that?'

'Intruders from across the border must have attacked.'

'To do this to a girl is unthinkable,' I said, trying to take in what was happening.

'You are in great danger.'

'Me?'

'They've killed a white girl. For certain a white man will be next.'

This was no longer funny. The thought of my head being shrunk to the size of a potato and stuck on the end of a stick wasn't how I'd envisaged ending my days.

'What do we do?' I asked, trying to control the tremble in my voice.

'You hide, me investigate.'

I looked around; these trees weren't English oaks or beeches that you could shin up. They were massive great columns – whose lowest branches were hundreds of feet from the ground.

'Hide? Where?'

Zadoc stared at me with pity and shrugged his shoulders. 'It's you they after, not me.'

ELEVEN

You people are so culturally insensitive.

From out of nowhere I heard a laugh. I turned, and standing right beside me was a small man holding a long, straight stave. He was just over five feet tall, slight of build, and, except for an ochre-coloured hessian cloth round his middle, naked. He had a round face with high cheekbones and a whisper of a moustache. He put out his hand and bowed his head.

'Welcome to our land.' He gave a wide smile showing perfect white teeth.

Half a dozen figures holding blowpipes taller than themselves appeared noiselessly from the bush and surrounded us. I was so taken aback I didn't know what to say. 'I come in peace,' was the first thing that came to mind.

The man roared with laughter. 'What did you say?' He spoke in unexpectedly clear English.

'I come in peace.'

'I thought that's what you said. You sound like Buzz Lightyear.'

'Pardon?'

'Toy Story. "I come in peace." That's what Buzz Lightyear says.'

'You've seen Toy Story?'

'Everybody has seen Toy Story.'

'I suppose so,' I said.

'But not yet Toy Story 2. I hear the characterization is delightful. So what can I do for you gentlemen?' the man asked.

I was confused. 'Yeah, well, as I say, we've come in peace.' Why did I keep repeating this idiotic statement?

'That's good. We don't like unfriendly visitors.' He pointed to the stake with the impaled skull. 'So welcome to the land of Macawaiwai.'

'That's an unusual way to greet people.' I said, trying to be diplomatic.

'What?'

'Shrinking heads.'

He strode over to the post and, to my horror, lifted the hideous object off the spike. As he tilted back the head its eyes rolled closed.

I could now see what it was. A doll. A dismembered doll's head.

The man giggled. 'That's not a real shrunken head. A missionary gave the doll to my daughter. She never liked it. It didn't feel right; the skin is as white as a turtle's egg, the eyes blue and the hair yellow. Why don't missionaries give brown dolls? You people are so culturally insensitive. My daughter put it on the boundary marker as a joke.'

'Well, it certainly made me laugh,' I said looking at Zadoc, who continued to eye the man with suspicion.

The man said his name was John Smith 'but all my friends call me Billy'. Billy was the headman and belonged to the Macawaiwai tribe. He seemed charming and polite, with a teasing sense of humour and the easy manner of someone used to visitors.

'You look in a bad way,' he said, scrutinising my cuts and bruises. 'You must come with me. It is not far.'

I looked at Zadoc to check if this was a good idea. He was talking and joking with one of the other men.

'Zadoc?' I called. I nodded my head in Billy's direction.

'They good people,' said Zadoc. 'This their land. They guide you for final stage of journey.'

We set off along a clearly-defined track and after forty-five minutes came to a cluster of half-a-dozen huts in a wide clearing. The rectangular buildings, which had deeply-carved wooden doors, were made of timber with palm-leaf roofs. There were several vegetable patches where maize, beans and some sort of gourd were being grown.

Naked children rushed to greet us, but otherwise the village was quiet.

'How long are you going to stay?' Billy asked as if he had been expecting me. 'We have a benab set aside for visitors. Our guests are mostly missionaries; otherwise we have visits from district officers and anthropologists.'

'That's kind of you.' After the horror of camping in the bush, a night in a benab sounded like luxury.

Billy showed me round the village. The wooden huts were built on stilts and smelled of smoke and dried leaves. Inside, women were cooking or lying in hammocks. I thought that I ought to be presenting gifts, beads perhaps, and was embarrassed that I had nothing to offer.

A wiry snake, as thin as a hosepipe, and perhaps ten feet long, pursued a frog through the short grass. The snake moved with its head in the air as fast as a man could run.

'Is it poisonous?'

'Whip snake. Keep clear as it can lash out with its tail.'

The frog didn't stand a chance. I watched, intrigued and horrified, as the unfortunate amphibian became a struggling bulge in the reptile's slender body.

A group of giggling children were clustered around a fire roasting something spiky on the end of sticks.

'Smells good,' I said.

'We will eat some for dinner.'

Billy pointed to massive silk-cotton tree, its immense fluted trunk soaring upwards hundreds of feet. It was sacred and would never be cut down, he whispered. A short path led down to a creek where half a dozen dug-out canoes were moored. A bare-breasted woman was soaping clothes. Beside her, a small child was stretching garments to dry on the polished river rocks. I would have dived into the gently flowing water if it hadn't been for the thought of piranhas, or worse, the terrifying toothpick fish.

'Where are the men?' I asked.

'I will explain later,' Billy said.

'As you see, we have no church. We like it like that,' Billy said firmly. I got the impression that he thought I was a man of religion. When I explained I wasn't a missionary he appeared relieved.

'I discourage missionaries as they fight with each other. For many generations they have visited and told us about Jesus and his magic tricks. They say they read from the same book, yet they argue about it. They stir things up and try to undermine our traditional leadership systems. I understand that for some people faith is a comfort. We don't want your God here, we are happy with our own life-view. We Macawaiwai like a peaceful existence. You foreigners make a big noise – if you were quiet for a moment you might find what you are searching for.'

'I am planning to visit the pork-knockers,' I explained.

I could sense a change in Billy's demeanor. 'You must be careful. They are dangerous men and give my people bad ideas. Many are murderers and thieves on the run from the law.'

Billy showed me to the visitors' shelter. It had a wooden floor, a hammock strung between two posts and a white plastic chair, missing a leg, propped against a wall. The mosquito net had more holes in it than Zadoc's T-shirt.

'Make yourself at home,' Billy said as he stepped out of the hut. 'I will see you at night-fall for supper.' A couple of seconds later, his head popped round the door again. 'I forgot to say. Just to let you know, we don't have a card machine, but we are quite happy to accept US dollars.'

We were sitting on grass mats on the stoop of a wooden hut, catching the last of the light, when Billy started talking about Manchester United. He seemed to assume that David Beckham was a personal friend of mine. 'David Beckham has Macawaiwai tattoos.

The next time you speak to him you must tell him to visit us.'

'I'll tell Victoria.'

A young girl sidled up to me and without saying anything touched my hair. Then, carefully she rolled up my sleeve and pinched my skin. She looked up at me and smiled and ran off giggling.

'So, let me guess about your work,' said Billy. 'I have a game I play with visitors – it's called twenty questions.

'Sounds fun. But you'll never get it.'

'So, if you are not a missionary, are you an anthropologist?'

'No, no, no.'

'Many anthropologists visit us. They don't want us to wear clothes and we have to hide the electricity generator. See over there,' he said pointing to the roof of one of the huts, 'underneath those palm leaves is a satellite dish. We keep it covered in case of unexpected visitors. We live the traditional Macawaiwai life but we don't spurn modern technology. We want all the stuff that everybody else has: flip-flops, phones, DVDs, and the women like epilators. But we also want to keep our culture.

'Of course, the worst visitors are the linguists. They ask us to say things again and again. Again and again.' Billy put his hand over his mouth and yawned. 'Linguists are very boring guests.'

Billy continued, 'So, if you're not a missionary, and you're not an anthropologist, I'm presuming you're from an NGO?'

'Pretty close.'

'And by the look of you, I'd say that you are not a frequent flyer.'

'The look of me?'

'You're more at home sitting at a desk.'

'There's some truth in that.'

'So, you are doing research, but I don't think you're doing environmental research. You'd need all sorts of heavy equipment, and you'd fly in by whirly-bird.'

'I certainly haven't done that.'

'In that case I'd say... I'd say you are ...' he held my gaze, and like a TV quiz show host announcing the winner of the million-pound jackpot, was silent for ten seconds '... I'd - say - you - are - a FREELANCE LABOUR FORCE CONSULTANT.'

I was astounded. 'How the heck did you know?'

Billy sat back with a beam across his face. 'Simple. It's obvious. First of all, I know you're freelance because you're travelling on a tight budget.'

'It's not that tight.'

Billy shrugged his shoulders and nodded towards Zadoc. He lowered his voice. 'You've not exactly gone for the top end of the range when it comes to guides.'

'That's not fair.'

'He is not a good influence on my people. I bet you spent your journey wandering around in circles.'

'Zadoc did get a bit stoned.'

'How long did it take to get here?'

'Three days.'

'Three days! We're a day's walk from Kaieteur Falls. At the most.'

'You've got to be kidding.'

'And when we had the horses it was just several hours.'

'Okay. But how did you know about the labour market?'

'It's the topic of the moment. Time magazine ran a feature a couple of months ago.'

'Really?'

'And only a few days ago we had a woman and her posse from the International Bank stay.

My heart jumped. Of course, this was the tribe Tallulah and Stilton had mentioned. 'Tallulah, I met her at the Falls.'

Billy smiled. 'She loved the jungle oysters, she couldn't get enough of them.'

'Stilton told me they were good.'

Apropos of seemingly nothing, Billy asked, 'Did you and Tallulah do jiggy-jiggy?'

I choked on my cassava. 'What!'

'Did you do jiggy-jiggy with Tallulah? The Kaieteur Falls is a sacred spot. Many Macawaiwai have been conceived there.'

'Billy, it's none of your business.' I really wasn't keen to talk to a stranger about my recent romantic liaisons.

'What's wrong? Billy said, raising his hands and looking behind him at the family-sized open-plan hut. 'We have an open society here. Anthropologists are always asking us about jiggy-jiggy. That's all they want to know. How often do I do it? Who with? Where? With animals? Can we film?'

'With animals!?'

'They always ask when I last had sex with a goat. No Macawaiwia has ever done it with a goat. We don't keep goats – we don't like goat meat.' Billy grimaced and made a retching noise. 'Do English men do jiggy-jiggy with goats?'

'No! Not usually.'

'That means yes.'

'No, it doesn't.'

Billy was laughing now. 'Well, as soon as I mentioned Tallulah's name I could tell by the look on your face you'd hammered her by the Falls.'

'That's not an expression I'd use.'

'English men don't know how to have sex in a hammock. Once you get the hang of it there's nothing like it. Sex in a hammock aids deep penetration and maneuverability.'

I didn't want to be talking about this. 'I'll take your word for it.'

'It's like riding a motorcycle, once you've learnt you never forget.'

'All I'm saying is that Tallulah is a very charming woman and maybe things got a bit intense. Okay?'

'No jiggy-jiggy then?'

'I'm not telling – one way or another.'

'I can see you are embarrassed. Is that why English men prefer pokie girls?'

'What?'

'Hookers.'

Did everybody in this bloody country think I was paying for sex? How did he know? Had Tallulah told him? But I hadn't even spoken to Tallulah when she visited here. And anyway, come to think of it, I hadn't paid anyone for sex.

'We do not prefer hookers,' I said. 'And it's politer to call them hostesses.'

'I don't understand why English people are so ashamed to talk about sex.'

'It not that... I hardly know you.'

'My friend, it sounds like you hardly knew her!'

We both laughed. I wondered if Billy had also slept with Tallulah.

TWELVE

The Indians are the cowboys.

We began our evening meal with a jungle oyster, which, according to Billy, who had now changed into cut-off jeans and a Manchester United T-shirt, was a Macawaiwai signature dish. I bit into some unidentifiable matter that expanded with moisture and filled the whole of my mouth – the more I chomped on this foul glutinous substance, the bigger it seemed to get. I had no idea what it was. From its musty, meaty taste I surmised it was animal. Testicle? Eyeball? Gallbladder? What part, who knows? I wanted to chew, but it was like biting into jelly. I thought I was going to suffocate and then I started to gag.

Billy masticated with great gusto. 'It's good, yes?'

'Hmmm,' I couldn't speak.

I thought of chocolate and swallowed the snot-ball down in one.

The jungle oyster was followed by more cassava – a bland, gloopy porridge that had the texture of wallpaper paste.

Billy raised his mug. 'Here's to Cherie Blair and the new heir to the throne.'

He pointed to the three boys who were roasting what looked like spiky marshmallows on sticks.

'Would you like?'

'What is it?'

'Amuse-bouche,' he chuckled.

'What sort of amuse-bouche?'

'Very succulent. We roll them in spices before we roast. Very tasty – like crayfish. You suck the jelly out of their legs.'

'But what are they?'

'What else could they be?' Billy looked at me as if I was daft.

'Tarantula.'

'No thanks,' I said, patting my stomach, 'the jungle oysters have filled me up.'

I was longing for a beer, or water even, to cleanse my palate and clear the film of bitter, viscous stickiness that clung to my teeth.

Over the meal Billy told me about his life. Village headmen, epuru, inherit their status from their father. A while back there had been a government scheme to educate future village leaders and he had received a scholarship to attend the prestigious King's College Grammar School in Georgetown. The college, with its cross-country runs, cold showers and pedophile teachers, was modelled on the English public school system. The dormitories were not unlike sleeping in a Macawaiwai family house, though the food at the school wasn't as good. After gaining top grade A Levels he had planned to get a job with the government but was repeatedly rejected by the civil service. He had a suspicion that this rejection was because he was Amerindian. Reluctantly, he enrolled on a City and Guilds HND in Catering and Hospitality, but had to rush back to the village when his father was shot by an arrow in a hunting accident and subsequently died of blood poisoning. It was then that he took over the role of epuru. He showed me a shimmering turquoise and scarlet feather headdress that he wore at ceremonies. Every year, headmen from all over the country were summoned by the Department for Amerindian Affairs to a convention in Georgetown. 'In Georgetown they've built a large benab for us to use for meetings,' he said. 'This is an insult. Across the road is the five-star Olympus Hotel with full conference facilities and a swimming pool. But we don't have access to any of that.' At the convention they discuss native Amerindian matters and also attend training lectures. 'The normal sort of things: first aid; risk assessment; health and safety; gender sensitivity.' The courses were interesting but difficult to apply. 'There is a clear gender divide in our village. The men hunt and fish, the women gather fruits, cultivate the gardens and look after the children and we all argue about washing the cooking pots. It's the way we've always done things. We're all happy about this – well, maybe not so much the women.'

More recently Billy had been on a UNESCO Equality and Diversity course. He was now well prepared for the reception of foreign visitors. 'I have a certificate to prove it,' Billy said. 'I assure you there will be no discrimination; you will be treated like anyone else in the village. If you misbehave we will take you to a high cliff and throw you off.' Billy roared with laughter at his joke.

Billy's wife had died a few years ago and he was now looking for a new partner. He'd got his eye on his cousin's daughter, but she wasn't ready for marriage yet. He'd wait a year or so until she was sixteen. Of course, he wouldn't marry the girl until she had presented him with a child.

'That would be illegal in my country,' I said.

'That is the best age for a young woman to have a child,' Billy replied. 'They are stronger then.'

I protested that this was too young, and young girls should have the opportunity for an education before they became mothers. Billy didn't think that motherhood was a hindrance to education. Far from it, this was the most important thing they would learn in their lives.

I asked Billy about head shrinking. The chief slapped his thigh; he seemed very entertained by this.

'There's not much of a demand. Trade is illegal.'

'But you used to?'

'My grandfather gathered monkey heads. He would carefully peel the skin off the skull and let it dry in the sun. He made good sales to ethnographic museums across the world. He told the buyers that these heads weren't human – but they didn't want to believe him.'

'There are shrunken heads in a museum in Oxford,' I said. 'They take pride of place in their ethnographic collection.'

Again, Billy found this hilarious. 'Many years ago an English lady came here. My grandfather sold her our tribal cast-offs,' he laughed.

'Yes, I've seen them.'

Billy looked surprised. 'So where do you come from, old bean?' he asked.

'Bristol - it's near London.'

Billy's eyes widened. 'Bristol! The home of Wallace and Gromit?'

'That's the place.'

'Of course Aardman's stop-motion technique is old-fashioned but it lends a charm to the film-making. I find the English patois difficult to understand, but Gromit is very funny. And, Bristol cigarettes are good.'

Billy stood up. 'Now, if you'll excuse me, I have to go and round up the cattle. We have to protect them at night-time from the tigers. Round here, the Indians are the cowboys.'

He handed me a cellophane package containing what looked like small twig.

'What's this?' I asked.

'Tooth stick – all part of the hospitality service. It tastes of peppermint.'

'Thanks, I'll see you in the morning,' I said. It was several hours after sundown and I was feeling exhausted.

'Do you still want to visit the pork-knockers?', Billy asked.

'I've come all this way. Why not?'

'They are not far from here,' he said somberly. 'Tomorrow, I will take you.'

THIRTEEN

For the first time in weeks I began to feel cold.

I was glad when a crowing cock heralded the dawn. I'd had another night of disturbed sleep, being woken repeatedly by the incessant whine of mosquitoes. The Macawaiwai didn't appear to be heavy sleepers either. From my hammock I could hear laughter all night long and at one stage there was singing and irregular flamenco-style clapping.

I stood at the entrance of my hut, poking my mouth with the tooth-cleaning twig, and took a few minutes to enjoy the scene before me. Dawn, with its slanting light and early morning mist, is the best time in the rainforest. The air was still and smoke from the night-time fires drifted through the palm-thatched roofs. It was difficult to tell where the settlement ended and the greenness of the bush began. There were uncountable verdant shades: bottle-green banana plants, sea-green palm leaves, sage-green grass and emerald-green parrots.

I'd fallen for the openness and hospitality of the Macawaiwai. It may seem unlikely, but I felt very much at home in their village. Billy, with his porridge-bowl haircut and loin-cloth, was always laughing and joking, and generated a profound feeling of friendship and honesty. I liked him a lot. It was as if some deep, recessed gene had been awakened in me, and I belonged. I'd once read about a group of early European explorers who had met a tribe, the Mandan, on the North Dakota plains. The Mandan paddled a boat like a coracle and spoke a language bizarrely similar to Welsh. I wondered if there was a possible link between the Somerset Levels and the Amerindians. Maybe, countless generations before, a fishing boat from Porlock had been blown off course and ended up on the South American coast and stayed.

Surrounded by these happy families, I realised I was fortunate to be here and, for a brief moment, I experienced a deep sense of contentment.

Billy appeared to be in no hurry to set off in search of the pork-knockers. He took me into a smaller hut, which contained a rough wooden table, a couple of plastic chairs and a stack of cat's eyes.

'This is my office,' he said. On the wall there were pictures of bare-breasted girls ripped from a magazine and also a calendar for 1992. 'Before we leave I would like you to fix my computer. I can't get it to print.'

I noticed a collection of wooden drums in the corner of the room.

'Was that your drumming I heard yesterday as we were walking through the bush?' I asked.

'Probably, we always have drumming practice on Tuesdays.'

Billy lifted a blanket and revealed an old IBM PC. 'Can you have look at this? I'm more of a Mac man myself.'

After he had cranked up the generator I pressed the power button on the computer. It fired up with the familiar Windows 95 musical motif. Billy stood behind me, watching.

'So, let's see...' I had no idea what I was doing, but I hated to shatter his confidence in me. I stared at the screen and made a knowledgeable clicking noise through my teeth. Tiny white mites skittered across the monitor. I wiped them off with my shirt sleeve. I went to the Control Panel and there, thank you Bill Gates, was Printers and other Devices. I was feeling like an expert. I remembered the annoying mantra that Adge would repeat: 're-install software'.

'Do you have the printer installation disks?' I asked.

Billy looked in a wooden box and brought out a plastic wallet of floppy disks.

I deleted, re-installed, and re-started. Jackpot. 'That wasn't difficult.'

That's the great thing about computers. The system used in the upper Amazon rainforest is exactly the same as that operating in the White House. The language is also identical. It does, of course, make the job of GCHQ and the CIA easier when they want to nose around your inbox. It also meant that the Y2K bug was truly global. Even the Macawaiwai would be affected.

By the time we set off it was nearly noon and I was already feeling exhausted in the ominous heat. The sky had clouded over and the air felt full of moisture. It soon began to rain. Until now I'd ignored the 'rain' part of rainforest but the incessant beating of drops upon the roof made it clear this was no misnomer.

Billy said in the past we would have travelled by canoe, but the river was now too shallow, blocked by sandbars caused by the mining up-stream.

'What about horses?'

'I haven't seen a horse for a long time,' Billy said and smacked his lips.

'You didn't eat them, did you?'

He ignored my question. 'Come on, let's go. To infinity and beyond,' he said, fist raised, chin held up.

We walked along a well-defined track through the bush. The sounds of the forest were so varied: a woodpecker hammered at a tree, a cicada screamed like a high-speed drill piercing metal, and an unseen bird gave its penny-whistle call. A couple of Macawaiwai men and a woman had joined us. They talked loudly and frequently laughed. Sometimes I felt they were laughing at me. With the racket they made they certainly ruined any chance of spotting wildlife.

As we walked, Billy pointed out flora that were used for natural medicines. The plants were good for the blood and the brain and manhood, of course. He broke off a fleshy leaf from a plant that looked like aloe vera and asked me to smell its fresh, unctuous sap. 'Next time you are at the Kaieteur Falls you could use this.'

'What is it?'

'It is a very good lubricant for jiggy-jiggy,' he said and laughed.

What Billy was most keen to talk about was films. Recently, he'd seen American Pie and Fight Club. He liked George Lucas and Steven Spielberg, but found some of the Teutonic existentialist directors baffling. Billy rattled on about Herr Herzog, a German film-maker who had visited and caused havoc. With his differential pay rate, Herzog had split the tribe's age-old equalities. 'He wanted us do stupid and dangerous things like fly a giant balloon over the Falls.'

Billy turned, looked me up and down and said. 'You are a sad, strange little man, and you have my pity.'

I thought I'd misheard him. 'Excuse me? What did you say?'

'You are a sad, strange little man, and you have my pity,' Billy said again solemnly.

I tried not to feel insulted. 'Why do you say that?' I remembered Stilton warning that Amerindians could be alarmingly forthright. 'You're not exactly tall yourself.'

A bright smile burst upon Billy's face.

'It's a quote!' By now Billy was hardly able to speak, he was laughing so much 'That's what Buzz Lightyear says to Woody.'

'Very funny,' I said, pretending to laugh.

'How long is this storm going to last?' I asked Billy.

At first I enjoyed the rain but I soon got tired of the persistent hammering of massive drops. I couldn't see clearly – my hat was saturated and beginning to droop and my boots were waterlogged.

Billy sniffed the air and looked up – the sky was hardly visible through the canopy. 'Maybe a couple of hours?' he shrugged. 'Maybe days. I didn't have time to check the weather forecast before we left.'

With the sun hidden, I had no idea in which direction we were heading. I've always had a good sense of bearing, but here I felt as if

I'd been blindfolded and spun around until I was dizzy. Not having a map continued to bug me. Maps offer freedom. Wherever I am, I like to be able to orientate myself, and I feel uneasy if I can't. In England I would spend many happy hours studying Ordnance Survey maps – imagining the patchwork landscape and the lie of the land, checking for villages with pubs, and churches with spires.

The air smelled of mildew and fungus. The rain got worse. Like everything else in the bush this was on a bigger scale than I was used to. Glutinous drops the size of grapes bounced off massive forest leaves. With the raindrops beating onto the vegetation it was difficult to hear what Billy was saying. Our walk soon felt like a version of water torture. We trudged on and for the first time in weeks I began to feel cold.

FOURTEEN

A diamond the size of a garden pea.

I could sense a change coming in the landscape. Instead of the rich odour of decaying vegetation a metallic taste hung in the air. Soon we came to a lagoon the colour of milky coffee. The usually rich vegetation overhanging the water was grey, limp and rotting.

'My people can no longer fish here,' said Billy.

'Kenaima?'

Billy gave a sarcastic laugh. 'The water has been poisoned.'

I didn't know how it could be possible, but the rain was now plummeting down even harder. The noise was terrific; I had to shout to be heard.

'See,' he said, pointing, 'the chemicals used in the mining have killed the plants.'

The bush had turned into something sour and unnatural.

'We're nearly there,' said Billy. 'Paradise Mine is just round the corner.'

The pork-knockers worked around a muddy lagoon. Apart from a nod and a 'morning, morning,' they paid little attention to us. The mining process was surprisingly low-tech. A home-made wooden contraption like a multi-layered sieve was used to filter the gravel. The remains were then inspected for diamonds. I watched half a dozen people pick through the residue looking for grey stones that had a certain translucent appearance.

It looked like hard, dirty work but was probably no worse than labouring in the fields, cutting cane. The atmosphere was relaxed, a couple of guys were drinking beer, a figure was asleep under a makeshift shelter.

Billy was known to them and despite his assertion that they were aggressive, they appeared happy to tell me about their work.

Miraculously, the rain stopped as suddenly as it had begun, and soon the sun appeared. An iridescent blue Morpho butterfly, so large I could hear the beat of its satin wings, flapped past. I wished Aurora was with me to see it.

'The spirits of our ancestors - the guardians of eternity,' said Billy. 'You must never catch them. It brings bad luck.'

'What would happen if I did catch one?'

Billy grinned. 'We would kill you.'

'Yeah, that would be bad luck.'

The simple panning process seemed to work well. One guy, the gang-master, emptied the contents of a small cylindrical canvas bag the size of a Smarties tube into his hand. In his mud-stained palm he held a small, greasy pile of peppercorn-sized stones. At this stage, he explained, before they are cut, rough diamonds don't sparkle.

'Have a go,' said the foreman as he handed me something that looked like a large garden sieve. I sifted through the mud and rubble. 'You have to get your eye in,' he said.

At last I saw something. I held it between my fingers. 'Look at that, it's a beauty.' It was enormous: I'd got a diamond the size of a pea. It must have been worth thousands.

'Beginners luck!' laughed Billy.

I passed it to the foreman. With hardly a glance, he chucked it into the pond.

'Why did you do that?'

'Quartz. Worthless.'

'Come,' said Billy, 'I will show you something else.'

'What?'

'Wait and see. It is not far.'

I was beginning to lose confidence in the value of the expression 'not far'. 'Not far' could be minutes, hours or days even.

'How many miles?' I asked.

'We don't talk about miles in the bush.'

We walked for an hour or so until our way was blocked by a high, galvanized-metal fence topped by razor wire. The undergrowth had been hacked back on either side for about five metres. Billy kicked the barrier with his bare foot.

'This should not be here,' Billy said. He had lost his generous smile and for the first time since we'd met he appeared distracted and ill-at-ease. 'How is this possible? This land belongs to the Macawaiwai.'

I could see the frustration in Billy's eyes. He pointed to a sign 'No Trespassing. Keep Out'.

'Tell me,' he continued angrily, 'how is this possible? This land has always belonged to the Macawaiwai. The government knows this. Our ownership is confirmed by treaty. Yet the government sells our land. They have no right to do this. This land is ours, it is our birthright, it is Macawaiwai land. For us it is like losing a limb. We need this land for hunting. We need this land for our physical and spiritual wellbeing – for our ancestral medicine. We should protect this sacred earth for our children and grandchildren. But we are powerless to stop these foreign thieves stealing and looting our territory.'

I peered through the metal fence. It felt so wrong. Snaking away into the distance, this cruel blemish defiled the purity of the forest.

'Can we see the mine?' I asked.

'We cannot go any further. They won't let you in. These people are not pork-knockers. They are very secretive.'

'Where's the entrance?'

'There's an airstrip, the workers come by plane.'

'Isn't there a road?'

'There are no roads for hundreds of miles.'

'But there must be an opening through the fence somewhere.'

'I don't think so.'

'Is all the labour imported?'

'A few Macawaiwai work here,' Billy said, his head bowed, avoiding my gaze. He looked tired: the energy had drained out of him. 'For some the lure of work is difficult to resist.'

'So how do the workers get in and out?'

Instead of answering Billy said 'For me it is very sad.'

'Why?'

'The miners leave their families.'

'But they must earn good money.'

'Maybe, but their families don't see it.'

'What do you mean?'

'It is painful for me to talk about this.' Billy told me how the mines disturbed the natural order of his tribe. These people, they stole their ancestral land and they stole their men. The men left their villages but rarely returned. The fields remained uncultivated, so the wives and children went hungry. The tribe should have benefited from this, but they were even poorer than before the miners came.

Billy started to walk back along the track.

'Billy, wait! Maybe I can help. We must speak to somebody. This could be an important part of my report.' Billy turned and looked at me. He shook his head and said nothing.

'But I could try,' I said.

He sauntered towards to me and put his hand on my arm and gave a sad, resigned smile. 'We just want to live in our own way, in peace and harmony. These forces of evil are too powerful. You can't do a thing. One day, maybe, but not now.'

FIFTEEN

Back-breaking, lung-busting, soul-destroying work.

I wasn't about to give up now. 'Let's see where the fence leads,' I said.

Billy and I began to walk along the line of the perimeter divide. Despite what Billy had said, I thought there must be an entrance.

The metal barrier was incongruous in such a vast natural landscape. Behind us a troop of howler monkeys was crashing through the tree tops making their mocking call. From further afield another family of howlers returned their sinister taunting cry. Although the rain had stopped and soft scuds of cloud filled the sky, the air felt as heavy and moist as a sweat lodge.

We followed the barrier in the full sunlight. The vegetation inside the enclosure was dense forest. Although there was no obvious evidence of mining activity I could hear the distant thrum of a generator. After fifteen minutes or so, we came to an entryway with a sturdy padlock on it. There was still nobody in sight. I rattled the gate. A shout came from down the pathway.

'Qué estás haciendo?' A man with a rifle casually slung over his shoulder strode towards us.

'Do you speak English?' asked Billy.

'Si.'

'We want to speak to the manager,' Billy continued.

'Who he?' the man said, ignoring Billy and looking at me.

'This is Billy, he's the headman round these parts.' I replied.

'Huh? So what you want?'

'I'm a researcher. I'd like to speak to your boss.'

'We no allow visitors.'

I felt in my pocket. I wondered how much I should give him.

'We've come a long way.'

'Me tambien,' the man replied sarcastically.

'It's important that I speak to the person in charge.' I put my hand through the fence and gave the guard two ten dollar bills. He put the money in his pocket without acknowledging the transaction.

'You wait. I see what I can do.'

There was the distant sound of a light aircraft. The noise got louder and soon I spotted a plane dropping low and disappearing out of sight to land, I guessed, on a runway.

Ten minutes later the guard ambled back and unlocked the gate.

'Come. But he stay here,' the man said pointing at Billy.

'No, he's part of the team. He's my executive adviser.'

'Why your executive adviser not wear clothes?'

'That's how the people dress round here.'

'Savages.'

Embarrassed and humiliated, Billy stared straight ahead.

'He comes with me,' I said.

We walked over a low ridge and before us was a pitted moonscape devoid of vegetation. The air was still and the heat tremendous; I could taste the gritty soil in my mouth. Swarms of people were excavating holes – there was mud and water everywhere. It was a monochrome world; everything was brown: the soil, the machinery, the vegetation, the people. Mixed with the smell of wet earth there was a not unpleasant bitter almond tang in the air. Unlike the orderliness of the Linden bauxite mine, this place had an unplanned and arbitrary appearance. It was like a human warren. Figures were scurrying about, digging, raking, carrying sacks of earth and pushing wheelbarrows. Apart from a few simple tools it seemed the miners relied on raw muscle and mental grit. This was back-breaking, lung-busting, soul-destroying work.

High-powered jets of water from massive hoses turned the soil into oozing sludge which was then processed through machines to draw out the gold. At the far end of the clearing was an opaque lake the size of two football pitches. The pond was eerily still – not even mosquito larvae disturbed its surface.

'Where do these people come from?' I asked Billy.

'They are from the coast and other countries: Brazil, Venezuela, Bolivia. They are violent. Some are criminals on the run.'

Billy strode over to a labourer who was covered in mud from head to toe. They began talking animatedly. Billy was shouting and gesticulating. The man then turned and walked away.

'Who was that?' I asked.

'This is a bad place. It corrupts people.'

'Do you know that man?'

There were tears in Billy's eyes. 'He is my son.'

'Your son? Why didn't you say?'

'I haven't seen him for over a year. He left his wife and my grandchildren. At first he sent them money. But now, nothing.'

SIXTEEN

You didn't see that, right?

I was shown to the manager's office, which was built out of a converted shipping container. Holes for a door and a couple of windows had been hacked through the steel. How the container got there, I couldn't imagine. I left Billy sitting outside on a bench in the shade.

The office was as hot as a furnace. There was a desk, two chairs, a filing cabinet, a safe and a stack of three boxes of Johnnie Walker Red Label. A thin film of brown dust lay on every surface. The manager, who introduced himself as Mackenzie, appeared to have just woken from a deep sleep.

'Who the fuck are you? Are you lost or something?' With his big square face and thick rugby player's neck he had the demeanor of a man who wouldn't back away from trouble – and might even seek it out. He rubbed his eyes and shook his head. He looked exhausted by the heat.

'I'm from DoDO. A British international development organisation.'

'Dodo. Bit of a dying species, eh?'

I'd heard it all before. 'I'm an economist. I'm undertaking a labour market survey.'

Mackenzie grunted. 'We don't get many visitors. You're not one of those whining eco-terrorists are you?'

'I've never been called that.'

'Well, I don't want people sniffing about, stirring up trouble.'

I couldn't place his accent. 'Are you from South Africa?' I asked.

'Fuck off, I'm Australian.'

Mackenzie looked at his watch. 'You've got ten minutes.' An

antique silver pistol was on top of a pile of papers on his desk.

'Does that thing work?' I asked.

Mackenzie chuckled. 'It's my most important piece of office equipment.'

'Yeah?' I wondered what he used as a stapler.

'Let's just say it can shout a lot louder than I can. Sometimes those blokes need to be reminded who's in charge. They're hard men doing a hard job. But they get some funny ideas. The local fellas don't seem to fully understand the concept of ownership.'

I was still pissed off with the way Billy had been treated. 'No offence meant, but they probably say the same about you, seeing as you're mining land that belongs to the Macawaiwai.'

'I don't know about that. The government gave us a licence. The local blokes need to wise up to the situation and get over themselves.'

Mackenzie got up and opened the filing cabinet. 'Have a drink?' He blew the dust out of two mugs and filled them half-full with whisky.

'It's only 2.30.'

'Strewth! We better get a move on then. Everybody here drinks bloody Tom Thumb. I can't stand the muck. It makes me hallucinate. Whisky's a better bet. The mosquitoes don't like it – that's a plus.'

'Is that so?'

'Too right. It raises your thiamine levels. The little bastards hate thiamine. Cheers! This'll put hairs on your bloody survey or whatever you're doing.'

'So when did you last use that gun?'

'Occasionally people ask for more money than they are entitled to. Mostly, I have to break up fights between the men when there aren't enough hookers to go round. Somebody's got to keep the law.'

Despite what he said about being busy, I got the feeling that he was happy to talk.

'This is a pretty remote spot, huh?'

'People see this virgin land and think that it's some kind of Eden.

It's untouched for a good reason. We're on the edge here. The heat, the rain, the racket at night-time. Those bloody laughing monkeys. You know what happened to that guy, Jim fucking Jones. That was a tragedy, man. He didn't heed the signs. Set up his Jonestown community in the jungle and went totally troppo. The jungle fever got him. He poisoned the lot of them. Kool Aid and cyanide, not a good cocktail.'

'It made grim reading.'

'Do you know how he did it? Every so often he'd say "We're going to make the ultimate sacrifice". He'd hand out the Kool Aid which was supposedly poisoned. Everybody drank it, but to no effect. "Just testing" he'd say. They did this several times. But then, one day, it was for real. Nearly a thousand dead – women and children, as well. And their dogs. Doesn't bear thinking about.'

'Tragic.'

'The government is very sensitive about it. It gave the country a bad name.'

We were both silent for a moment. Mackenzie emptied his mug. 'So tell me about the mining process,' I said.

'Rare metals, that's what everybody's after these days. Promethium, neodymium, dysprosium, there's a whole list of the bastards. That's where the big money's made. The I.T. industry can't get enough of that stuff.'

'So I hear.'

'This isn't mining as such, here, at Paradise Mine we're more open pit. I've worked around the world - Canada, Alaska, Wales, Colombia...'

'Wales?'

'Yeah, big mistake. Worse than the boongs – they were always on strike. I soon whipped them into shape though. You name it, I've worked there. Compared with some places, this is a bloody holiday camp. There are mines in Brazil that are the far side of your worst nightmares. Take Sierra Pelada. Some kid pissing in the river found a gold nugget the size of a Malteser and wham, bam, there's a gold-rush from hell. Thousands of people made their way to this hill and just dug it away. Suddenly, you have this shanty town in the bush and all the mad-dog craziness that goes with it – stores and whores. They dug away a whole fucking mountain.

'Here, at Paradise Mine I'm just managing an extraction process. We use a process called hydraulicing which doesn't need much equipment. Just dynamite, high-jet hoses and a few chemicals. We blast the rock, wash the overburden into a sump, take the slurry through a sluice and extract the gold. Simple as that.' Mackenzie smiled. 'And my bosses laugh all the way to the bank.'

'That sounds straightforward.'

'It usually is. The soil can be a bit of a worry, though – the land can slip if you're not careful. But if you get the right plot there's money to be made. The problems are caused by the remoteness of the site and the lack of a skilled workforce. The local blokes are a bit unsophisticated. They make stupid mistakes.'

'Is this a good plot?'

'That's confidential information, mate. This isn't a honey hole, but it's not a piece of crap either. Let's just say that my bosses don't have to piss into a jar.'

'Who are your bosses?'

'I couldn't tell you.'

'But you must know.'

'Slopes, probably. It's best not to ask.'

'Is this set-up legal?'

Mackenzie shrugged. 'I've got a permit.'

I looked out of the door of the container over the pitted landscape.

'So what are those ponds?'

'They're the reservoirs for waste water.'

'What happens to them?'

'We let nature take its course. One day you'll never know we were here. The water eventually evaporates and the jungle grows over.'

'What about the chemicals?'

'They're mainly neutralised by the sunlight.'

'So what chemicals are we talking about?' I knew I was pushing it, but Mackenzie didn't seem to care.

'A bit of a mash-up.'

'Like?'

'It's a tad technical. Cyanide, mercury, they're the main fellas.' From outside, I could hear the sploosh of water and men shouting. 'Anyhow, as I was saying, we provide everybody with respirator masks.'

'I didn't notice anybody using them.'

'If they choose not to, that's their concern.'

'So when the water evaporates what happens to the cyanide?'

'That's not a problem. It breaks down pretty quickly in this intense sunshine.'

'And the mercury?'

The atmosphere was getting edgy. Mackenzie filled his mug again, but didn't offer me a top-up.

'Mercury is the bastard. You have to be more careful with that one.'

'So how do you make sure the mercury doesn't get into the river?' I could sense I was pushing his buttons but I wanted to press him as far as I could.

'You're not an eco-terrorist, are you? You're not one of those whack jobs from Greenpeace?'

'No, as I said I'm just writing a report on the labour market.'

Mackenzie sat back in his chair and stared at me. For a few seconds he said nothing.

'Look mate, we're not making bloody chocolate bars here. There's no such thing as Fair Trade gold. That's not how mining works.'

'I appreciate that.'

'We've got the support of the International Bank, you know.

Mining brings into this country four times as much money as sugar does. The I.B. reckon that mining is the way forward for Guyana.'

'I'm sure they do.' I wondered, though, if this was the sort of operation the I.B. had in mind. 'I'm just interested.'

'This is a poor country. It needs the revenue, right?'

'But at what cost?'

Mackenzie shifted in his chair and leant forward as if he was about to stand up. 'Right, I've just about had a gutful of this.' I feared he might hit me if I squeezed him any further. 'Like I said mate, this is a lawless place. We're not here to fuck spiders. My advice is that you might want to go and be interested in the labour market somewhere else.'

Our conversation was interrupted by a siren blowing.

'That's our alarm system. One blast, stand by. Two blasts, assistance required. Three blasts, get your arse out of here.'

The siren had sounded twice. I could hear yelling and the sound of people running.

Mackenzie stood up and put the gun in his holster. 'Now, if you'll excuse me I've got work to do.' He offered his hand. 'I'm sure you can see yourself out.'

While Mackenzie sauntered off, I stood in the doorway and looked at the scene before me. Billy was no longer sitting on the bench. The landscape, which was dotted with stagnant pools, was poisoned forever. Without a doubt the polluted water, heavy with sediment and cyanide would eventually make its way back to the river with horrible consequences. Fish would die and water sources for the Amerindians would be poisoned.

Mackenzie walked towards a group of miners who were shouting and gesticulating. The power jet that had been blasting a river bluff was now just a trickle.

'Why have you stopped work?' Mackenzie roared.

People were digging frantically at the bottom of the cliff. Some were scraping with their bare hands. An arm was sticking out of the mud.

Mackenzie's manner changed. 'Get a stretcher,' he shouted.

Slowly, painstakingly, the man was unearthed. Somebody leant over and pumped his chest, another gave him mouth-to-mouth resuscitation. By now a crowd had gathered. I couldn't tell whether the man was still alive, though I could see his limp body was twisted in an unnatural shape.

I noticed Billy pushing his way through the group of men and then I heard a howl so deep and grief-stricken it could mean only one thing.

'Okay, that's it,' Mackenzie said. The body was put on a stretcher and taken away. 'Switch on that hose. Get back to work you bludgers.'

Mackenzie turned and walked back to the office.

'I thought we'd said goodbye,' he said as he pushed past.

'I got sidetracked.' I nodded in the direction of the landslip. 'What was that all about?'

Mackenzie stood with his hands on his hips and was silent.

'How is he?' I asked.

'He'll be all right, he's good.'

'I'm glad to hear it.'

'You didn't see that, right?' Mackenzie gently tapped his fingers on the handle of his revolver.

I shrugged and didn't say anything. From where I'd been standing the crushed man didn't seem all right at all. In fact, he looked pretty fucking dead to me.

SEVENTEEN

I walked into the dark water.

That was the last time I saw Billy. I walked to the gateway, past the pools of stagnant water, and waited for a couple of hours but he never turned up. The guard promised to tell Billy we had gone back to the village.

It was a grim return journey. Zadoc led the way, neither of us spoke. I walked for hours in a daze, glad of the silence between us. Not even the filthy heat bothered me anymore. I had to keep going, the anger pushing me. Without even noticing I scratched the insect bites on my skin so my arms were raw and bleeding.

Thunder rattled around the grey sky, though strangely it didn't rain. I was unravelling in the climate. Reality was shifting and bending in this alien environment. The steaming heat, the lush and monstrous vegetation, the wall of noise from the tree frogs was closing in on me. I could sense the plants growing and rotting – I could hear the constant shuffle of insects. The weight of the moist air was pushing down on me; there was pressure on my chest, I couldn't breathe. This felt malicious and personal; the rainforest was attacking me.

It was dusk by the time we got to Billy's village. A pack of angry barking dogs announced our arrival. I left Zadoc to hang up the hammocks while I went straight to the creek. What the shit, I thought, I need a swim. I didn't care. Just let those caimans try. I'd clamp their fucking jaws together so hard they wouldn't know what had hit them. I hung my clothes on a bush and walked into the dark water. I lay on the burnished rocks, and allowed the fast flowing river to wash over me. The cleansing action of the water gradually washed away the layers of dirt and sweat. It took a while for my head to clear. I opened my eyes and floated on my back in the black river. For once I could see the stars. For a moment it put things into perspective, but then I remembered Billy's cry, and the hopelessness of that terrible place came flooding back.

As I stood on a rock, drying myself, I looked around. All along the river bank I could see red eyes in my torchlight, glowing like hot embers. Several caimens had already slipped into the water and were gliding towards me. I walked quickly back to the village.

The next morning we set off early. It had rained all night and I had hardly slept as water seeped through the grass roof and dripped onto my hammock.

News of the death of Billy's son had spread through the village. I had considered staying, to try to make amends, but people looked at me with the fear of kenaima in their eyes. It was as if his death was my fault. I knew that there was nothing I could say that would help. I was a foreigner, the bringer of bad omens, and as far as they were concerned I was the cause of all this trouble.

EIGHTEEN

Don't fuck with me, you bastard.

I found Da Silva sitting in the lounge at the Kaieteur Lodge.

'Where have you been?' I said.

'What do you mean where have I been?' Da Silva replied. 'Where have you been?'

'You disappeared. When I wanted a lift back to Georgetown, you'd gone.'

'You should have got up earlier. You're not the only person round here who wants a flight.'

'Yeah, well, so can I get a ride back with you today?'

'I'm already booked.'

'Don't fuck with me, you bastard.' I wasn't in the mood for messing about. I wanted to get to Georgetown as soon as possible.

'An American couple, the Briskets have reserved the plane for the day,' said Da Silva.

'Oh com'on. I could fit on the back seat.'

De Silva held his arms out as if he was hugging a tree. 'The Briskets are a large American couple.'

I couldn't be bothered to argue and walked away. I went to get a drink from the bar. The place was empty. I grabbed a warm beer from a crate and put the money on the counter. I thought of Billy and his son. This trip had suddenly become too real, too serious. Until now I'd treated the project as a bit of a joke. But something had to be done to protect the Amerindians and their indigenous culture. Were the I.B. really colluding in the destruction of the forest? Maybe mining is a good thing, and would help the country's economy, but not if conditions were like this. The price these desperate and decent people were paying was too high.

I wanted to get back to Georgetown with a minimum of delay. I was at Da Silva's mercy and realised I needed to take a more conciliatory approach if I was to secure a ride.

Da Silva was pushing a large suitcase into the plane's tiny luggage compartment. 'If you want to read your book, I'd be happy to steer,' I said.

Da Silva laughed. 'We're already near the weight limit. I'll ask the Briskets if they don't mind sharing. It'll be a squash getting them in the back seat.'

'I can offer you an incentive.' How much extra should I give him? I had no idea how this baksheesh dodge worked. $50 felt about right.

Da Silva was unmoved by my sweetener 'That's appreciated, man, but it doesn't make the plane any bigger.'

'So what time do we leave?'

'We're expecting storms this evening. I don't want to be flying in the dark.'

'Fine by me.'

'I will be leaving at about four. And, Mr Radstock, I haven't said yes, yet.'

'I'm relying on you.'

'That's not advisable.'

Zadoc was sitting on the veranda in a fug of sacramental fumes. 'Are you sure it's okay to do that here?' I asked. He muttered something about Babylon having no jurisdiction over the righteous.

'Thanks for everything,' I said. 'It's been an enlightening experience.'

Zadoc gave a beatific smile. He attempted to stand up but seemingly thought the better of it. 'Rastafari!' he said, as we bumped fists.

'Jah!, Haile Selassie, I and I,' I answered, hoping that I'd picked up the right response.

'No extra service charge for bald head.'

'Thank you.' I put my hand to my hair; thankfully it was still there. I had no idea what the man was talking about.

'Sent my regard to Xavier,' he said. 'Nephew plenty good at book-learning but he not practical man. He afeared of bush.' We both laughed knowingly.

'Yes, I hope Xavier got back to G.T. okay', I agreed. After all I'd been through, I was concerned about Xavier. His journey down the river couldn't have been any easier than the extreme nightmare I'd endured.

'Yeah, man,' Zadoc beamed, 'Travel safe, cool runnings.'

I still wasn't sure whether I'd been ripped off or not by Zadoc. But I didn't care – good luck to him.

How we got airborne with the Briskets on board – both weighing at least 280 pounds – I will never understand. The Cessna limped along the grass strip and only when it looked as if we were about to plough into the bush did the aircraft reluctantly leave the ground.

Sheet lightning lit our way as the little plane was tossed and buffeted by squally winds. 'Lucky you're here. The extra ballast adds stability in a storm,' shouted Da Silva. Ballast in a plane? Really? After the trip here and now this, I was rapidly going off flying.

'Have you read this?' Da Silva held up a slim and battered volume - Wind and the Sand and the Stars by Antoine De Saint-Exupéry.

'Yes, it's good.' I had read it. As far as I could recall, De Saint-Exupéry was an early French aviator who flew postal missions across the Sahara. He crashed his plane several times – once he was rescued by a Bedouin only to be put into slavery.

'The Sahara is similar to the rainforest,' said Da Silva. 'Remote and often featureless.'

'Remind me, what eventually happened to De Saint-Exupéry?' I asked, already knowing the answer.

'He wrote 'The Little Prince'.'

'Yeah, I know that, but what happened to him?'

'Oh, he disappeared.'

'Disappeared?'

'Without trace. During the Second World War. Neither he, nor his plane, was ever found. It is thought he may have gone down into the Mediterranean.'

'Not such a good role model then.'

'His identity bracelet was found off the coast of Marseille by a fisherman only last year.'

'That must be fifty years after he crashed.'

The Briskets, unaware of the danger, talked non-stop about their life in Cincinnati and how much they missed their 'dawgs'. When I told them I was a labour market researcher they laughed. 'What labour market?' they asked. They were disappointed by the Kaieteur Falls and its lack of shopping facilities.

'Niagara has six shopping malls,' said Mrs Brisket.

'And a Factory Outlet and a Duty Free,' said her husband. 'Until they build a casino at Kaieteur, forget it.'

'And a Planet Hollywood,' added Mrs Brisket.

The Briskets depressed me, so I spent the remainder of the journey gazing out of the window. Below, a delicate quarter-moon ox bow lake, straight out of my school geography text book, lay alongside the twisting Demerara River. There were occasional blemishes on the unbroken greenness where pork-knockers had set-up their mines. I found myself thinking about Tallulah. My emotions had been messed by our happy-pill cavorting. It had been fun, but I needed to move all that to the back of my mind and focus my thoughts on Aurora.

I thought about Aurora's slim limbs and her curvaceous figure. I thought about the time she cut her shoulder-length blonde hair. I had picked up a lock and put it in a little plastic stash bag which I kept in my wallet. 'That's the most romantic thing you've ever done,' she said. There was a distant look in her heavenly eyes. I wanted to remember her from those early days before I began to doubt her. I wanted to remember us from those early days. She said we might get a dog, perhaps we could have kids or something.

To avoid the bubbling storm clouds we were diverted to Ogle Airport, a smaller facility to the east of Georgetown. The Briskets said goodbye to me as if I was an old friend. They insisted I should visit them one day in Cincinnati and see the Finlay Market, a proper market – not like that third world shanty, the Stabroek. The Stabroek had real character, I protested. 'Yeah, real BAD character,' Mr Brisket boomed.

I caught a taxi from the airport back into Georgetown. I was glad to be away from the racket and claustrophobia of the forest. The electric storm had passed and the air on the coast, refreshed by the Trade Winds, felt less enervating. The streets were busy with cyclists and pedestrians. Suddenly, from behind a parked truck, a young girl was pushed straight into the path of our car. My driver swerved and swore. 'Cash for crash! Insurance scam. Parents claim for their children's accidents.'

'That's appalling.'

I hoped there was a room at the Stabroek Lodge. I didn't want to stay in that Silent Night hell-hole again.

As soon as I got to the hotel I would contact Gordon and arrange my flight to London. I'd then phone Aurora and tell her I'm on my way home. Meanwhile, with the events of the last few days still fresh in my mind, I was eager to start knocking out my report.

I also had one last official duty. I'd got my appointment with Lucas on Friday afternoon for my debrief. Payback time. What did that mean, exactly? Should I admit I'd never been able to track down a source for 'top notch' statistics? Should I let him know about my trips out of Georgetown, and risk his formidable wrath? Did he know about the treacherous working conditions of the miners?

More than likely he'd ask about the computers. I was anxious about his threat that I wouldn't be allowed to leave the country. An image of his deep-freeze, stuffed with staring, decapitated heads kept appearing in my mind.

As we drove through the security gate of the Stabroek Lodge and into the courtyard I was pleased to see the Land Rover outside the hotel entrance. I wondered how Xavier had survived the ordeal of his trek back to Georgetown. The car was parked alongside three Toyota Land Cruisers.

NINETEEN

The computers have been diverted to Sierra Leone.

Xavier was waiting in the foyer and greeted me like an old friend. I was glad to see him, too. He appeared in good health, and was wearing a blazer, a blue linen shirt and sharply ironed chinos.

He looked me up and down and frowned. 'A few days of recuperation in G.T. and the scars will heal,' he said.

I didn't like to tell him he had been right. The bush was a nightmare and best avoided at all costs. But then again I'd learnt a lot. Sometime it pays to go off-piste.

'How was Uncle Zadoc? Did he look after you well?' Xavier asked.

I didn't want to spoil the moment. 'He could have been worse. His sense of direction was erratic but he was a genius with the Cup-a-soup.'

'No iguana stew then?'

'He's vegetarian.'

'I forgot. I don't see that side of the family often.'

'Zadoc's a very spiritual guy. He got me there – in a roundabout sort of way.'

'Did you visit the pork-knockers?'

'Yes, and I've gathered some very important information for my report. Something has to be done.'

'I'm glad you found it useful.'

'I hope your boat trip wasn't too difficult?' I asked.

'In the end, I never went by river.'

'You walked? That must have been horrendous.'

'No, I caught a flight back.'

'But I thought...'

'The river trip sounded worse than flying. Those canoes often capsize. Three days in the bush – no way, man. One bottle of Five Star did the business.'

'I thought you didn't drink.'

'There are always exceptions. I took a flight with Da Silva a couple of hours after you'd left the lodge. He even let me steer.'

I had a feeling I wasn't getting the true picture. Had I been tricked by Xavier into going into the bush unnecessarily?

We walked outside. 'So is the car fixed?'

'I have the car for this afternoon. And then it has to go back to the garage for the final stage of its service. They need to make adjustments and do some fine tuning.'

I stood under the shower and let the powerful jets massage my scarred and battered body. I avoided looking in the mirror; I knew I was covered in bites, bumps, scratches and sores. After trimming my nails and putting on clean and freshly ironed clothes I felt comfortable for the first time in days and was ready to call Gordon.

It was a bad line to London with hisses and crackles. Gordon sounded miffed.

'I've just seen Mr Zeeland's expense claim. Who does he think we are? Flights, camping equipment, guides. Where have you been? Up the bloody Orinoco? I'll be hopping mad if I find you've been bird watching.'

'The Orinoco is in Venezuela.'

'Don't get smart with me.'

'I've gathered some important information.'

'So where the heck have you been?'

'In lieu of statistics I've been doing field research.'

'Where?'

'Up-country investigating the gold and diamond mining.'

'That's not in the contract.' Gordon didn't sound as enthusiastic as I'd expected.

'I haven't read the contract.'

'Why not? I faxed it to you.'

'I never got it.'

'How do you know what you're supposed to be doing?'

'I'm using a standard paradigm.'

'Okay, I'll email it to you again.'

'I thought first-hand empirical evidence to back-up the anecdotal accounts would be useful. I've got some significant information that is going to cause waves.'

'I want to know about Linden and what's going on with Al Int.'

'I've got all that.'

'Good. Generally mining comes under the remit of the I.B. but Al Int is different.'

Gordon didn't get it. I'd write my piece – he would be so blown away, he'd have to take it further. 'I'm going to tie up a few loose ends and then I'll be ready to fly back to England. A couple more days should do it.'

'Too bloody late, mate!'

'What!? I thought you said I'd got an open ticket.'

'You have. But the flights are all booked-up. The news about the Y2K bug is out. The only seats available are for departure on the 31st December. That means you'll be flying at the bewitching hour – I don't want your death on my conscience.'

'But you promised.'

'You shouldn't have gone off radar.'

'You promised you'd get me out of here before Christmas.'

'I will, but not by plane.'

'How?'

'There's probably a banana boat chugging along the coast. And the British Fleet has some frigates in the West Indies doing counter narcotic operations.'

I could never tell whether Gordon was joking or not. 'Guyana is on the South American mainland,' I said.

'You have a point. Diverting a gunboat might be a bit extreme. I'll sort something out, don't worry.'

'I don't want to miss Christmas with my girlfriend.'

'You've only got yourself to blame, Felix. If you wander off into the jungle without telling anybody, what do you expect? I know how obsessive you bird watchers can be. But really!'

How dare he? The pompous bureaucratic oaf. What did he know, sitting on his great spreading arse five thousand miles away in London?

'Look, I put my life on the line for this project. I could have had my head shrunk to the size of a grapefruit.'

'We don't want to be causing waves. That's the last thing DoDO wants.'

Something Jim Bucket had said in the Greenheart flashed through my mind. I wondered if I was getting the full story. Was there some other information – information so important that Gordon couldn't tell me – that he was really after?

'Gordon, one final thing, I need to ask you about the computers. When are they arriving?'

'Oh, I wouldn't worry about them.'

'I'm not. I just want know if they are on their way.' For a moment I thought the line had gone dead. 'Can you hear me? Are you there?'

'Yes, I can hear you.' Gordon said, eventually.

'So, are they on their way?'

'Not exactly,'

'What does that mean?'

'They've been diverted.'

'Diverted?'

'To Sierra Leone.'

'Right. So what sort of delay are you talking about?

'I'm not. The computers are staying in Sierra Leone.'

I hoped I'd misheard him. 'Can you say that again? The line's bad.'

'The computers are staying in Sierra Leone.' Gordon's voice was loud and clear.

'But people are expecting them here.'

'Tell Lucas they weren't suitable for the climate.'

'Isn't Sierra Leone's climate similar?'

'They'll all be worse than useless after the 31st December, anyway.'

'But Dr Professor Lucas said I couldn't leave the country until the computers had arrived.'

'Did he? Hmmm. That might be a bit awkward.' Gordon was silent for a second. 'I'm sure you'll think of something,' he added cheerfully.

'But…'

'Must go, I'm working on the final draft of the post Y2K risk assessment. It doesn't look good. The machine's stopping. The Chinese were right, we should have stuck to the abacus. Take my advice, Felix, as soon as you're back in the UK buy a can opener.'

'Gordon, you need to know, DoDO needs to know, what's going on out here. They've got to do something about it.'

'I'll be the judge of that.'

Ellis had been right – Gordon was such a prick.

Aurora answered the phone.

'Darling!' I said. This time there was no drilling or hammering in the background.

'Oh, it's you,' she sounded surprised.

'How are the shelves?' I asked.

'What shelves?'

'The new ones.'

'Oh, them. They're very useful.'

'What are they like?'

'Well, you know, like shelves. I've put books on them.'

'And CDs?'

'No, not CDs.'

'Oh!'

I asked about the weather. It had been wintery. She said things were fine. It had been quiet, but she was keeping herself busy. She was thinking of getting a tattoo.

'Are you sure?'

'Only a small one.'

'A tattoo of what?'

'I'm not sure. I'll draw something that can be copied.'

'Where will it be?'

'I was thinking on my neck.'

I thought of her elegant yielding neck. 'Don't do that, Aurora.'

'Why not?'

'You might regret it. Wait until I get back.'

'Okay. Maybe. What's Guyana like?'

'It's good.' I suddenly felt guilty.

'How's the butterfly book going?' I asked.

'I've had an argument,' she said.

'That's not like you.'

'They wanted me to draw a Silver Y.'

'That's ridiculous! The Silver Y is a moth.'

'That's exactly what I said.'

'But you're illustrating butterflies.'

'They want day-flying moths as well.'

'Be true to yourself, Aurora. Stick to your principles.'

'I will.'

I told her I was arranging my return trip but the details weren't clear, as yet. I didn't want to worry her. 'I'll definitely be back before Christmas' I said.

'Oh!'

'I've got to go now.' I said.

'Okay.'

'Love you,' I said.

'Felix, we need to talk,' Aurora replied.

'Of course. We will soon.'

I felt unsettled. Everything was happening far too quickly. The scars on my body had already started healing, but my mind was still warped from the bush nightmare. Aurora sounded remote, detached. Perhaps it was the phone line. Maybe, she was picking up on my twinges of guilt about Tallulah.

TWENTY

Caymans have voracious appetites at this time of year.

I walked past a security guard and up the steps into the Ministry building. Apart from a woman on her knees, buffing the wooden floor, there appeared to be nobody around. I wandered from room to room. The Ministry building smelled of dry timber and synthetic lemon spray polish. A constant high-pitched bleep came from a smoke alarm whose battery had run low. From along a corridor there was the distant clack-clack of a typewriter. I knocked on the door.

'Hello.' A woman looked up from her typing, startled. 'Excuse me. I have an appointment with Dr Professor Lucas.'

'It's Friday afternoon.'

'That's when I'm due to see him.'

'Nobody works on Friday afternoon.'

'I don't understand.'

'The Minister goes home to New Amsterdam for the weekend.'

'I'm due to give him feedback.'

'He'll see you on Monday afternoon.'

'I might not be here.'

'Who are you?'

I told her my name and that I was writing a report.

'Leave your report with me. I'll see that he gets it.'

'I'm still writing it.'

'What's it about?'

'The labour market.'

'A couple of days ago Dr Lucas had a presentation on the labour market by the International Bank.'

'The I.B. has its own perspective.'

'Isn't the labour market all the same? The exploiter and the exploited?'

'Did you train in Moscow?'

She gave a broad grin and took my letter of thanks which I'd written earlier and placed it in an in-tray on the top of a tottering two-foot-high stack of papers.

I felt both disappointed and relieved that I wasn't going to meet Lucas.

'Please make sure he gets it,' I said.

She patted the pile. 'These are all for Doctor Lucas. I can assure you it will get the attention it deserves.'

Someone was walking up the stairs.

The door opened. 'Doctor Lucas!' The receptionist appeared surprised. 'I thought you'd left. I have a visitor for you.'

Lucas was wearing Ray-Ban sunglasses and was dressed for the weekend in jogging bottoms, a Lonsdale T-shirt, and a multi-coloured African kufi hat. He looked annoyed.

'Come!' he said nodding towards the door.

Lucas turned to the receptionist. 'Violet, you can go home now. I will lock up the office. Have a good weekend.'

It was the tidiest office I'd seen in Guyana. A glass cabinet contained an array of gleaming silver cups and medals. In the centre of the display was a picture of Lucas embracing Muhammad Ali.

'Thirty-seven knock-outs in his career,' said Lucas. 'Do you know what Ali said? "I ain't got no quarrel with the Viet Cong – no Viet Cong ever called me Nigger." He's the greatest, yes.'

'Good looking man,' I said.

Apart from two phones, one red, one white, his desk was clear. He strode over to a refrigerator and took out a bottle.

'Would you like a Cherry Cola or something?'

'No thank you.' What sort of wind-up was that? I was gasping, but I didn't want to be seen sucking on a kiddy drink.

'So Mr Radstock, Friday afternoon, just you and me.' I didn't like the way Lucas said this. There was a mean edge to his sonorous voice: the suggestion of a threat.

'Thank you for giving me your time. I won't take long,' I apologized.

'You have had a successful visit, yes? I hope our Department for Statistics has supplied you with all the data you need.' He said this as a statement rather than a question.

'I've gathered some useful information.' I didn't want to be the person to break the news that his Department for Statistics had closed three years ago.

Lucas stared at me through his dark glasses. His muscular presence, seated behind a desk, seemed incongruous – it was easier to imagine him in a boxing ring or working as a bodyguard.

'Tell me about your analysis?' he asked. 'What conclusions have you come to?'

I wanted to explain about my trip to the interior, and the scandalous mining conditions. I owed that to Billy at the very least. But I knew I'd have to save that for my report. Lucas could only know I had disobeyed his orders once I was safely out of the country.

'I have yet to write the full account.'

'I would like a summary. I would like a summary, now.'

'Well, the figures show there are challenges for Guyana on the world stage...'

'Stop!' Lucas slammed a massive, scarred fist on the table. 'Challenges! What sort of language is that?'

'Yes, but ...'

He was clenching and unclenching his hands. 'Every so often I have people like you visit. But you have no idea. Absolutely no idea.

'We are a country under pressure – our borders are disputed and our political parties do not trust each other and cannot work together.' Lucas paused and took off his sunglasses. 'For a while, with independence, we thought we were free. Free from the shackles of Britain, free from imperialists. That was in way back 1966. We nationalised our industries, GuySuCo, GuyRiCo, GuyMineCo. At last, we were in charge of our destiny. We had a fair chance. Or so we believed. But we were naive. The imperialists were cunning, they bought elsewhere. Our sugar was exactly the same quality as before independence, our rice was exactly the same, but the imperialists cancelled our contracts and purchased from other unscrupulous countries. We dig, we grow, but nobody wants our harvest. This is a worse tyranny. They are punishing us...'

With a soft clunk, the air conditioning cut out. 'Friday afternoon power cut, it always happens,' he explained with a tone of exasperation.

Lucas continued: 'We called Britain the mother country. But once we'd left the family she didn't want to know. We'd become an embarrassment to them, a bastard child. They ground us down until we cried for mercy. For a while we looked to Russia for help. But like everyone else they had their own agenda. We are a rich country, we have great mineral wealth, yet the International Bank say we are one of the poorest states in the world. This is not acceptable.'

He was right about this; I wasn't about to contradict him. About the only home grown industry that appeared to be on the up was security. I looked straight at Lucas and gave a submissive shrug. 'Perhaps, with the data from my analysis you can argue for extra support.'

'What use do I have for data? Look around you. People work their fingers to the bone. Go to the Stabroek market. There is great energy, but for little return. That's all you need to see.'

'You can use these figures to your own advantage.'

'Mr Radstock, the only organisation that has data is the International Bank. And they use this against us. Cleave here, cut this, save that. That is all they say. It is always less, never more. We need more. We need more education, better education. How can we improve this country without better education?

Lucas gave an exasperated laugh. 'The I.B. advise that we should raise more revenue from taxes. It'll help you meet your spending commitments, they say. But sixty per cent of the economy is informal. Most people live at a subsistence level – few are fortunate enough to have a fixed salary at the end of the month. We work on a different system here. It doesn't fit the I.B.'s so called state-building framework. The data is always used against us. I don't trust your data.'

'DoDO wants to help,' I said.

'Help!' he snorted. 'We don't want help. There is no quick fix. Foreign companies come and take what they want. Until we control our own means of production we are powerless. In your own country the poor get poorer. Here, the whole country is getting poorer. All we ask for is an even playing field.'

'I appreciate that.'

Lucas shifted in his seat and leaned forward. 'Mr Radstock, there is an important matter I wish to discuss with you.'

The room was quiet and the building empty. I sat with my knees together and my hands clasped on my lap. I feared what was coming next.

'Where are our computers?' he said with calm menace in his voice.

'Ah,' I flinched, 'I will need to check.' I could feel sweat dripping down my back. 'I hear they have been dispatched, but I'm not sure when they will arrive.' I wondered where Lucas did his butchering? Surely not in the office?

'But they should be here by now.'

'As I said, I'll find out what's happening.'

'There could be serious repercussions if they do not arrive. Dangerous repercussions. Caymans have voracious appetites at this time of year. Disappearances in the bush are not uncommon.'

Was that a joke? 'But I'm not in the bush,' I said.

'That's a mere technicality. Who knows where you are?'

'I spoke to Gordon Jones only an hour ago.' I wanted Lucas to believe DoDO kept a close track of my movements. 'DoDO know exactly where I am.'

'Without those computers your situation can change rapidly. You understand what I'm saying?'

'I have no intention of visiting the bush.'

Lucas gave me a sly, knowing look. 'Of course not.' He was weighing me up. Was I worth bothering with? What sort of prize was I? 'And your flight home,' he asked. 'When are you hoping to leave?'

'DoDO is still arranging it.'

Lucas smiled and nodded. 'So you will let me know about the computers, yes?'

'As soon as I hear.'

'I do not like people abusing my hospitality.'

'I'll let you know.'

Lucas said nothing. He stared at me for a while, grunted, and then leant sideways and slowly opened a drawer of his desk. I wondered what he was going to do. For a moment I thought of Mackenzie's 'office equipment'. To my relief he pulled out a sheaf of papers which he nonchalantly flicked through. He seemed to have forgotten I was sitting directly in front of him.

I sat with mounting fear listening for heavy footsteps in the empty building. Was this the moment the Tonton Macoute came to take me away? But the building was silent.

He looked up. 'When you write your report give them the full story, Mr Radstock. How miners grab land illegally; that we do not have the manpower to adequately police the interior. The I.B. tell us we are in "economic stress" and will have to make some difficult decisions. We are in this situation BECAUSE of the I.B.'

His voice slid away, his anger seemed to have left him. 'One day they might care, but not now.' He took a mouthful of his Coke and stared at me, slowly nodding his head.

'It is Friday afternoon,' he said, 'is there anything else you want to tell me?'

'It'll all be in my report.' I wanted to tell him so much, but I knew I couldn't.

Lucas sat back in his chair, his powerful frame looked strangely deflated.

He took a deep breath. 'You are free to go.'

For a moment I didn't believe him. 'Free to go,' his voice echoed in my head. I was still waiting for shouting, the slam of doors and a hessian bag being shoved over my head as I was dragged away to ... to who knows what horror.

Standing up in a daze I offered my hand. 'Thank you for your time and your hospitality. You have a wonderful country. I promise I will do all I can to spread the word.'

Yet again I had misjudged: my first impressions had been clouded by preconceived ideas, rumours and untruths. It took a while to clear the tangled picture. Lucas was battling for resources for his people in an upside-down world. He was no monster: no Idi Amin tyrant, no Mugabe despot. But he did mention caimens, didn't he? I hadn't imagined that, had I? I was confused.

He heaved himself from his chair and walked over to the door. 'Mr Radstock, I am sure you are a good man and doing your best. I've got no kick against you personally, but you have no idea.'

Maybe. But I was learning.

TWENTY-ONE

All I wanted to do was to walk through the night with Tallulah.

I had eaten my last chunk of Toblerone and was now sipping twelve year old El Dorado rum in the hotel bar. (The chocolate had slumped out of shape in the heat – the nuts and nougaty bits were now on the surface. It was quite a good look, actually.) I was light-headed with the thought that my trip would soon come to an end. The I.B. team were playing a drinking game that involved rolling a dice, everybody shouting 'Banzai' and then some unfortunate sucker knocking back his drink in one. They had been at it for quite some time. Several of the group were holding their head in their hands while a couple of the guys were stripped to their underpants – though they still had their shoes and black socks on.

Tallulah was wearing a figure-hugging, all-systems-go green dress that accentuated the delicious curves of her breasts and hips. 'Let's get out of here,' she said as she gave me a welcoming kiss.

'Sure.' I could see the I.B. squad would soon be reaching a tipping point that could only head downwards.

'I'd like to go for a walk,' said Tallulah.

'A walk? I thought you didn't like walking.'

'I'm interested to see what an Englishman does on his wanderings. In the U.S. you could get arrested, you only walk if you're a burnout or a bum.'

'That's so sad. Walking is good for creativity.'

'Man, where I come from even taxis are only for out-of-towners or prostitutes.'

'All the best thinkers walk. Charles Dickens was a raving insomniac and spent all night tramping the streets of London. There's an artist called Richard Long who walks for a living.'

'How do they hang that on a wall?'

'He's created a whole new genre. He's a genius.'

'So, does walking help your labour market research?'

'Of course. I think of it as my laboratory for ideas.'

'Wow, the sidewalk is your laboratory. Crazy.'

'Think of it as a meditation. You listen to your body, you feel your feet and hear your breath.'

Tallulah put her hand on my arm. 'If you walk with me, will that be a distraction?'

'Not at all, having a companion helps confirm that you're not dreaming and the world exists.' I thought Tallulah would appreciate a bit of metaphysical bullshit thrown into the conversation.

She whistled. 'Lordy! You Brits!'

At the next table Stilton, who was now down to his dirtied boxer shorts, had fallen off his chair. He was lying on his back with his arms and legs waving in the air like a giant beetle struggling to right itself.

'Oh God!' I said.

'So where shall we walk?' Tallulah asked. 'To a shopping mall?'

'Walks aren't usually retail focused. I walk where I fancy. The best walks are done on a whim.'

'Don't you get lost?'

'I've got a good sense of direction.' Though, to be honest, after my circumambulatory trip with Zadoc, I was beginning to doubt the reliability of my homing instincts. 'You can learn a lot about people when you walk with them.'

'Let's go.' Tallulah stood up. 'For Christ's sake, Stilton, put some clothes on.'

I liked Georgetown at night. The street lighting was intermittent and apart from the occasional grumble of a motorbike the roads round the hotel were empty.

'So where are we going?' Tallulah asked.

'We might end up by the sea.'

'It would be good to see the ocean.'

'Do you get turned on by the ocean as well?'

'Maybe. A little bit,' she added, coyly.

'I've always liked the sea. Its smell, its movement, the mystery of what lies beyond. I think it's something to do with being brought up on an island.'

'Are we going to be safe?'

'Just don't look like a lost American. Walk like the English. Fast.'

'How did you get on with Billy?' I asked.

'Sweet dude. Love at first sight.'

'What! Really?'

'Did he give you a jungle oyster?' she asked.

'I've never eaten anything like it. They're certainly an acquired taste.'

Tallulah grimaced. 'Not something I was going to acquire. While nobody was looking, I threw it into the corner of the hut. The dogs seemed to like it.'

There was no pavement so we walked in the road which ran parallel to a canal with a grass verge and trees on either side. The tree frogs squeaked their nightly chorus. Three laughing boys on a bicycle – one on the saddle, one on the crossbar, one on the handlebars – glided past. The darkness blurred the town's rough edges and it seemed altogether rather beautiful.

'We've got to do something to help the Macawaiwai,' I said. 'They're being shat upon.'

'Stop thinking you're mister nice guy,' said Tallulah. 'Overseas development is about plugging into new markets in fragile economies.'

'But I saw a man die,' I said.

'You can't do anything about that.'

'I saw Billy's son die.'

'I know, I heard. But it's a local issue.'

'Oh, come on.'

'Look, I'm sorry. Truly sorry. I liked Billy a lot.'

'It's not right. Surely you, the I.B., can put pressure on these people.'

'No, listen, it's not our business to enforce health and safety thousands of miles away in the jungle.'

'It was dreadful, Tallulah.'

'The country is financially challenged, the economy is sliding backwards.'

'Is that what you told Lucas?' I said.

'In so many words.'

'I bet he didn't like it.'

'People don't like to hear the truth. Especially if it hurts.'

'Truth! Whose truth?' I said. 'That's so subjective when it comes to economic development.'

Everywhere I went I had heard the same old story. The economy used to be stronger, life used to be better. But, I wondered, did it? The good old days. Don't people always say that? Was it just me harking back to the days of the British Commonwealth? Yet, some schools looked well built. In the dining room at Princess Elizabeth Technical College the Principal had shown me boards on the wall listing the achievements of former pupils. Scholarships to universities in Great Britain and Canada; going by the dates on these faded plaques, things seemed to have come to a halt in the mid-1960s. Perhaps, once, there was a golden age? But a golden age for whom? The children of the rich? The plantation grandees and enterprises owned by British companies? Had I fallen for the myth of The British Commonwealth? Common wealth! The old lie.

We walked on. The smell of wood smoke and jerk chicken hung in the warm air. I was attempting to retrace my previous route to the seafront, but was unsure of the way. Behind peeling picket fences, ramshackle wooden houses were lit by dim yellow lights. Families were camped out on verandas talking and laughing. Someone was practicing on a tenor saxophone – the sound of loneliness, the sound of lost love.

Tallulah continued: 'You know what I'm saying. It's pump-priming investment. We get a foothold in, and they feel morally obliged. One day we'll reap the rewards.'

'That's such a cynical view.'

'I call it realistic. You Brits fall for your own propaganda.'

'Maybe. But meanwhile, can't we make people's lives easier?'

Tallulah shrugged. 'By imposing western culture? Half the world lives in poverty. The gap between rich and poor is widening.'

'Alleviating shortages, clean water, health, education, sustainable energy – that's got to be worth something.' I remembered what Ellis had said. 'Give a man a sandwich and feed him for a day, give him a chicken and feed him omelettes for life.'

'Maybe. And in the process destroy their unique social structures. These people don't need us. Once you've got the basics of life sorted the rest is in your head.'

'You're talking from the luxury of a western perspective. Don't you ever give presents without expecting a pay back?'

'That's different.'

I didn't understand Tallulah. Why was such a smart, sassy woman working for the I.B.? Did she have no scruples?

'So, if the I.B. are such a bunch of bastards, why do you work for them?' I asked.

Tallulah stopped walking. 'This isn't exactly what I planned.' There was a sadness in her voice. 'I took a path and didn't know which way it was going. When I started with the I.B. I thought everything was going to be straightforward. Wham, bam – I'd save the world. Ah, the naivety and sweet idealism of youth. Of course, it's not like that. But I hang on to the thought that there's got to be other, better, ways of doing things.'

'Huh! So you do think there's hope.'

'Sometimes hope is all we've got.'

A pack of free-range dogs was heading towards us. Tallulah tugged my arm. 'I don't like dogs.'

'They're okay. Round here, it's the cattle you have to worry about.' I slipped my arm round her waist. She felt smaller, slighter than I remembered.

There were half a dozen of the animals, all nasty hyena brown.

'They could be rabid.'

'Rabid dogs don't go about in packs,' I said confidently. It seemed a reasonable assumption.

'Let's cross the road.' They were now within twenty feet. I could feel Tallulah's body tense.

'Relax.' I didn't want to make any sudden movements.

The dogs slowed down. I wondered if we should shift off the sidewalk and let them pass. The leader moved forward and sniffed with his wet nose. He gave a low, drawn-out growl. I was waiting for him to pull back his lips and bare his fangs. I looked into his yellow, unemotional eyes and held out my open hand. I knew I had to show no fear. 'Good boy.' He stood still for a moment, sizing me up, then shuffled forward and licked my palm with his rough tongue. 'Good boy,' I repeated. He sneezed and sauntered on. The rest of the pack trotted past without so much as a snuffle.

'So, what were we saying?' I asked.

Tallulah put a finger to my lips. 'Honey, this is our last night together. Let's talk about something else.'

She asked the usual clichéd questions. Why did the British love toast? What caliber gun did I have back home? And was the Duke of Edinburgh immune from prosecution for his predatory behaviour?

'You seem like the sort of guy who has a library of leather-bound books,' she said.

'I do have a bit of a book habit, and I love the smell of furniture wax,' I laughed.

She told me about her childhood on the Connecticut coast and the unbroken New England summers. 'Daddy was an orthodontist to the 5th Avenue elite,' she said smiling, showing her immaculate teeth. She would make crazy drunken trips in a speed-boat, borrowed from her parents, across Long Island Sound, narrowly missing the lobster-pot markers. In comparison, I felt so unsophisticated, but she listened with polite curiosity to my stories anyway.

I told her about my adolescent dismay when I exchanged the mystical Somerset wetlands for life in the London suburbs and charmless streets of Ruislip. I described catching the 711 bus to London, lying on bean-bags, listening to Purple Rain in the Virgin record shop in Tottenham Court Road, under-age drinking and my first spliff in the car park of the Antelope Inn.

'Your life sounds like something out of Oliver Twist,' she said.

'Really!? I don't think Prince was around in Charles Dickens's day.'

Tallulah put her arm in mine. 'I don't mind what you say, I just love the sound of your voice.'

'I think we're lost,' I said.

The ocean was doing something to me as well. I hadn't felt as good as this for a long time. I was enjoying Tallulah's company. I liked her confidence and her intelligence. I remembered the Kaieteur Falls. For a few moments the world had closed in on us. It had been just Tallulah and me, surrounded by the deep magic of the rainforest, the thrum and hammering of the Falls vibrating through the rock. I'd never in my life felt anything so intense.

And then I thought of Aurora. I missed her so much. When I got back to England, we'd start over again. I'd watch her draw exquisite pictures of Adonis Blues, Clouded Yellows and Meadow Browns. We'd visit the tropical house and kiss under the palm trees and go back to my flat and make love in the late afternoon.

Tomorrow I'd be leaving Guyana and everything would change. Now, all I wanted to do was walk through the Georgetown night with Tallulah.

TWENTY-TWO

I'd touched the impossible dream.

There's a couple of things for you, here,' Festus said, as he put my keys in the pigeon-hole.

Fortunately, I wasn't travelling back to England by banana boat. Gordon had been able to organise a last-minute flight to Barbados, and from there I'd get a connection to London, Gatwick.

Festus handed me a printed email. I looked at the heading, it was from Gordon. I'd read it later. 'Is this for you?' Festus also gave me a couple of sealed envelopes, one with 'Merrick' written on it.

Outside, Xavier was waiting for me by the Land Rover.

'So you've got it back?' I said.

'All fixed.'

'What was the problem again?'

'It would take a while to explain.'

'That complicated, eh? The only Land Rover Discovery in G.T., eh?'

'The only one in the country.'

We looked at each other. I nodded and smiled. Maybe it was for the best that I didn't know the full story.

We were now on the edge of Georgetown. I gazed out of the window at the jungle of shacks and shanties. Radio Guyane was playing the usual mix of reggae and middle of the road music between adverts for restaurants, beauty products and mining equipment. It was another burning day – but I was beginning to enjoy the heat. It slows you down and gives you time to appreciate things, to lime. In the British temperate climate you have to be busy, busy, busy just to keep warm.

While I was pleased to be on my way home for Christmas, I was sorry the experience was coming to an end. I had that sad, last day of the holidays feeling, and was starting to realise how much I liked Guyana. I would miss the laid-back ambience, the kindness of the people and their good nature in the face of adversity. This country could be strange and annoying, but there hadn't been a day when I hadn't been enchanted by it.

I took Gordon's email out of my pocket. It was too late to do anything now. I contemplated tearing it up and throwing it out of the window where it could join all the other roadside garbage strewn by feral dogs. Instead, I opened the envelope with Merrick written on it. Inside was a postcard with a picture of a bright red bird. Cock of the Rock. I laughed and turned it over to read,

'Felix, I never say goodbye, the word upsets me. Tallulah XXX.'

I looked out of the window and shook my head. I didn't have Tallulah's address, I didn't even know her surname. To my disquiet a tear rolled down my cheek.

'Can you turn up the air-con?' I said.

'It's as high as it can go.'

I'd touched the impossible dream – I loved her so much but enjoyed the realisation that I'd never see her again. You can't maintain that level of passion for long.

Xavier looked at me. 'Are you okay?'

'Yeah. Hey, thanks for your help, Xavier. I've learnt a lot.'

'It's been a pleasure, boss.'

'It's Starsky.'

'It's Hutch actually.'

On the radio Bing Crosby was singing 'White Christmas'. It was such a ridiculous song to listen to in the searing heat.

'I'm glad you got the car back,' I said.

I opened the final letter. It was an invitation from the British High Commissioner in Georgetown to attend drinks and a poetry reading, courtesy of the British Council, by an 'exhilarating up-and-coming' British poet. At least I'd learnt how to tie a Windsor knot.

At the airport we stopped in a busy car park. A jet was on the runway – the smell of kerosene hung in the hot air. I looked around for any sign of Lucas's henchmen ready to abduct me and turn me into freezer fodder.

Xavier and I shook hands. He pulled me towards him and hugged me.

'There's something I've been meaning to tell you,' he said.

'Yes?'

'We may be down but we're not out.'

'I'm sure you're right.'

'You can't crush the spirit of the people. We've always been a people of struggle. Wait and see. One day the brilliance of Guyana will shine forth.'

His unfettered optimism was inspiring. 'It can't come a day too soon,' I replied.

There were difficult times ahead for sure, but I hoped these kind and generous people, living in a land rich with resources would one day prosper. Extraordinary things can happen. Maybe, not before long, people would stop leaving, the country's talent would return and Guyana would establish its rightful place in the world.

I was grateful for Xavier, I'd learnt a lot from him. He was a good man. While most of his compatriots had abandoned the country to earn the Yankee dollar he'd remained at home looking after his family.

'Xavier, did you say your middle name is Yolanda?'

'Yolando, it's Dutch.'

'I thought Yolando was a girl's name.'

'Not in Guyana. It's a very macho name. If you ever have a son, you should call him Yolando.'

'It's a pretty name. If I have a daughter I will call HER Yolanda.'

Xavier stared at me. For a moment he said nothing. 'And you will remember me!' he said.

'I'll never forget you. You must visit me when you come to London.'

Xavier nodded. 'To Tooting.'

I looked at my ticket. I was already late for check-in.

'Xavier, if anybody asks you about the computers, just say they are on their way.'

'I always do. Perhaps, one day they will arrive.'

'Maybe.'

'I doubt it, my friend.'

Before I joined the long line of people waiting to leave the country I put my straw hat in a waste bin. I never did get to meet Roxy. But then again – remembering the dream I had at the Silent Night Guesthouse – maybe I had.

PART FOUR

ONE

A poem for Aurora.

There was little excitement in Aurora's home-coming kiss. 'It seems like you've hardly been away,' she said. Her eye-liner was smudged and her dyed raven-black hair longer. She was pale, and even more ravishing.

'I've been gone for ages,' I said.

'You've lost weight.'

'The cheese toastie and Toblerone diet – I can recommend it.'

'You've painted your nails black,' I said.

'It's not black, it's midnight blue.'

'Looks black to me.'

'Do you like them?'

'I'm not sure.'

I gave her a bowl turned from purple-heart wood and a T shirt with a macaw painted on it. 'They didn't have any with butterflies,' I apologised.

'Thanks.' She put the gifts down without looking at them.

'It was difficult to find anything to buy. They don't do souvenirs in Guyana.'

Aurora shrugged. 'Didn't they have a duty free? Chanel is always welcome.'

There was so much I wanted to tell her: the cloud of butterflies on the rock in the bush, the immense forest and the racket of the night-time. For a day or so, she was interested in my tales. We laughed about my retreat from Corriverton hidden under a blanket; I described the drunken pilot, the tarantula in the roof, my stay with the Macawaiwai. I told her about Billy and his tragic son. I also briefly mentioned Tallulah and the I.B., but only in passing. Aurora asked questions, but

I found it difficult to find the right words.

'So you think overseas aid is a waste of money?' she enquired.

'No, no, no. I'd never say that. Absolutely not. At the right time, in the right place it's a lifesaver. I just wish aid could be distributed more effectively. A bit more fairly.'

'Life isn't fair, Felix. You ought to know that by now.'

I realised ever since I'd proposed to her (had I?), something unsaid and tissue thin had come between us. The magic had been broken. It seemed like I couldn't reach her any more, we no longer connected.

'I'll read your report when you've written it,' Aurora said.

We talked about her tattoo. 'A butterfly on your arm would be nice,' I said.

She grimaced, 'I was thinking more of a skull or a bat or something like that.'

It took me a while to adjust to the grey skies and monochrome British winter. Once, in the middle of the night, I woke and did something I'd never done before. I wrote Aurora a poem. But in the morning I tore it up without giving it to her.

The office was quiet. I'd never noticed before how small and drab the room was.

'So how was Africa?' Adge asked, as if I'd just nipped out for a coffee and doughnut.

'Guyana is in South America.'

'Are you sure?'

I looked out of the window across the yard to a towering, concrete wall. If I tilted my head upwards I could see a patch of grey sky.

'Certain. I flew across the Atlantic to get there.'

'How do you know that wasn't the Mediterranean?'

'Look, it's in bloody South America – I've just been there, right?'

Adge shrugged. 'I must have been thinking of somewhere else

then.'

I checked my emails. There were several requests for labour market assessments, mostly for out of the way, rural counties – Radnorshire, Rutland and North Somerset. A terse email from Gordon merely specified the date by which my report should be delivered. Apart from addressing a couple of specific questions about my visit to the mine at Linden, he said he would leave the format and content to my professional judgment.

'Any calls?' I didn't like to ask Adge what he'd been doing over the last few weeks. Not much, I guessed. He hadn't even watered the pot plant, which was now a stick surrounded by brown leaves.

'A few.'

'What did you say?'

'I mostly told them to fuck off.'

'Well done.' Why was I stuck with this thug? I would fire him at the earliest convenient opportunity.

The city night felt too quiet. Sometimes I found myself thinking about Tallulah, but pushed her to the back of my mind. I slept little, and when I did I would find myself lying at strange angles as if I was sleeping in a hammock.

I was constantly turning over in my mind all I'd seen. I felt strangely disconnected. Sometimes it can be a good thing to wander in the wilderness and confront fears and uncertainties. Even if I was led into temptation.

I had experienced some kind of catharsis. Although I didn't know the answers at least I had some questions. I'd aged and grown up; the world was a more serious place. I was beginning to see how clichéd my views had been. We do it all the time – without knowing, we assemble and formulate national and racial stereotypes. In England it pisses down all summer, the food is inedible, and we adore the royal family and the ever-increasing number of freeloading hangers-on.

With Guyana I didn't start with any specific image, I did, however, have a laid back, rum, roots and reggae view of the Caribbean. I had to discard my prejudgment and dig beyond the cliché. I thought of Billy and his village. Even now, months later, I have nightmares about that gold mine, and wake up, with a sour mouth, drenched in sweat. I was sure Billy's son wasn't the only victim. I had a responsibility to tell the story of a country whose resources had been laid to waste and its indigenous people debased.

But what could I do? Who else cared about this forsaken country at the edge of the world? Sure, there were people like Ellis doing their best and dedicating their lives to bettering the opportunities of the poor and disadvantaged. But in the end, I wasn't sure who really benefited from 'overseas development'. It seemed to be a cynical way of propping up exploitation by industrialised countries. I vowed that the young man, Billy's son, wouldn't die in vain.

I was curious about Gordon and wanted to meet him. What sort of man was he? Did he have any real idea about the complexity of the project, or was he just another keyboard clicker in an anonymous civil service department?

For the next month, while I wrote my report, I answered no phone calls and ignored emails. For the first time in my life I had the opportunity to do something useful. But I had little hard information: I was searching the data for the Hallelujah Chorus but all I had to work on were a few bum notes. I was left with no other option but to use the entry-level version of the Radstock Framework©.

We were on the brink of the Millennium. The Earth seemed increasingly fragile. I used to believe that as time went by things got better. But the future didn't look so positive. Voracious banks and unpredictable weather didn't bode well. I saw people in Tesco filling their trolleys with mineral water, Pot Noodles and toilet rolls; preparing for the big shut-down. I feared after the Millennium the clock would go backwards.

As teenagers we had talked about revolution - there would be peace and free love. John Lennon, Bob Dylan and Gerry Garcia would be the new world leaders. It was a preposterous idea but they gave us hope and slogans to shout. Then we were punks. Thatcher was a hate figure that we could all rail against. We'd rip up everything and replace it with, well, I'm not too sure. Blair bounced in, but it soon became clear that New Labour was frighteningly like the old Tories. Certainly, there was no stopping the deregulated city barrow-boys, while honest manufacturing was sneered at – it couldn't be got rid of fast enough. Leave mass-production to the low-wage-paying Chinese.

I was glad when the celebrations were over. There were fireworks across the world, the Queen and Tony Blair linked hands awkwardly and sang Auld Lang Syne in the Millennium Dome, but not a whimper came from the Y2K bug. As the clock hit midnight on the 31 December 1999 there wasn't so much as a bleat as computers seamlessly switched to the new millennium. If there were any problems they could be fixed by merely turning the computers off and on again. The Millennium Bug turned out to be a global, billion-dollar swindle stirred up by nerds who saw the opportunity for a quick buck and a laugh at our expense. Millennium Bug consultancies quietly closed as we realised we'd been taken for an exorbitant ride with no destination.

By the end of January I was ready to dispatch my report which was the thickness of a telephone directory. I had one last thing to do.

TWO

The lies just got bigger.

Gordon was unenthusiastic about meeting. He said he couldn't see the point. The project was finished. I'd been paid, hadn't I? He'd been up to his neck in it, busy tying up loose ends after 'the Y2K fiasco'. Reluctantly, he arranged to rendezvous in a pub, not, as I had expected in Slough, but in London, near the Tate Gallery, across the road from the Thames Embankment.

It was a wind-whipped day, with flurries of wet sleet. The pub was noisy with lunchtime trade but we grabbed an empty table by the window. Gordon was shorter and rounder than I had imagined. His receding hair made his plump face look perfectly round. Under a shabby tweed overcoat, his piggy body was crammed into a grey suit that was too small for him. His plump face had the florid complexion of a committed lunchtime drinker. And after all he had said about neckwear, I was disappointed that his paisley tie was stained and had the look of polyester about it.

'Fascinating little boozer this. Over there,' Gordon pointed to a side street, 'used to be London's largest prison. They say there are secret passages running to the pub's cellar.'

'Really?'

'Millbank Prison. It was used as a holding-pen for convicts waiting to be shipped to Australia.'

'Interesting.'

'You probably knew that already.'

'I think I did,' I lied.

'So how was the wildlife in Guyana? Did you see any macaws? I'd love to see macaws in their native habitat. Stunning birds. Always fly around in pairs, mate for life. And what about toucans?' he smiled.

'Did you see any toucans?'

'They're ridiculous animals, they're top-heavy. With their stubby little wings and massive beaks, it's a wonder they get airborne.'

'Is that so?' Gordon leaned forward with interest. 'I bet you had some good food. The Stabroek Lodge is reputed to have one of the best restaurants in South America.'

'I think that might be overstating it.' I thought of the iguana eggs, and felt a lump in my throat.

Gordon looked at me as if I was a kill-joy. 'I hear the street food is good. Great rotis.'

What did he know? Gordon scoffing humble street food was as likely as me chowing down in the Ritz.

'What about the Y2K bug, then?' I asked. 'We all fell for that one, didn't we?'

His baby face hardened. 'Ill-informed people say the department over-reacted. Maybe we did, but there are always unexpected by-products from these projects. Those cyber bombshells are out there. You can bet somebody in the early days of computing inserted an Armageddon Meltdown Bug into a basic programme which has subsequently been cut and pasted all over the shop. Our detectorists have already found dormant viruses in nuclear reactors, which override safety mechanisms and heat up to oblivion. Sometime, there's going to be a global internet crash, but maybe not just at the moment.'

'But why? Who's doing this?'

'You'd be surprised. Nation states, crazy dictators, religious crackpots, spotty teenage hacktivists. There are loads of Maoist mummy-boys and anarchist bed-wetters who want to de-stabilise society.

'Anyway, the teams have been re-allocated. We're now studying the effect of violent solar flares on communications. Every two hundred years, or so, the flares peak. If we get a coronal mass ejection anything could happen. The last one was in 1859. Technology wasn't so sophisticated then. But even then, the telegraph wires became so hot that the operators were making toast at their desks. Imagine the damage today?'

'Is that a good use of resources?'

'At least we're prepared.'

'But why? It's as likely as earth being hit by an asteroid.'

'You may joke, but that threat was raised in Parliament only the other day. There's a unit looking at that as well.'

'Oh God!'

'It's going to happen. It's happened before. The last big impact didn't do much for the health of the dinosaurs. As recently as 1908 an asteroid exploded over Siberia – hundreds of miles of forest were reduced to match-sticks. A few hours later it could have been Paris.'

Gordon pulled out a cigarette and lit it. 'I've read your report with great interest. In some places you have overstepped your remit. I wasn't expecting you to actually visit the gold mining region.'

'There were a lot of issues to address. I did as well as I could under the circumstances. It was very challenging. As I was nearby I thought you'd appreciate an eye-witness account.' At this stage I didn't see the point of saying what a lousy manager Gordon had been.

'And what was all that nonsense about waterfalls stimulating parts of the frontal lobes. Where did you get that idea from?'

'It's scientifically proven. Fluffy bunny syndrome. That's why hotels are built near waterfalls. They provide, as any psychologist will tell you, subliminal stimuli that release pleasure giving hormones.' Thoughts of a gloriously naked Tallulah flashed into my mind. 'The reaction can be unexpectedly powerful.'

Gordon looked at me as if I was loose in the head. 'Forget psychologists. Futurologists are what we're after these days. Anyway, I won't let your unauthorised peregrinations affect your final payment.'

'What will happen next to my report?' I asked.

'It's difficult to say.'

'What do you think will be done about the gold mines?'

'Done?'

'Will there be pressure to regulate them?'

'The gold mines are not within our remit.'

'But they're an important part of the report.'

'I have had to delete that section.'

'What do you mean?'

'It was leaning towards the subjective. We are in no position to lecture the Chinese. You could cause an incident.'

'I saw a man die in the bush.'

'Such emotive language doesn't help international relations. There's no point in upsetting the new world order.'

'But those mines, they are the most awful places imaginable.'

'Power is shifting. China, India, Brazil – these are the nations we have to cosy up to these days. And Saudi Arabia, of course – we won't have a bad word said about those hand cutting, public flogging, misogynists.'

Gordon looked at his empty glass. 'Fancy another one?' He stood up and walked across the room. The air was thick with cigarette smoke and lunch-time conviviality. Above the bar, left-over Christmas decorations were gathering dust. I shifted my gaze and stared out of the window. Across the grey Thames was the green and cream ziggurat that housed MI6.

Gordon returned with two pints of Young's Special and an additional whisky chaser for himself.

I was so pissed off. Had Gordon really deleted the most important part of my report? 'So which of my recommendations do you think the Guyanese government will act on?' I asked.

Gordon gave a derisive snort. 'None of them.'

'Why not?'

'My guess is that they won't read it.'

'What exactly is wrong with my report?'

I watched Gordon's Adam's apple quiver in his great crimson wattle as he knocked back the final drops of whisky.

'You have to realise, Felix, that you are a tiny nut in a big and complex engine.'

'Meaning?'

'Overseas development is a convoluted business. The government doesn't just hand out money for the fun of it.'

'I understand that.'

'Sometimes we have to approach things in a roundabout way.'

'So?'

'We hide our true intentions so they can't be seen. To put it bluntly your little project was a bit of fancy wrapping.'

'What do you mean? That totally undersells the importance of my recommendations.'

'Your survey was a small part of a package that just happened to be on the table when we were talking about something much bigger. It was a diversion.' Gordon nodded towards the decorations hanging above the bar. 'A stocking filler.'

This was insulting. I could still hear Billy's terrible cry; I thought about those grim-faced managers in Linden and my promise to highlight their predicament.

'You're a bunch of cynical, manipulating bastards!'

Gordon didn't even flinch. 'I wouldn't put it quite like that myself, but that's the way things are, Mr Radstock.'

'But you're messing with a country that needs help.'

'The situation is not that bad. They're not starving in Guyana!'

'They may not be starving, but everybody comes in and rips the country off. The UK, the US, China, multi-nationals, you name it. It's open season for ripping the shit out of Guyana. It's appalling.'

'You're beginning to sound like Miss Deane. Seems like we got you out in the nick of time.'

'Ellis is doing a good job.'

'And you, Mr Felix Radstock, are part of that process. You were happy to take your pound of meat.'

'But I didn't realise.'

'You're not so innocent. It was a good fee. What did you think you were being paid for?'

'I'm not like all those other people. I produced a clear and practical in-depth report that you will find valuable for taking matters forward.'

'You promised something that you knew you couldn't deliver.'

'I did not!' I was indignant.

'Look, I got our computer nerds to give the Radstock Framework© the once-over. You know what they said? "The architecture is full of errors." The Radstock Framework© is a sham, and you know it.'

'Nobody has ever said that before.'

'Maybe, nobody has ever given it a rigorous testing. It's structurally unstable, the whole kaboosh goes round in an eternal loop. It blue-screened. So, Mr Radstock, who is ripping off who now?'

'Okay, the algorithms may need recalibrating for this set of conditions, but what about the empirical research? I had to make the difficult switch to Flexible Thought Planning mode.'

'What's that then? Sounds like the well-known bullshit method of making-it-up-as-you-go-along.'

'But the colours!' I said.

'What colours?'

'I see colours, textures and patterns.'

'The School of Tropical Medicine is not far from here. Drop in and see them later. They're always looking for unusual ailments. I expect they don't get many referrals from Guyana.'

'You misunderstand. I see patterns in figures.'

Gordon said nothing and gave a thin disbelieving smile.

I squirmed. Maybe, he was right. I'd flattered myself that I could help, but I'd been part of the rip off process as much as anybody.

All my life I've been a fraud. I make stuff up, I pretend to understand

and know things. Throughout my career I've bluffed my way, giving the appearance that I know what's happening and how. I must have carried out this pretence well as, to my surprise, colleagues appears to find me plausible. I've been waiting for people to see through me, but it has never happened. The lies just get bigger.

'But I visited...'

'Huh! I could have got all that information from the International Bank.'

'Why didn't you then?'

'You don't get it, do you?'

'What?'

'Do I have to spell it out? Your project was part of a package, a phantom package. You were like an annoying little wasp buzzing around a honey pot.'

'Why?' I stared out of the window and across the Thames. Suddenly, I understood. I felt sick. 'You work over there, don't you?' I asked.

'Felix, in case you haven't noticed, it's a bad world.'

'No. It's a good world! It's just made bad by people like you.'

'Easy there, Felix, easy.'

'So do you... do you work for MI6?'

'I couldn't possibly tell you.'

'So that's a yes, then?'

'I'll let you come up with your own conclusions.'

'But why me?'

Never in my life had I been taken for such a fool. They must have been laughing their rocks off. No wonder the money was so good. I was such a mug.

'Outsourcing. As simple as that. Government diktat. Even the undercover services have to do it.'

'Why don't you use your own people?'

'You answered the phone, you assured me you could do the work and you were available. It was no big deal.'

'It was a big deal for me.'

'For a business support project like this, it's much cheaper to use a one-off low level snoop. We call them butterflies – very beautiful but not around for long.'

'That's insulting.'

'Yes, well, I can't help that.'

'I don't like being thought of as disposable.'

'Maybe that's the wrong word. It's so much easier to sub-contract human agents.'

'I don't get it.'

'Official channels take too long. We have to put in travel applications, swear affidavits, draw up quality standards, check core technical competencies, show outcomes – and all that other fuck-wittery. These days it's 95% paperwork. Low-level undercover investigations have come to a virtual standstill. Using sub-contractors for covert commercial operations means we get value for money and can gather strategic information with impunity. If it's any consolation, Felix, you did a good job. You provided us with the intelligence we needed on vital raw materials. You checked out Ellis and, most important of all, you gave us crucial information about Aluminium International. The maps were particularly useful; how you got those I'm not going to ask. There were rumours about rare-earth metals. We can't get enough of them. Unfortunately, the Chinese have cornered the market. A UK blue chip company was about to acquire the Linden mine. Even with the new road coming through from Brazil we weren't so sure. Thanks to you, they've not wasted their money.'

'But I promised I would help.' I thought of those despondent men, sitting in their dusty boardroom, pleading for assistance.

'You confirmed that they are a dead duck.'

'They need somebody to buy them.'

'Not a British company, they don't. Don't worry; the Chinese will snap them up.'

'But the rest of my report, what about that?'

'Listen, Felix, we were interested in two things, two things only.' There was a tone of frustration in Gordon's voice. 'First of all, crazy girl Ellis. We were concerned about her state of mind, that she'd gone loco in the jungle.'

'They call it the bush.'

'Whatever. Anyway, you confirmed she's not as flaky as we feared. But more important, much more important was the intelligence on IntAl. IntAl was the big bucks question. Was IntAl a swan that was going to make lots of money? Or a dead duck? Got it? Capisce?'

I nodded. I got it. I didn't like it, but I got it.

'And the computers?' I feared what was coming next.

'Ah, the promise of computers!' Gordon leant back in his seat and raised his hands to his chin as if he was about to pray. 'That always gets them going. It's a great way to kick-start the local black economy.'

I couldn't believe what I was hearing.

'Well done, Felix, you've saved the British tax payer billions.'

I looked out of the window at the monotonous grey London sky. Large unhurried snowflakes were settling on the pavement. How had I got mixed up in something as underhand as this? I'd met many decent people in Guyana, all doing their best, working against odds constantly stacked against them. I swore to myself that I would never again answer the office phone after 2.30 pm on a Friday.

'Felix, you have a very naive, uninformed, view of life. Nobody is innocent in this game.'

'Well, I prefer my view to yours.'

THREE

Our love was slipping away.

Aurora's pictures became darker: dystopian Blade Runner images, giant blood-sucking spiders, a screaming Dalai Lama. 'The new millennium,' she said, 'nobody wants the pretty stuff anymore.' She bought a pair of Doc Martens.

We drifted back into the same old habits. There was always an argument threatening. We'd stopped bringing each other cups of tea in bed and started bickering and saying cruel words to each other. Things, small things, had changed. There was extra spicy chilli sauce in the kitchen cupboard, the toothpaste, a new brand, was in the wrong place. We manoeuvred around each other in a polite, but passionless, routine.

Aurora complained that since I'd returned from Africa I'd become unbearable. She'd once said I was agreeably attractive – time, I felt, had diminished this attractiveness.

'How many times do I have to tell you,' I said, 'Guyana is in South America.'

She accused me of being aloof and preoccupied. I told her that for the first time in my life, I had found something that mattered and motivated me. For the moment I had to concentrate on writing my report.

'What's the point?' Aurora asked. 'What can you do? What can anybody do?'

I was in a unique position to tell the world. I was drafting feature articles for the Guardian and the New Statesman. I hadn't contacted them as yet, but I was sure they'd be interested.

'Knowledge is power,' I said.

Aurora waved her paint brush. 'Yeah, and this is my sword,' she said sarcastically.

'I can't give up.'

I thought of Ellis, so far away from home, teaching people to read and write and her belief in making a difference. Ellis, bless her, was doing the right thing, however small.

Meanwhile, Aurora talked about the inequalities of the world, the melting of the ice-caps, the lack of butterflies in the summer, and how dreadful things were. But we did nothing.

Aurora's increasing negativity was getting to me. I'd always thought she and I would grow together, that our differences would fade and the cracks disappear. We'd been in love certainly, but the intensity was short-lived. In hindsight my proposal of marriage was an act of desperation. I was clinging to the debris of something I was losing.

We were drawing apart. She didn't want to see Crouching Tiger, Hidden Dragon with me. She was at a crucial point with her illustrations and couldn't afford to interrupt the flow. Instead, one afternoon she went to the cinema on her own. Despite my hopes, our love was slipping away.

'You're such a nerd,' she said. 'Look at you, counting on your fingers. You're like a child.'

Just as I was picking myself up, Aurora and I didn't want each other anymore. There was fight in me now and with my new found enthusiasm for my work I needed to shift up a gear. I was hopeful for my future; a new dawn without Aurora. But I'm no good at finishing, I play safe and let matters drift. We fought, we laughed, we fucked. For a moment I was optimistic things would get better. But we were both faking it. There were too many things unsaid; I had a stifling guilt about my betrayal.

I couldn't get Tallulah off my mind. I would dream of the curve of her breasts, the warmth of her smile, the grace of her movement. My secret, never to be disclosed, never to happen again. I knew Tallulah was unobtainable, but her memory made me restless. I didn't want to settle for less.

Who knows what Aurora thought? Had she guessed? Maybe, I'd shouted secrets in my sleep. But we never spoke about my betrayal.

Aurora made whispered phone calls. There were unexplained absences; she smelled different. Despite the evidence I wanted to hang onto my sweet, naïve vision. Eventually, I could no longer ignore the hints of Aurora's own infidelity.

But she beat me to it. Aurora's parting words came as no surprise. 'I've moved on from butterflies,' she announced one morning as she was eating her muesli. 'I'm into moths now.'

FOUR

At least, this time, I know where I'm going.

One year later.

It's Friday afternoon on a dull October day. The low clouds have sucked all colour from the urban landscape. The phone rings. Adge picks it up. 'Futurology Solutions', he announces. That's our new name.

After a few brief words he transfers the call. 'A woman wants to speak to you.'

I answer, yes, yes and yes to her questions. I tell her about the upgraded Radstock Formula© and assure her that it is cross-continental.

'So, are you available to fly to Lahore in two weeks time?' the woman says. The survey is straightforward enough, it'll take a couple of weeks, at the most.

'Lahore? Pakistan?' I ask.

'I'm not talking about the Lahore Kebab House in Brick Lane,' she replies.

It's the sort of job with a sizeable payment I've been waiting for. I need the extra money to pay for my new flat now Aurora and I have gone our separate ways.

'There may be some additional tasks, but our person on the ground will explain this when you get there.'

I ask no more. And at least, this time, I know where I'm going.

Thanks

Thanks to: Fay Weldon for support and inspiration; Richard Jones of Tangent Books; Sue Gent for the beautiful cover; Dr Edson Burton for contextualization; Nicky Coates and Hilary Arundale for proofing and intense scrutiny; Steve Tanner; Glenn Carmichael; Bristol Writers Group for food, feedback and friendship; Marian de Luca (for a joke I borrowed from her); Cecilia Caio, Liz Dowse and Josephine Tsui for advice on international development; Paul Waldren for guiding me through Suriname and Guyana; fellow students and lecturers at the Bath Spa Creative Writing MA course; and Maggie for being there, and journeying with me.

Also by Mike Manson

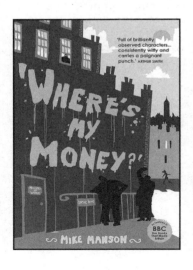
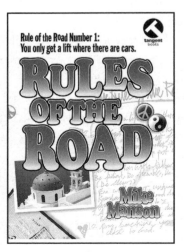